DISCARD

D1221767

STUART BRANNON'S
FINAL SHOT

**Center Point
Large Print**

Also by Stephen Bly and available from Center Point Large Print:

The Land Tamers
Creede of Old Montana
Cowboy for a Rainy Afternoon

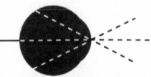

**This Large Print Book carries the
Seal of Approval of N.A.V.H.**

STUART BRANNON'S FINAL SHOT

STEPHEN BLY

With Janet Chester Bly, Russell Bly, Michael Bly & Aaron Bly

CENTER POINT LARGE PRINT
THORNDIKE, MAINE

This Center Point Large Print edition is published
in the year 2012 by arrangement with
the author.

First Edition March 2012.

Printed in the United States of America
on permanent paper.
Set in 16-point Times New Roman type.

ISBN: 978-1-61173-354-9

Library of Congress Cataloging-in-Publication Data

Bly, Stephen A., 1944–
Stuart Brannon's final shot / Stephen Bly...[et al.]. — Large print ed.
p. cm. — (Center Point large print edition)
ISBN 978-1-61173-354-9 (library binding : alk. paper)
1. Large type books. I. Title.
PS3552.L93S79 2012
813′.54—dc23
2011045932

DEDICATION

To the doctors and many other staff members of St. Joseph's Hospital & St. Joseph's Cancer Center, Lewiston, Idaho, who ministered mercy, aid & comfort for our father, grandfather, brother & husband in his last days.

ACKNOWLEDGEMENTS

A note from Janet Chester Bly and her sons, Russell, Michael & Aaron—

Grateful thanks to those who helped us complete this project:

To James "Jim" Grueter, who gave advice on firearms.

To Michelle Bly and Jan Grueter who critiqued the full manuscript.

To author Kathleen Y'Barbo who critiqued the first two chapters in the early stages and offered encouragement.

To the staff of the Seaside (Oregon) Museum, especially Judy Decker.

To Gretchen Baker of the Gearhart (Oregon) Ocean Inn, who connected us with research resources.

To Karen Emmerling, who lent us her Gearhart historical booklet.

To Liisa Penner, archivist at the Clatsop County Historical Society in Astoria, Oregon, for taking time to share her knowledge and provide resources.

To Gail Como, Gearhart City Hall.

To Roger Hemingway, Gearhart, Oregon, who shared oral history, as well as provided many written resources.

To the rangers and staff of the Fort Clatsop Visitor Center who provided copies of Smith House family interviews and other resources.

To editor Diane Hull for providing an extension for the deadline and allowing the family of Stephen Bly to finish the project he had started.

To God be the glory, great things He has done.

PROLOGUE

Early Monday morning, June 5, 1905, near Seaside, Oregon

At twilight, twelve-year-old Hack Howard lined his cot with a couple lumpy pillows and covered them with the thin blanket that was his orphan farm issue. He picked up his worn leather shoes with only one gap in the right sole so he could slink quietly through the room.

None of the dozen of his male roommates stirred or stopped snoring.

He slid the door open, then closed it to a slit as his face warmed, his breath quickened. Miss Penelope Tagg left her station, slipped down the hallway in her sleek nightgown and pink, silky boudoir cap over long strands of brunette locks for her early morning coffee break. Hack sidled past the opening with his lanky frame, then stole to the front door. He unlocked it with the key he'd made out of a spoon in the blacksmith's shop.

"Hack, you're slow in some ways. Some call you a simpleton," Mr. Smythe, the orphan farm director had told him on several occasions, "but you're not dumb."

He slinked down the steps, threw off the

branches from a bicycle he had hidden in the woods, then rode hard and fast to the dock at the beach.

Like he'd done many times before.

He was borrowing one of the smaller orphan farm canoes to row out to Hack's Hideaway, his own secret cove on the huge Tillamook Head cape that jutted out to sea, to check on the wildlife and rule over his domain. He had discovered an accessible route to this place during an orphan farm field trip—a secluded, small cove with a very narrow, winding entrance, and a canoe length's ride from the dock.

But this time when he untied the canoe, he heard his name called: "Hack!"

He whirled around.

"It's me, Bueno. Please, let me go too. I won't tell, honest I won't."

Hack considered his options and figured he had no choice. Either he took the younger boy with him or risked being detected by the orphan farm director. That would mean no more trips to his special place.

So the two boys canoed west to the rock and forest cliff outcropping that Hack loved to explore. He noticed that Bueno rowed as heavy and even as he did. Maybe stronger. The younger boy, though shorter, had a stockier build, bigger, tighter muscles on his arms. They made fast time. He hid his canoe in a tiny cove and tied his shirt to a tree to rustle in the wind and lead him back to the right cove. Like he always did.

They had been at Hack's Hideaway for more than an hour, to listen to owls hoot, watch curious flocks of crows caw and circle them, see hawks and gulls soar, collect fuzzy orange and black caterpillars and long, slimy slugs. They chased various creatures that scurried over fallen tree limbs through ferns. Several small thrushes, bright-eyed birds in the upper reaches of the tallest spruce, sang their hearts out in a swelling melody.

Hack even showed Bueno his private fort, a hole down an incline in a circle of tree branches, with pine bedding and room to play or munch snacks. They rough-and-tumbled for a while.

Then they heard a motor's roar.

They climbed out to scan the sea and spied a boat headed to a much larger cove around the bend. They skimmed on hands and knees up to a higher overlook, behind a trio of stubby spruces.

The boat landed on the far side, on a wider stretch of beach. Three men got out. The hands of one of them were fastened behind him, some cloth tied over his mouth. The other two men shouted at each other and hurled a few punches, then one of them began to climb up the incline in their direction.

"Run," Hack said, as intense as he could in a whisper.

They scurried down to the canoe and rowed away as fast as they could, leaving the shirt to swing in the breeze, clinging to the needles. They looked back once when they thought they heard a rumbling sound like thunder. Or was that a gunshot? They couldn't see the men and only hoped the men could not spot them to chase them with the motor boat.

It seemed longer getting back to the dock. Their arms ached with the strain of the racing speed. The waves skipped higher and the horizon lightened enough to reveal them in full view for miles around. They stooped low as they rowed. At long last, they bumped up against the dock. Bueno jumped out and pulled the rope tight to tie on the railing. The canoe bobbed and the rope slipped out of his hands.

Hack kept throwing it back to Bueno. After a half dozen attempts, Bueno got the canoe moored. Then they heard the motor of a boat and detected a gray blob of movement behind them. Hack stood like a statue in the canoe. He couldn't move.

"Jump," yelled Bueno. "Quick!"

After a couple deep gulps of air, Hack took a flying leap towards the dock. But he crashed against it and splashed into the water that pulled him a few yards towards the sea. He screamed in panic. His arms and legs flailed.

"I can't swim," he hollered.

While Bueno scooted closer to the dock's edge,

the motor boat pulled up to the end. A single male got out. Bueno couldn't tell if it was one of the men from the big bay or not, but he was desperate.

"Please," Bueno called out. "Can you help my friend?"

"What are you doing here?" The man's brown woven hat was pulled down over his ears. His brown gloved hands clenched into balls. His dark eyes pierced into Bueno's.

While Hack floundered in the water, Bueno made another plea.

"Please, sir, help my friend."

"What have you boys been up to?" the man demanded. "Are you from the orphan farm?"

Desperate to save Hack, Bueno blurted out his first thought. He had never told a fib and he didn't know how.

"We rowed out to Hack's Hideaway and just came back. We meant no harm."

"Hideaway? Do you mean Tillamook Head?" The man shook Bueno until he got too rattled to think. "Where did you go? What did you see?"

"We saw three men and they seemed mean, so we came back."

Now Bueno couldn't bear it anymore. He tore away from the man and jumped into the salty water. He could see his friend going under again. He swam out and pulled Hack up by the chin to keep him afloat for several minutes, then slowly swam with him back to shore.

When he got there, the man he had talked to was gone, but both Miss Penelope Tagg and Miss Henrietta Ober, aides from the orphan farm, had arrived. Each held a switch. They scolded the boys as they revived Hack.

Later, Hack told Mr. Smythe, the director, they had been crab-trapping on behalf of the orphanage and he had slipped on the deck and fallen into the water.

"And you caught no crabs?"

"No, sir."

"I'm not surprised. The river's the best place for that. And Bueno saved you? From drowning?"

"Yes, he did. I cannot tell a lie."

"You owe him a debt of gratitude and so do we."

It would be a long time before Hack ever tried to visit his hideaway again.

CHAPTER ONE

Sunday afternoon, June 11, 1905,
south of Portland

"I thought you was dead." The words rumbled out of some deep, dark pit of tales told at late night campfires and smoky saloons. Thick drops of dirty sweat careened down the bearded man's face. A ripped-in-shreds shirt sleeve exposed a long, jagged old scar on his left arm. Bloodshot brown eyes glared into the future as if forecasting bad news. Very bad news.

"A common mistake."

A faded, red bandana brushed the man's bulging neck. His bronzed face held to the tight expression of a man looking for an advantage. "No foolin'. Argentiferous Jones said he shot you dead over a poker hand in Bisbee. I believe you was packin' three queens."

"He was wrong." Every eye in the dining car watched the trigger of Stuart Brannon's drawn Colt .44 revolver, ready to witness a sudden blast.

"I can see that now and would like to be given a chance to atone for my erroneous assumption."

"I'm sure you would. You stopped this train on a tall trestle in the middle of a river, cold-

15

cocked the conductor, stole the possessions of all the passengers and whatever else of cargo you found on board, and in the mix scared the women, children, and most of the men near to death. Out West a man can hang for such offenses."

He tried to straighten his bow-legs, puffed out his huge chest. His good eye glared at Brannon like the headlight of a locomotive. "What do you get out of this? Surely you don't expect to shoot me in front of these delicate ladies. What if I just put down my pistol and . . ."

Brannon glared right back. "And what do all of us get out of that?"

The man croaked out the words. "A clear conscience?"

"Already got one." Brannon shoved the muzzle closer to the man's ripped ten-gallon-hat with the creased crown and molded brim.

"What if I return the money and goods to all these fine folks on the train?"

"That's a start."

He dropped a leather sack to the carpeted floor, stepped back, and raised his hands. "What else can I do?"

"Hike down the track to the next town and turn yourself in to the sheriff for robbing this train."

"You mean, turn myself in on my own accord?"

"Yep. You can do it. We'll just ride on up ahead and let them know you're on your way."

"No one does that, especially Slash Barranca."
He studied Brannon to watch for the reaction.

Brannon didn't blink. "Well, Slash, here's your chance to stand out from a crowd of no-goods."

"So, you know who I am?"

"Nope. Never heard of you."

"Are you sure you're the original Stuart Brannon?"

"The real question is, do you trust that I'm Stuart Brannon? If you aren't certain, then make your move and see what happens. And if you still wonder, then say goodbye to these nice folks. I'm pullin' this trigger right now. So, what's your choice?"

The man looked over the crowd. His gaze stopped at two men in their fifties in brown suits. One of them glared a kind of warning. The other looked down. For a moment, Brannon wondered if Barranca was going to make an appeal to them. But his chin drooped to his chest and his words blurted out with such force, the windows almost rattled. "Yeah, you're Brannon, all right."

"Good. Leave the stash, your gun and your boots in the car. Then, start walkin'."

"Now, how do you expect me to make it to town without boots?"

"Very slow. By the time you get to the other side of the bridge, there should be a nice little posse gathered. And don't think about diving over the edge. You've got one foot of water and a fifty foot drop."

Slash Barranca pulled up his pants' legs as he climbed out of the train and stepped onto the rough track surface. Applause and "hurrahs" rocked the car as the train rolled away without the bootless outlaw. The staff seemed eager to return order and routine for the passengers as quick as possible. Announcements of supper followed with beefsteak, fried eggs and fried potatoes wheeled out to the dining car. A little overdone, but no one complained.

A huge sign made of logs greeted them at the next stop when they transported the injured conductor off the train.

100 Miles to Portland, Oregon
Home of the world's famous
Lewis and Clark Centennial Exposition

Brannon stretched his arms and legs and tried to remove the dust from his travel suit. No amount of brushing or shaking made a dent. He pulled out a copy of *Treasure Island* by Robert Louis Stevenson that his daughter-in-law, Jannette, had given him before he left Arizona, but his mind wandered. He ran through the recent events once more.

It started at the Prescott Post Office with one of those rosy-smelling letters from Lady Harriet Reed-Fletcher.

When Lady Fletcher sends you a scented letter, it's a dangerous omen.

The answer he gave her was "no."

At fifty-eight years old, Stuart Brannon had no intention of leaving his beloved ranch or Arizona Territory, not even for a long-time, good friend like Harriet. No matter how many times she offered her appeal—"I need one more celebrity . . . It's for the Willamette Orphan Farm . . . It won't cost you anything." But she could not convince him to go to Oregon, especially to participate in a golf tournament charity event in conjunction with the Lewis and Clark Centennial Exposition.

What was she thinking?

Yes, Captains Lewis and Clark were his heroes.

Yes, they deserved a gala celebration.

And yes, from what he heard, the Oregon coast promised a refreshing change from the desert landscape.

But he had never once picked up a golf club.

An old rancher and retired lawman playing on a golf course? What a ridiculous idea.

And the Triple B ranch needed him.

Or he needed the ranch, since his adopted son, Littlefoot Brannon, could oversee and do most of the work.

Life had become a peaceful routine. L.F. and his wife, Jannette, provided him with four over-active grandchildren, who played tag, leapfrog, hopscotch and occasional simple card games, but more important, listened to his stories.

No more evil men to track down. No one trying to shoot him in the back. No lawless gangs preying on the innocent . . . not near his ranch anyway.

Then the telegram came from another friend, Theodore Roosevelt. *Stuart, I need you in Portland. Tom Wiseman is missing. I think there's a cover-up going on. Say you're going to the Exposition. Find out how a U.S. Marshal can disappear and no one knows why. T.R.*

If Tom Wiseman had vanished, Brannon suspected the marshal initiated the event. But why? And where?

But he was too close a friend to ignore this plea. As a government worker, as well as an Arizona rancher, Tom Wiseman had aided him with personal and legal problems. And many times Tom Wiseman had stood with Brannon against lawbreakers, when no one else could or would.

And how could he refuse a request from the President of the United States?

Still, Brannon wondered how much help he could contribute. He could track Wiseman through the hills of Colorado or the deserts of Arizona. But searching the coastal environs of Oregon? A local might do better.

The boy who tugged on his pant leg looked a bit older than his grandson, Everett, but he had similar big, brown eyes that looked at the world like a ball of mystery that had to be pounced on, juggled and unraveled anew each day. "Mr. Brannon, you're famous like them two explorers, Lewis and Clark, aren't ya?"

Brannon tussled the boy's copper-colored hair. "Son, some Arizona outlaws know my name, but few others."

"My daddy says . . . he's the man sitting way over there by that window holding his hat between his knees. The pretty lady next to him with the red hair and reading a book is my mama." The boy swallowed and wiped his nose with his sleeve.

Brannon guessed the man to be in his thirties, dark-haired, but already starting to bald. Next to the woman was a young girl with auburn hair, fresh into puberty, holding a squalling baby. "What does your daddy say?"

"He told me you done cattle drives all over South America and brought more than a thousand Mexican beef into Arizona Territory, all by your lonesome, and kilt off a hundred horses in the bargain, run 'em right into the ground."

"Now, son, that's what mountain man Jim Bridger called stretchers. I want you to get it right, tell it straight. I did have the privilege of helping out with several of the great cattle drives, but that was to Kansas. And I entered Arizona Territory with two hundred head."

"You oughta know and you can call me Drift. That's the name I'm going by when I'm all growed up and carryin' a Colt revolver, just like yours. Then I'll be a brave captain in the U.S. Army and kill over a thousand . . ."

"Well, Drift, I did some scouting for them. That's all."

"And you built your ranch out of all the gold you prospected at the Little Stephen Mine. At sunrise it shines like heaven's streets."

"I'm afraid I didn't wind up with more than a small poke from that mine and my Triple B house is made of wood and very rustic. In fact, it's gotten a tad rundown over the years. Your daddy's tellin' you some mighty huge windies." He winked at the boy.

"But how about that time you was a U.S. Marshal with Wyatt Earp and Buffalo Bill Cody as your deputies and you three saved all those drowning women from a terrible flood in that huge canyon?"

"Why, I do believe I've never heard that one before and don't even know an event close to make it an exaggeration. That one's an outright lie."

"Mama says honest men always become famous. But Daddy says most that try to be brave end up dead. And here you lived through that shootout with the train robber, so you must be one of the honest ones. I do know you're famous.

My whole family knows you, even the ones back home in Dinuba. That's in Calyfornia." He hitched in a deep breath after his bigger-than-boy-sized soliloquy.

"Now remember, Drift, there was no shootout on this train. No gun was discharged." Brannon tried to give the boy something of importance to tell. "I have shaken hands with the President of our country and so did Lewis and Clark, only for them, it was President Jefferson instead of President Roosevelt, and they surely are famous."

The boy's face brightened and he ran off towards his parents, who kept looking in his direction. He did a kind of wave and nod, but they quickly turned their heads.

Brannon browsed the fields and hills they passed, filled with town sites, barbed wire fences, painted barns. A landscape both frontier and modern. One scene portrayed a slipshod claim shack with a brand new motor car parked outside.

Farmers and their families had come in droves at the enticement of railroad advertisements to fill up and fertilize the land, with promises of low prices and ownership. One way to populate the West in record time. Otherwise the tracks were laid on vast expanses of empty prairies and wilderness.

Before the railroads, those were the days. Vacant . . . wild . . . free.

Back when men like Stuart Brannon and Tom

Wiseman established ranches, raised their families, tried to tame the borderlands by self-protection and the Code of the West before official law ruled.

In 1898 Wiseman called at the Triple B with a request, "We're starting a volunteer cowboy regiment. Can you help us get some recruits?" Brannon didn't hesitate. He did his part to enable them to be one of the first in the West to fill their quota to fight in the Spanish-American war.

Some mighty excellent men have been part of A Troop and Roosevelt's Rough Riders. Tom has served his country well.

Now Tom Wiseman needed someone in this country to come to his aid. How, exactly, Brannon didn't know. He couldn't believe that anyone could get the draw on his friend.

When Lady Harriet Reed-Fletcher learned that Brannon was headed to Portland, she hurried back a telegram of her own. *You're needed in Gearhart. The orphans need you. Besides, Tom Wiseman last seen near here. We can help. Will meet you at Gearhart depot. Your friend always, Harriet*

CHAPTER TWO

The train made a stop at the crowded Portland depot. Brannon took time to admire the impressive Italian Renaissance style in brick, stucco and sandstone, built in a graceful curve that confronted downtown. He craned his neck at the tall clock tower that he figured rose to a hundred fifty feet or so.

Posters everywhere advertised trolley lines, steamers, and exhibits for the Centennial Exposition. Brannon detected languages spoken from every conceivable country, a gibberish of noise. He expected to see the Tower of Babel rising to the cobalt, celestial sky. Or flames, tongues of fire, to appear and settle on their heads.

An excited, but orderly, procession of humanity buzzed and milled around him. Families rushed to coaches or ticket booths. Suited businessmen gathered in groups. Peddlers pushed carts full of soap, produce, flowers and amenities of all kinds. Free enterprise in its purest form.

Brannon gazed at signs that pointed out directions to the recently constructed baseball stadium at Vaughn Street Park and Guild's Lake, the setting for the huge fair. One billboard boasted the motto: "Westward The Course of Empire Takes Its Way."

Brannon opened one of the back cars. Tres Vientos reared up at the sight of him and pawed to get out. "I dread letting you out here in the public square, boy, but I know you're gettin' stiff and rank. You need some exercise. Ignore all that noise and confusion." The big black horse tossed his head, shaking his ebony mane.

Brannon led him out for a short walk, then gently eased up into the saddle. Tres Vientos reared up again and veered into the traffic. Horns blared. Brakes squealed. Drivers yelled as they veered around and past them. Tres Vientos shook his head side to side in jerks and tosses. He pulled hard against the reins.

"Hey, you!" a man shouted. "Mr. Brannon, stop! We want to talk to you."

Brannon yanked the reins on Tres Vientos and turned him around. Three in the crowd rushed towards him. Two of them he recognized as the brown-suited men on the train.

Brannon tried to steer the horse in their direction, but he galloped down the street the other way, weaving between pedestrians, bicyclists, motorists, flower carts and fruit stands. Hats flew. People fell. Screams echoed everywhere.

Tres Vientos galloped past ticket booths and rumbled towards a huge colonnade entrance. Brannon groaned as he wondered how the big horse would choose an opening quick enough not to crash into one of the columns or visitors to the Exposition. Brannon tried to signal with his thighs, his knees, his heels, his shouts. Tres Vientos was too far gone.

They squeezed through an opening under the words "Westward The Course of Empire Takes Its Way," but not without a painful scrape on Brannon's left leg. Tres Vientos plummeted down a path headed to the Bridge of All Nations. The horse pounded across the wooden structure built to imitate solid masonry. More than two thousand feet long, it crossed Guild's Lake dotted with manmade islands and singing gondoliers. A huge hot air balloon flew overhead with arms waving over the side. Tres Vientos refused to slow until they heaved in front of a building with two tall towers at the end of the peninsula with the title, *United States Government.*

"Whoa, boy, you've got us in a heap of trouble." Sweat soaked Brannon's shirt. He reached up to straighten his cocked black Stetson hat.

Plaid jackets and striped pants don't make a quiet fashion statement. Neither do they calm a nervous horse. A man dressed like this crept close and opened a mahogany Commodore camera on the walk in front of them.

Surely he is not dumb enough to try to take our photograph.

The black horse kicked and wheeled around to

circle a bronze statue of Sacagawea with baby in cradleboard, hand raised high to the west. But Tres Vientos shot east across another bridge to the other side of the Exposition.

Round they went as they streaked by parks, benches and gardens. Brannon strained forward to keep his balance. Flashes of gleaming white structures with archways, fluted columns and red roofs, manicured landscapes, domes and cupolas blurred on either side. Crammed squares of vendors hawked their wares. Street musicians and a team of acrobats performed on the walkway.

Far beyond the striated, fat cone of Mt. St. Helens, Mt. Hood, Oregon's highest mountain, loomed. Brannon almost slowed his steed beside a Centennial Park, but Tres Vientos trotted to the amusement center and the whirlwind ride. A loud boom startled the horse into full gallop again. Parasol-twirling ladies gawked. Bespectacled gentlemen backed away. This world fair may have been constructed as a fantasy land, a fairy tale for visitors, but at the moment, it was a full-blown nightmare for Brannon.

I so want to be back at the Triple B ranch in Arizona! "Whoa, boy, whoa!"

Brannon re-centered himself, body upright, to get in rhythm with the horse. He focused to stay on, to keep riding no matter what. "Relax, boy, it's okay. Stay calm," he said in his best mono-tone. He tried a squeeze and release motion until Tres Vientos began to slow way down.

Brannon finally got him stopped near a huge log cabin building, very different in style than the other Spanish Renaissance architecture they passed. Walls were made of massive logs and fronted by a portico of tree trunks. A black canvas-covered wagon pulled by two teams of gray, braying mules was parked in front. One of the mules gave a half-hearted, sideways kick at Brannon. The others looked him over in that curious, quizzical way typical of the dim-witted brutes.

As Brannon tied Tres Vientos to a post, bells and whistles, loud clops of hooves and a whir of wheels squalled behind them. With white horses in the lead, three fire engines surrounded them. Brannon held tight as his horse attempted to whirl and buck.

At least six uniformed men from each red truck jumped out, plus a man in a black suit, starched white collar and harsh part down the middle of his hair above a stern, in-charge face.

They've got a fire department? This is an exposition in full party mode, but equipped like a city.

The dark-suited man about Brannon's height called out, "What's going on here?"

Brannon began to apologize when a gray-haired, gray-bearded man from the log building interrupted. "Good afternoon, Mr. Goode, you do know who this man is?"

A murmur rose up from the firemen as they whispered. Mr. Goode didn't reply. "Stuart, this is Mr. Henry Goode, President of the Board of Directors for the Centennial. Mr. Goode, I'd like to introduce you to the one and only, Stuart Brannon, the real live hero of The Wild West Series dime novels. He's here to help us promote the Exposition and did a better job than I expected."

"Miller!" Brannon spewed out. *Hawthorne Miller! Out of this big, wide world, how did he and I get connected again? I'm not here to do anything for him. And what does he mean our dime novels? I've never seen a single dime. Not that I care about that.*

"You're supposed to apply for special events. I don't have any paperwork concerning this display. It's not on our records."

"That's true," Miller blurted. "I did not know exactly what day Mr. Brannon would appear. He is as big a surprise for me as he is for you. But I do vouch for his identity."

"Very good, Mr. Miller. We do appreciate any legitimate entertainment. But we also have a protocol. The men will ride back to the fire station and I'll get busy with the business of the Exposition. Stop by and fill out the proper papers, please." He tipped his hat first to Miller, then to Brannon.

With much noise and bluster about who

followed whom, the fire trucks caravanned back down the street.

Brannon offered a quick word of thanks to Miller, then reached for Tres Vientos' reins. "Not so quick, Mr. Brannon. The least you could do is come in and sign some books for me."

Brannon started to protest and wondered how much longer until the train pulled out for Gearhart. He sighed, tied up Tres Vientos, and followed Miller into the huge log building.

Inside Brannon gazed at an interior like the nave of a cathedral. Colonnades of tree trunks supported a high ceiling. Multitudes of displays exhibited samples of lumber, dioramas of wildlife such as elk and panthers, plus galleries of Indian photographs and artwork. He admired one of a youthful barefoot Indian sprinting the length of a hilltop at dusk, holding high a lighted torch. Below, villagers being attacked by another tribe, craned their necks up to the torch-bearer. The painting was captioned "Catcher-Of-The-Sun Runs High."

Then, he stared in stunned amazement at a large framed image of himself with school-teacher Rose Creek in her beaded buckskins, moccasins, and her long, raven hair braided.

That day at Paradise Meadow.

"I don't like this any more than you, Stuart," Rose had told him. "Posing as a trinket in these buckskins for some promoter like Miller is not my idea of dignity. But he did help us when we needed him."

As compensation for his secreting an infamous prisoner out of town . . . whom vigilantes wanted to hang. Appreciated, but I wonder if he would have done it otherwise. He always has an angle for everything . . . and it usually means exploiting me.

Brannon hurried past the gallery of photographs and followed Miller to a table display of yellow-paged, paperback dime novels, small enough to fit in a soldier's or sailor's pocket, all of them with Hawthorne Miller's name prominent on the covers. Each of them purported to be adventures of Stuart Brannon, illustrated and fantasized. A large circle surrounded the figure of ten cents.

"Be much obliged for your autographs," Miller said.

"I don't know if I could copy the signature that you use all the time," Brannon commented. "Folks might think I'm forging my own name."

Miller's face turned a shade of crimson.

Brannon glanced at some of the titles: *Brannon Blasts the Collectors, Brannon of the Wild West Series.* He noticed the lithograph of himself and Rose Creek on the cover of *Stuart Brannon Tames the Town.* He picked up one entitled *The Man Who Killed Stuart Brannon,* flipped the pages and stopped at number 32:

"You think you're going to kill me?"

Stale sweat hung thick as cigarette smoke as the startled occupants of the long, narrow saloon faded into the walls like a cheap backdrop curtain for a traveling stage play.

"I've got a gun. You have a knife. Seems unavoidable at the moment." The tall, broad shouldered man with the drawn gun didn't flinch. "Turn Jenny loose and we'll renegotiate."

The girl stumbled as she was yanked one step closer to the front door. "Back away, mister, and I'll let her go unharmed."

"Make your play." The man with the gun inched his way to the right of the overturned table. "I'm tired."

The man waved the knife like a painter at a grand easel. "You can't kill me. Do you know who I am?"

"No, but your mama does." He scooted to the right and slid another step closer. "I don't think this is her proudest hour."

As if unveiling a statue, the knife-wielder shouted, "I am Argentiferous Jones. I'm the man who killed Stuart Brannon."

"So, you're the one?"

"Yep. Causes you to pause and ponder, don't it?"

"Not really. I'm Stuart Brannon and I'm very much alive."

Brannon laid down the book with care, brushed it off with his hand as though to clear dust and

33

germs, raised that same hand into a clenched fist . . . and punched Hawthorne Miller in the nose.

Hawthorne Miller screamed and grabbed for a handkerchief, blood gushing down his white shirt.

Brannon stormed for the door, untied Tres Vientos' reins, and climbed in the Visalia saddle. "I have information about what happened to Tom Wiseman," Miller yelled after him. "But I won't tell you. Not ever. Never. No matter what. You're no hero, Stuart Brannon. You're a coward. That's what you are. And I can make you into a villain anytime I want. I've got the power. You better believe it."

Brannon kept riding until he couldn't hear Miller's rants anymore, afraid to turn his horse around and get himself, Miller or Tres Vientos riled again.

How on earth did that man even know I was looking for Tom? I shouldn't have hit him. I should have stayed calm and friendly, fed into his confidence. Maybe he does know something. Perhaps I'd be going to find Tom right now. But I can't be dishonest like that. However, I didn't hesitate to do him violence. Am I a violent man? Oh, Lord, me and my temper. Help me.

Just as he approached the French exhibit, several men on horseback dressed as Swiss Guards rode beside him. They handed him a card and returned to the entrance.

He turned over the Official Mailing Card of the Lewis & Clark Centennial with a picture of the exhibit by France on the front. On the back it read: *Stewart: Meet me in the Louis XIV Drawing Room. Wear your hat. Tom*

CHAPTER THREE

Tom Wiseman had helped Brannon with several legal wrangles and filing of papers through the years, such as the adoption papers for Lightfoot when their friend Judge Quilici died. Tom knew the man who directed the Bureau of Indian Affairs. Or what about the Spanish Land Grant fraud over his Arizona property? Tom Wiseman knew how to spell Brannon's given name. Second, that cursive handwriting . . . Tom preferred to print. This note wasn't from Tom.

But Brannon was curious . . . and anxious to solve the mystery that surrounded his old friend Tom. He didn't want to miss another opportunity, however suspicious. Perhaps some clue lurked in the Louis XIV Drawing Room.

He saluted at the Swiss Guards and stepped into an opulent display of European flourishes and centuries-old artifacts, now being viewed by crowds of vacationers. He weaved in and out of a throng of onlookers to follow a sign to the Drawing Room. *How am I supposed to know who sent me that note? This place is crammed with people.*

Decor of gold and silver brocade on crimson formed the backdrop to many world famous paintings on rich wood paneling.

Lord and Lady Fletcher would know the names of these works of art and their creators, I'm sure.

On several mantels sat porcelain vases, a bust of Louis XIV, a barometer clock and four candelabras. A bed had been shoved into an alcove. A carved and gilded wood balustrade separated the alcove from the rest of the chamber. Over the bed hung a stucco allegory of France.

He gazed at a narrow plush dark brown and cream chair with white pillows studded with crystal gemstones and gold tassels.

How could anyone be comfortable sitting on such a thing?

A sudden creaking movement from the ceiling caused him to reach for the revolver under his coat. He looked up to gawk at a woman who swung straight at him from a chandelier. Black sausage curls and a swirl of forest green and burgundy dresses over a hooped skirt swayed. She smashed against him and he sprawled across King Louis XIV's bed, crashing it to the floor.

"So sorry. I was cleaning the light," the young lady whispered at him. "I meant only to get a peek at you. Quick. Dash across the room to the sword display before they come get us."

Brannon struggled to untangle himself from the woman's wardrobe, both their legs and arms flailing. He bruised his hand against something hard.

"Ouch," she said and slugged him in the back.

Brannon felt at a distinct disadvantage in this war of escape as her dress was cut low both in the front and back and off the shoulders. He had nothing to push or pull, so he shut his eyes and rolled hard to the right and banged against a burgundy wall that collapsed. Screams filled the room as he raised up and scooted through the crowd to a wooden panoply of crossed swords. Just as he reached them, a man in full mustache and beard pushed a blade against his side.

"Stay right where you are, mister," he growled.

Brannon yanked at one of the swords as he elbowed the man's arm but the weapon wouldn't budge. *I don't know how to use it anyway.* The knife slashed his jacket. The people around them scattered away while four Swiss Guards moved in. The chandelier woman grabbed his arm to pull him down a hallway and into a side door . . . a room full of mirrors.

"Who are you, lady?" he demanded. "What's this all about?"

But the woman disappeared. All he could see was himself in a hundred different images. He felt all over for a doorknob. Not finding one, Brannon pulled out his Colt revolver and shot the glass into splinters and falling panes. When he glimpsed the woman bolting between dark exposed walls, he chased after her. Only when he tripped over boards and mystery objects was he forced to stop.

No sign of the woman.

Brannon shoved his hands around to feel the narrow passageway. He kept walking until he bumped against a wall with a latch. Pulling on it, he shaded his eyes against the streak of sunlight. *I'm in an alleyway, but where?*

He thought he recognized the corner of the Forestry Building down to his far left. He scooted the opposite direction, turned a corner, but didn't find Tres Vientos tied to the front colonnade of the French exhibit.

Brannon sprinted up and down the streets looking in every nook and square of landscaped lawn. He finally found Tres Vientos chewing grass and gnawing blooms at the Centennial Park and Experimental Gardens. He grabbed the dragging reins, scolded the horse as quietly as he could, then maneuvered onto the Visalia saddle.

With many bows and apologies, Brannon made his way around the Exposition, past park benches, a whirlwind of acts and rides, and light fixtures. They trotted through the packed bridge, then eased back through the looming colonnade where he raised up in the stirrups and reached into his pants pocket to pull out some coins. He found two silver dollar pieces, one for him, one for his horse. He tossed them at the ticket booths and yelled, "Keep the change."

They returned to the depot as the whistle signaled departure. He wasn't the only one in a suit and hat hustling to the train.

He crammed a cantankerous, unhappy Tres Vientos into the back car and as he tried to be dignified, rushed to board himself when he was accosted again by the brown-suited men. One man with them that he didn't recognize wore a badge. "Mr. Brannon, you're wanted for questioning."

"About what?"

The young deputy knotted his face into a stern frown. "For harassing patrons of the Centennial, for intruding into the protocol of the Northern Pacific line, so that they're almost two hours off schedule, and for taking the law into your own hands."

"You mean, for stopping a robber from getting away with loot he stole from Northern Pacific passengers?"

"Duly appointed officers could and should have taken care of him. Your . . . your misplaced chivalry, your interference, terrorized and endangered the lives of every passenger." The deputy paused to take a breath. His whole body shook with fervor. "We're a civilized country now, Mr. Brannon. We don't need aging gunmen saving the West anymore. Take the train out of town or go to jail. Your choice."

Stuart Brannon took a quick study of the young lawman, hand hunched over his weapon, eyes darting everywhere to see who might be watching his bravado. "What's your name, son? I'd like to commend you to your superior for a job well done."

The deputy's eyebrows raised. He hesitated in a brief fit of confusion, then swelled his chest. "I'm Harvey Kliever of the Clatsop County police force, but I also work for the railroad part-time."

"Well, Deputy Kliever, I heard you got your outlaw. Now, I've got to get to the coast. Some people are waiting for me."

A glint of triumph shined in his eyes. "Okay, Mr. Brannon. We'll let it go this time," he said loud enough for any on this car to hear. "But you watch yourself. You've stepped over a line. It's not like it was in the old days."

Deputy Kliever got on the train with him, but sat in a front car.

Brannon thought he noticed the passengers doing a lot of whispering when he walked by. Some reached out to shake his hand. A few shot glares his way. Most ignored him. That suited him fine. He was much relieved to find his duffles still under the seat, with his new-fangled take-down Winchester rifle in the leather case tucked inside.

The train rolled out of the depot on the single track and began the long trek west, across Young's Bay to Astoria, then south along the coast to Gearhart. Brannon closed his eyes, let his mind go blank and his body unwind for the four or five hour trip. *What's a Clatsop County deputy doing in Portland? He said he also works for the railroad . . . guess that's why. That's his business and none of my own.*

After a brief nap, he admired the lush groves with stubby and tall trees that lined the narrow track . . . firs, maples, spruce, cedars, pines. Moss hung from branches like door curtains. Fronds and ferns covered the ground with beds of undergrowth. Thick. Almost a claustrophobic feel. The striking contrast of multiple shades of green so different from the Arizona desert.

In the old days, Brannon would have wondered who hid in the bushes.

The conductor made odd stops, waited for stragglers, backed up for forgotten items and once a lost child. A leisurely four-dollar trip.

A few deer and elk grazed in vast meadows of deep purple. Brannon could almost hear the ring of the bluebells as they went from pastures, over hills, through thick glades, across creeks and bridges that spanned bays. Finally an expansive view of the ocean and the first scent of that lingering fishy, tangy air.

Brannon noticed the deputy got off the train at Astoria and pulled his horse out of a back car, who handled the sights and sounds of the city just fine.

Brannon snoozed off and on the rest of the way to Gearhart, with snatches of forest, beach and shoreline views.

After the short jaunt south, he was greeted at the Gearhart Depot by Lord Edwin Fletcher and Lady Harriet Reed-Fletcher with their Buick Model C Touring Car, even though the hotel was within walking distance.

"We had to come greet you." Lady Fletcher flung her arms around him for a long hug. "We've been to Seaside to buy some petrol."

And show off your auto car.

Brannon grasped Fletcher's hand and nearly wrenched it.

He was glad to be free of the constant rock and rumble of the train and couldn't help admire the yellow top and wheels, black upholstery and gold-rimmed headlights. The sort of transportation he'd presume for the Fletchers, although he halfway expected a Rolls Royce or Renault. He also treasured the reunion with his old friends.

I'm already glad I came. He marveled at the parts of the auto car again.

His New Mexico friends, Doc and Velvet Shepherd, owned a Ford Model F. In fact, there were a number of those wheeling around the streets of Prescott, as well as Thomas autos and Oldsmobiles. L.F. wanted a motor car for his growing family. But Brannon so far had refused to even consider one for himself. *So hard to fix, to ride over those bumpy roads, to keep gas in the ornery contraptions. Of course, horse transportation had its negatives too.*

Tres Vientos tagged along behind with worried eyes and a very fast trot.

"Suit, tie, hat and boots . . . you look good, Stuart," Lady Fletcher said. "But did you have to include the rip in the jacket? Just like the old days?"

"It was a long, long ride to get here."

"I realize that. We have so enjoyed our touring around this part of the U.S."

Lord Fletcher tossed his walking stick in the back. "Yes, but it's bittersweet to explore territory that Britain once owned. We British have given up so much land all over the world. It's a pity."

Brannon glanced at the fancy cane—T-style handle, jade and enamel with ruby borders on an ebony shaft. "You can't rule it all," Brannon remarked. "Your country needs to learn to share."

"We are a generous lot, too generous at times."

"Did you get a chance to visit the Exposition?" Lady Fletcher asked.

"Yes, you might say I did. Quite impressive."

"An achievement, to be sure," Lord Fletcher replied. "Could be a huge turning point for Portland, if not the whole state of Oregon. But all the lathe and plaster structures, meant to come down. Nothing permanent. Meanwhile, this state can leave its rugged frontier days behind and move into the modern era. That's what I've heard the committee claim."

Lady Fletcher patted his shoulder. "Too bad you didn't get to view it at night. Hundreds of thousands of lights on the site, I hear. They want to burn some sort of red powder mixture on Mt. Hood and make it seem to be wrapped in flames . . . with massive statues of Lewis and Clark. They lack nothing in vision, I do say. You must see that on your return."

Brannon tamped down his blowing hat. "Why haven't you been there?"

Lady Fletcher chuckled. "Oh, we will. We didn't dare go there first or we'd never get Laira to come here to Gearhart. That's promised to her on our way back to England . . . a sort of reward. Perhaps a bribe."

"Your daughter's here? How about my namesake, young Stuart?"

Lord Fletcher sighed. "I'm sorry to say the lad's played hooky again from Oxford and ventured to Africa . . . or is it Asia? I can't keep up."

"Edwin, you know perfectly well it's Asia. Your chest swells so much you've stretched all your coats."

"Sounds like young Stuart's a lot like his father," Brannon said.

"Yes, quite. You've already gotten some mail." Lady Fletcher handed him two postcards.

Brannon patted his pocket, then opened it wide. His face twitched as he stretched to feel all over his jacket, down his pants and into the seat. He checked the floor of the car. His heart sank as he realized that the new eyeglasses that he needed to see close-ups, some extra gold and silver coins, and especially the gold locket with his late wife's picture were all gone. *Lisa!*

"I take it that something's missing," Lady Fletcher replied.

"Nothing's there. I've lost them all."

He thought back to the last time he'd viewed those items. He'd pulled them out of his duffle this morning on the train . . . or was it yesterday morning? He'd bought his ticket with one of the coins. Then, he required the glasses to read his train ticket and later a newspaper. When was that? And he never parted from the locket . . . not once these last thirty years since that Christmas Day that she and the baby died.

Maybe that rough ride on Tres Vientos through the crowd at the Exposition had emptied his pocket. Somehow he got jerked around enough that they fell out. Or . . . or that chandelier woman at the French exhibit. Could she have stolen them in the chaos of that tumble on the bed?

Brannon groaned as Lady Fletcher looked back again to study his face. "Are you unwell?" she asked.

His chest tightened so he couldn't breathe. It was impossible to gasp out a word. *This is almost as bad as the day Hank Jedel fired the cannon at the Piñon Pines and the graves of Lisa and the baby. Lord, help me gain control. I can't get diverted by personal business. I'm on an important mission.*

The three-story plus dormer Gearhart Hotel with its winding stairs and wrap-around decks offered plush rooms, wicker chairs everywhere, and a lobby that reeked of Havana cigars. An evening array of lighted Chinese lanterns decorated the grounds.

Brannon delivered Tres Vientos into a well-stocked and cared-for stable and barn on the hotel grounds, then slipped into his room, pulled off the beaver felt Stetson and laid it, crown down, on a mahogany table. He tossed his duffles on the blue, canopied bed and searched them several times without finding the coins, glasses or locket. He slapped his hat back on and slammed the doorframe with his fist.

CHAPTER FOUR

Lady Fletcher met him in the lobby and handed him a telegram. He reached for his glasses, then remembered. He had to ask her to read it and the postcards from his precocious four-year-old granddaughter, Elizabeth, who asked him to describe "everything he possibly could" about the ocean. "To be there with you would be so fun," she had related to her mother, Jannette, who wrote the note. She also drew heads of her whole family . . . papa, mama, grandpa, brother Everett, five years old; brother Edwin, two years old; and baby brother, Jenner.

The other postcard stated: "Everett made me play cowboys and Indians. He was the cowboy. I was Sacagawea. He had a stick gun, but he wouldn't let me have a weapon because I am a girl, so I never could win. Got a new hat to wear to the Sunday picnic."

Neither he nor Lady Fletcher could prevent a full smile as he tucked the cards in his pocket.

The telegram, however, was cryptic and left them both puzzled. *Verify everyone. Report anything suspicious. T.R.*

• • •

Hawthorne H. Miller dabbed his bloody, throbbing nose as he cursed the hero of his dozens of novels that had brought him fame and fortune across the country and in many places foreign to the western U.S.

"What an ingrate. That Brannon doesn't deserve one whit of the adulation that my books have brought him. I'll destroy him. I built him into what he is today. I practically created him from scratch. Now I'll tear him down. I'll tell the world the truth about Mr. Stuart Brannon, that he is a vile man, not worthy of their esteem. It will be my life's mission, a very satisfying one. A worthy one. To point out the evil of those unduly revered."

Miller rushed to his wagon to pull out a clean shirt, sheets of paper and his typewriter. He carted them into the forestry log cabin and over to the desk by his display of novels. He crammed a sheet of paper in and began feverishly to type: *The Private Life of Stuart Brannon, An Exposé.*

He ignored the squeals so common from passersby as they recognized the book titles.

"Stuart Brannon dime novels . . . right here at the Exposition . . . and they're already autographed."

"I'd pay anything for these."

"I'd pay more for a glimpse, a handshake from the man himself."

You'll pay more for what I'm about to reveal.

Miller's hands flew over the keys. *"You think you're going to tell the world? No one's going to know about you and me and all the kids I abandoned years ago."* Brannon cocked the revolver and aimed at the woman's forehead. She held her baby boy tight, trying to keep him safe from the bullet she knew would end her life.

Miller paused. He started to doubt himself, but it quickly passed. *Yes, yes, they'll believe me. They'll never look at Brannon the same again. He'll be the black cockroach crunched under their grimy boots. He'll be the over-sized maggot crawling in their outhouse sludge. He'll be the scum of their pitiful piece of earth.*

"Sir, can we pay you for these books?" Her brunette pompadour shined under a peacock-feathered hat. A gold and emerald broach sparkled. She dropped a dozen novels on the table and pulled out a wad of bills from her purse. "And how about that picture on the wall . . . of Stuart Brannon and the Indian girl? Do you have posters for sale? My relatives in St. Louis would all be thrilled to own such a memento of our trip."

Miller shot a surly scowl at the woman. He was in the throes of his most important work. *Wait. What did she say?* His blurred eyes fixed on the money stack. A faint quiver stirred his being. His head cleared. His nose stopped throbbing.

"Oh my, have you been hurt? Is that blood all over your shirt?"

Miller rubbed at the stains. He yanked the paper out of the typewriter and wiped his shirt with quick jerks of his hand. "It's nothing. I . . . uh . . . what can I do for you?" Miller plastered on his finest fake smile.

Miller took care of his customers and analyzed the profit he made in a matter of minutes. Deep in thought, he gazed at the poster on the wall that advertised the celebrity golf tournament in Gearhart, Stuart Brannon's image spliced between William "Wild Bill" Cody's and Wyatt Earp's. His mind churned full speed.

Stuart Brannon's legend intact means more fame and fortune for me.

He rushed to find the director of the Forestry Building. "Can you spare one of your workers or volunteers to take care of my display? I've got to be gone a few days. It's all a part of the Exposition. I'll hurry back as fast as I can."

That arrangement settled, he gathered up the typewriter and the rest of the paper, then changed shirts. In the back of the wagon, he restacked boxes of dime novels and copies of the enlarged photo of Brannon and Rose Creek. Then he arranged the wet-collodion-plate, the black bellows camera, the field and stereo cameras with the silver nitrate, plus the glass plates and paper around the hand-fashioned, traveling darkroom.

He whipped the horses around and headed them down the street past skipping children holding balloons and eating multi-colored fluffs of sweet fairy floss. Women whirled parasols. Men in plain suits lounged in groups over flasks of beer. Stripe-suited men stood in line with women in batiste and lace at the French Exhibit.

"*Bonjour*," Miller called out to the guards as he pulled off his hat. Then, he stopped to whip out a pencil and paper. He wrote: *Going to Gearhart. H. H. Miller.* "To Darcy," he instructed. He felt light, relieved of a heavy burden. He had regained his life's mission. *You know, Brannon's not really a bad chap. There's been a misunderstanding, but we'll get it squared away. And if we don't, it won't be wasted. Every situation that involves Stuart Brannon provides me writing material.*

Excitement grew from his crimped toes to the sprawling hair of his gray head as he realized that he'd done an awesome thing. He, Hawthorne Miller, had bestowed grace upon the great Stuart Brannon. In one magnanimous sweep of his will, he had given a very unworthy man back his reputation, his honor, his life.

CHAPTER FIVE

Monday, June 12

Brannon woke up grumpy, disoriented.

He tried to sleep in the four-poster, canopy bed. He sprawled all over the double bed, stretching the length and breadth. He spent half the night bumped up against the carvings of acanthus leaves, garlands and ribbons in the headboard. Then he tossed and turned on the too-soft mattress while a group of late arrivers partied in the hall and slammed doors way past midnight.

After another pitch and roll session, he got up to stretch the kinks in his back. He decided he might as well get dressed for the day. As he hobbled around barefoot looking for the shirt and boots he wore on the train, he stubbed a big toe on the bed's ball and claw feet, then stumbled over the spittoon. Limping out to the hall, he almost collided into Lady Fletcher, who was alert and ready for an early morning walk.

She gave him a quick hug. "It's so good having you here, somewhat of a miracle, I'd say." She tugged on his arm. "Come get some fresh air with me."

As soon as they ventured outdoors, Brannon

realized he'd forgotten his revolver. He stewed whether to return for it. *Relax. It's a stroll on the beach. No one dangerous will be up this time of morning.*

They strolled on the fine sand grains of the almost level beach. Waves could easily push this sand towards shore while prevailing winds blew it farther inland. Constant movement. Shifting, growing and shrinking.

Lady Fletcher reminisced about their memories long ago in Arizona, then concluded with, "It's hard to believe I'm actually staring again into the Atlantic Ocean–hazel eyes of a wide-shouldered, gray-haired man who still wears a dusty, black cowboy hat. After so many years apart, those creases around your eyes hint at hundreds of tales I may never get to hear."

"I've never been to the Atlantic Ocean."

Lady Fletcher chuckled. "Well, if you ever go, you'll find out the true color of your eyes."

"You said that Tom Wiseman was last seen in these parts?" Brannon thought he caught the movement of a silhouetted figure far behind them. He casually turned his head to get a better look.

"Yes, here in Gearhart. The hotel manager said he had an important meeting and that he reserved two extra rooms next to his and paid for them too. Three or four U.S. civil engineers and a few foreigners arrived. They had supper together, then several of the group left for a late walk out on the beach. Never saw Tom again."

The other morning hiker kept at a distance, stopped and stepped forward when they did. "Foreigners, you say? What nationality?"

"From what I could tell . . . Edwin and I happened to be sitting across the room from them . . . at least one was a Frenchman. Another was Latin descent . . . certainly South American or maybe Mexican."

"Harriet, I'm shocked. You're losing your touch." Brannon heard the scrape of a shoe on a rock and regretted leaving his gun in the hotel room. *Don't be so leery. It's a man dawdling on the shore, just like you and Harriet.*

"He was very much trying to hide who he was and where he came from. He wore a costume." She paused.

"Well, what was it?"

"Buckskins, moccasins and a band with feather. He wanted everyone to think he was an Indian."

"Maybe he was."

"Perhaps . . ." Lady Fletcher's voice was tinged with doubt.

The loitering man halted to light a cigarette and tossed what might be a match into the water. "Show me where Tom was last seen," Brannon requested.

Rain began to sprinkle in spurts and fitful splats as they skirted the water's hissing edge.

"It's not far from here." Lady Fletcher led him down the beach.

Brannon tried to take in the immensity of the vast ocean, to imagine the teeming multitudes of creatures below and the apparent chaos of living things above the surface. Yet a rhythm ruled in the cycle of life.

"I've found the beach to be an elixir to the senses," Lady Fletcher mused.

He closed his eyes to have his being resonate with thundering breakers, rolling waves, the odors of salt, fish and seaweed. When he opened them, he noted the undulating snakes of pattern on the wind-swept, water-whipped sand and that the man behind them had vanished.

The tide washed in again, spilling driftwood of a variety of shapes onto the rocky shore. Somewhere near this spot, one hundred years before, Captains Meriwether Lewis and William Clark first saw the restless breakers of the Pacific Ocean and the lush land that would supply them with fuel. But no ship on the horizon.

"Right about here," Lady Fletcher announced. "Tom Wiseman and several others . . . who, I don't know . . . were spotted beside a fire across from these boulders."

Brannon studied the stacked wood, ashes and rim of rocks from a recent campfire. "Who saw them?"

"Some hotel employees on their way home

after their late shifts. They recognized Wiseman because he called out, 'Good night, be careful of the jelly fish,' to them."

"Jelly fish?" Brannon spied the man with the cigarette again. He emerged from a rain fog that seemed to hug the ground and made no pretense that he had his focus on Brannon and Lady Fletcher.

"Yes, I guess there's been a lot of them washed up on the beach. They can sting, you know. About golf," Lady Fletcher was saying. "It's a royal and ancient game where you hit balls with sticks and it can be quite fun. Poor children do that in slums. I play it myself once in awhile."

Brannon tried to catch up with the conversation, though he hadn't noticed how the topic changed. "I hear tell it's only fit for unemployed Scotsmen. I've never played it and you know that. I'm goin' to look mighty foolish. Why did you think of me to compete in a tournament?"

"Well, first, I take exception to the Scotsmen remark. Perhaps if you referred to Englishmen. Edwin plays, you know. And it's not exactly a competition. You show up as a celebrity . . ."

"A very minor celebrity . . ."

"You're the most infamous man I know. Meanwhile, you will be given your own clubs, bag, caddy and . . . free lessons. It's for the orphans, Stuart."

They listened to the rhythm of the break of

surf, the billows of foam that rushed and roared against the rugged, rocky coastline. Ducks floated in a long row off the shore.

Brannon scoured the area where Wiseman had been for any signs or clues. He kicked the moist sand with the toe of his boot, then patted it flat. "I'm trying to determine why Tom agreed to come up here for this assignment. I checked with his two daughters in Prescott. He told them it was to be his last. But why this place?"

"Perhaps no other reason than the President ordered it?"

"That's logical, but he was often given choices. I'm wondering if it had to do with his admiration for Captains Lewis and Clark." Another person joined the man behind them . . . a woman wearing a dress of flowing, deep purple. They conversed a few moments, embraced, then she quickly strode away. The man remained and lit another cigarette.

"To think, we're walking the same ground they tramped," Lady Fletcher remarked.

"After that long, exhausting trek across the country, the fight for survival, then the tense waiting, hoping for some sign of a ship. That stirred up quite a controversy among them and later with historians."

"Stuart, speaking of controversy, about that train robbery. Some think as a citizen you had a right to defend yourself and the other passengers.

Others charge you jumped over some bounds."

"There's no way I could sit there and let that guy ride off without a challenge."

"I know that. But these are different times."

"Harriet, it's always right to fight evil. But let's change the subject. I'm wondering what it felt like to be camped out right here one hundred years ago."

"Tell me, which one are you most like? Captain Lewis or Captain Clark?"

"Not sure I have what it takes to be either one. I wish I could be more like Captain Clark . . . the negotiator, master of frontier arts. He had the greater gift of the two for making friends with the Indians."

"How long would you have waited?"

"A little bit longer than they did. I never was very good at breakin' promises. I was born to the land and raised by the code. Share your fire and food with whomever comes into camp. It's better to lose your life than your good reputation. If I said I'd be a certain place, that's where I'd be until the cows came home."

Lady Fletcher tugged her wool shawl around her neck against the coastal cool air. "But why didn't President Jefferson send a ship?"

"Ah, you're getting too political for me."

"But didn't he make a promise? Being President doesn't exempt him." She reached down and picked up a pearly pink shell. "I know you're here mainly to find Tom Wiseman, but I do ask you to attend at least three events."

"Which are?"

"The banquet tonight . . . the director and workers for the orphan farm will be here, along with some of the orphans."

"Where does that name Willamette derive from?"

"Sam Smythe's father started an orphanage in Salem by the Willamette Valley and Willamette River. This one's connected somehow."

"And the other events?"

"There's a pre-tournament social Friday evening. And, of course, the tournament next Saturday. That gives you a bit more than three days to solve this mystery."

"Okay." Brannon pursed his lips, wondering whether to say more.

"Oh, dear," she sighed. "And you really must sneak in some golf lessons too."

Brannon began to get that tight feeling that he was being controlled . . . and he didn't like it. He had two causes to champion. He needed to spend earnest time chewing on one, which was difficult for a man of action. The other he'd prefer to avoid altogether. But he also knew Lady Fletcher had her project, her benefit, and she followed through on every commitment she tackled.

This will certainly be no holiday, as Edwin would say. But Lord, I believe this is Your leading.

You want me here. So here I am. Help me do this with joy. Help me not fight Harriet or You.

Lady Fletcher tugged his arm once more. "Edwin will want me to bring you back to the hotel. What shall I tell him?"

"Tell him the salt hasn't boiled yet. He'll understand."

"But it's time for tea," she teased. "Oh, I know you like the dregs at the bottom of the pot of cowboy brew after it's been over the campfire four hours or so. Well, I can make you some tea every bit that strong."

"I'm sure you can."

She scanned his attire with a frown. "Please remember you're supposed to dress up to meet some dignitaries tonight."

"Ma'am, I truly don't know how you talk me into these things."

"Brannon!" The bass voice startled them. The former dusky figure appeared in full view.

Was he the man earlier on the beach?

Brannon's hand moved for the revolver that wasn't there.

CHAPTER SIX

He wore glasses with smoked lenses, top hat, diamond tie pin and carried a gold-headed cane as though he used it for a club, not as a walking aid. "Mr. Stuart Brannon? I'm Tally Rebozo."

"Are you from the orphan farm?" Lady Fletcher intruded before Brannon could respond.

"Orphan farm? What makes you think that?"

She scrutinized him more closely. "You show up out of nowhere, on this particular part of the Oregon beach, at this time of morning, wearing an expensive three piece silk suit. I say . . . you're a Serbian spy."

To Brannon, he looked more like a professional gambler.

"Who is this woman?" Rebozo said.

Brannon kept his eye on him and made the introduction. "This is Lady Harriet Reed-Fletcher."

"You mean, as in Lord and Lady Fletcher, the Ambassador?"

"That's the one."

"I did not know." Rebozo gave a deep bow. "Forgive my impertinence."

Lady Fletcher held out her hand. "You are forgiven. But the fact is, you could be a Serbian."

In the haze of early morning light, Rebozo pulled off his glasses and seemed to play with his smile. "Perhaps."

"Oh, good." Lady Fletcher clapped with delight. "That will make conversation around our supper table much more interesting."

Rebozo pulled out a white handkerchief, wiped his glasses and bent down to swipe at his shoes. "How does my pretending to be a spy . . . ?"

"A Serbian spy . . ."

Rebozo rose up. "How does that make excitement for your guests? I presume that portends I'm invited to your banquet."

"Why, most certainly." She curtsied to an imaginary lady. "Oh, Marguerite, did you happen to get a chance to visit with the Serbian spy? He's such a delightful man."

Lady Fletcher, not some weak, trying-to-please woman, knew what she wanted and she was good at what she did . . . the consummate hostess.

"Well, I am sorry to disappoint you. I am but a . . ."

"No, no, no. I refuse to listen. You will be my Serbian spy. Now, if I can find a Turkish diamond merchant, I'll be set."

Rebozo turned to Brannon. "Does she jest?"

"Oh, no. Harriet will not tolerate a boring party."

Rebozo shoved on his top hat. "My lady, that is my cue to entertain at your beckoning. Whatever the occasion, I will concoct intrigue for you."

"Good. Now, I must return to the hotel. Are you coming with me, Stuart?"

"I have some important issues to discuss with him," Rebozo said.

"Then my presence is no longer needed." Lady Fletcher lifted her skirt, raised her parasol, and walked back over the footsteps they had stamped in the moist sand.

Rebozo turned to Brannon. "The President wishes me to partner with you."

"Oh?"

"To help you find Tom Wiseman."

"Why didn't he tell me about you?"

"Hard to say. But I am well-trained. I know how to wield a sword." He pulled a dagger out of a small scabbard and swished it next to Brannon who lunged out his leg and tripped the man. He sprang up and replaced his dagger. "Bravo! And I'm adept at poisons . . . as well as international intrigue."

"How do you know Tom?"

"We met opening day of the Exposition, but I was called away on another assignment soon after that. The President ordered me to return."

"Well, Mr. Rebozo, no offense intended, but I like to pick my own partners. I'll go this one alone."

"You can't. My commission is to keep you alive. Thought it fair to warn you."

"Telegrams aren't totally private. They can get intercepted or confiscated."

Rebozo pulled out a cigarette from a Murad package, lit it and blew circles that lifted in the slight breeze. "True. What are you saying?"

"Nothing . . . yet."

"I do know that the last communiqué the President received from Wiseman indicated that he possessed important information and that he'd send an updated telegram following a scheduled meeting."

"And that message never arrived?"

Rebozo flicked an ash from his Murad cigarette and bowed his head. "I was involved at that moment in solving another case. That's why you were contacted. T.R. knows you, trusts you, and you're a good friend of Tom's."

"And why are you on this case?"

"The President knows me, trusts me, and I'm a good friend of his sister's."

Who is this guy really?

They headed back towards the hotel together, an awkward lack of rapport between them, though Rebozo offered several attempts at light banter.

"Who's the woman?" Brannon finally pried.

"Which woman?"

"The one on the beach."

"A good friend, one of many." Rebozo's smile had a hint of man-to-man.

Does he expect me to cooperate or compete? Maybe he's testing me.

As they arrived back at the hotel, Lady Fletcher hailed him from the front deck. "Ted Fleming's getting ready for your first lesson."

"But I haven't had breakfast yet." *Or done my own planning for the day.*

Rebozo waved goodbye and headed upstairs.

"I've got some hot coffee and warm blackberry pastries waiting for you inside," she said.

After he finished the passable coffee and the delicious scones, Lady Fletcher escorted him several blocks down the street to the golf course. She pointed out the wooden golf clubs in a bag leaning against a rattan chair.

A slight shiver shook Brannon's spine, like the time Victoria asked him to dance with her around a hat in front of all her hacienda residents. Or when Lisa begged him to sing with her in the church choir. "You've got a good voice, Stuart," she had said. "With a little practice, you could sing bass."

He had made attempts to communicate to each of them how their requests petrified him, to no avail.

"You'll be in good hands," Lady Fletcher assured him. "Ted Fleming can teach anyone to hit a ball."

CHAPTER SEVEN

Brannon had donned the wool twill jacket with khaki breeches and belt that Lady Fletcher insisted he wear, but he added his Stetson and boots too.

"We need to get you a lounge or reefer coat for the tournament," Harriet said.

She waved to a man who wore a dinner jacket, knickers and lace-up shoes. The gentleman motioned them over.

What good is an outdoor sport if you can't wear ranch clothes? A pair of broken-in denim jeans? When's the next train to Arizona?

Pot-style bunkers, mounding and beach grass distinguished the seaside links course. Several young men, including an Indian youth, clipped hedges, raked and pushed mowers over sand dune–shaped fairways and greens.

Lady Fletcher introduced him to Ted Fleming, a huge, burly man who didn't look like a golf professional. His curly, salt and pepper hair and infectious grin promised a friendly exchange. "This is the legendary Stuart Brannon who knows absolutely nothing about golf, but with your expertise he'll come around."

Ted Fleming reached out his hand. "I'm

charmed. Truly. A man like you should take well to this game. It's a gentleman's game, built on honesty and the integrity of each player. I know we'll get that from you."

Brannon clasped Fleming's hand with a quick shake. "I think you'll need lots more."

Brannon deliberated several nagging factors, each which tugged him away from this place: his fervor to find his friend; the alien atmosphere of the course; and the brief amount of time to master the sport.

He tried not to look Fleming in the eye as he asserted, "Harriet, I have decided not to do this. If you recall, I never promised I would. It's not my expertise."

"I know that. Everyone will know it. Don't you see? That's the attraction. The old time cowboy accepts a new challenge."

"You mean people will donate to the orphanage to watch me make a fool of myself."

"Yes, they will," Fleming assured him.

"And you won't be the only one," Lady Fletcher concurred. "Bill Cody and Wyatt Earp will be here. I had a cordial conversation with Mr. Earp already. He is traveling with his wife and will also visit his niece and her family in the Portland area whom he's never met before. I believe her name's Nellie Jane and she's the daughter of Wyatt's brother Virgil. In addition, the Portland outgoing mayor, a state senator, Oregon's governor and some vaudeville folks have agreed to come . . ."

"Any trained or wild animals?" Brannon interrupted.

"Of course not. But we will have a few top amateur and professional golfers. Harry Vardon, the famous English golfer, is a friend of Edwin's, you know. He helped Edwin make the contacts. This is going to be a first class tournament."

Ted Fleming's face got as speckly as his hair. "You mean, Harry Vardon the Stylist? Harry Vardon of the Vardon Flyer ball? Harry Vardon of the Vardon grip?"

"Yes, that's who I mean, but he won't be in Gearhart. He's in London to attend a wedding." She picked up a club, swatted it hard and Fleming's hat went flying towards a tree. "Stuart, give it a try. Maybe it won't be as bad as you think."

"What if it's worse?"

The loud, brash voice drew Brannon into his confidence. "I've never failed to make a golfer out of anyone yet . . . don't guarantee tournament-winning status, but you won't be put to shame."

"Hear that, Stuart? Besides, no one's watching you now and you've got one of the best teachers in the West. Why not take a few swings and get a feel for the game?"

"Or why not climb a sharp cliff barefoot?"

"I cannot fathom that a tiny, white ball can

stymie the man who backed down the King of Arizona all by himself."

"And I cannot believe the queen of sophistication, Lady Harriet Reed-Fletcher, would use such manipulation."

"My goodness, Stuart, when have you ever known me *not* to manipulate? Which reminds me, what would it take to convince you to carve your name on the big tree at the Willamette Orphan Farm?"

Brannon forced a grin at Lady Fletcher, then picked out a club from the bag Ted Fleming gave him and used it to clean off the bottom of his boots.

With patience, much bravado, step-by-step instructions and many puffs on his pipe, Ted Fleming opened up to Stuart Brannon the world of golf . . . at least the concept of the goal to swing a club and connect to a ball. His first attempt at the driving range missed the ball. So did the second. The third shot shattered a window at a small storage building on the far side of the street.

"I do better hunting squirrels with my Winchester," Brannon muttered and swung again. The ball skipped a dozen short bounces and landed a few feet away.

Lady Fletcher convulsed in laughter. "You won't have trouble finding that one."

Brannon began his list of excuses. *I got a*

*contagious disease from a train passenger. I
broke my arms, both of them, and need to
keep them in slings. Tom's been found . . . in
Portland . . . and he insists I join him for a grizzly
hunt in the Coast Range . . . now.*

Brannon sighed. *I can't make things up . . .
and I can't play golf. What a bind. Any suggestions, Lord?*

Soon after, he tossed the mashie club all the
way to a nearby corral and stampeded some
donkeys. The Indian youth helped him settle the
angry burros with shouts and stern glares.

Hope began to glimmer when one of his shots
soared, then bounced off an ash tree. Mr.
Fleming told him to aim for a practice green in
the middle of the range. The next few shots
sprayed to the right, but then he glided one
straight and high towards the center of his
target. Brannon yee-hawed. "That little ball rolled
up on the green near the mug," he boasted to
Lady Fletcher and Ted Fleming.

Mr. Fleming beamed with pride too. "It's not a
mug. Each hole has a number. You hit the ball
into a cup. It's a simple game, really."

"Then why do they have a two hundred page
rule book?" Brannon asked.

"Scotsmen can get picky."

Ted Fleming got out a club of his own and
made the same shot, not once or twice, but three
times and each ball arced much lower than the

previous one, though they all landed within feet of each other.

"You'll have to admit, Mr. Fleming is quite good at it," Lady Fletcher said. "Now you should go play nine holes."

"Nine!" He looked over at the first fairway. "I'll never last that long." Brannon wiped his brow. "So, I go out next Saturday . . . make an idiot out of myself . . . and all the professionals get a trophy."

"And you raise hundreds of dollars for the Willamette Orphan Farm, a refuge for orphaned and friendless children anywhere in the state," Lady Fletcher reminded Brannon.

"You're confident there will be plenty of paying customers who will want to view this game?"

"You've already proved that. When you started, how many watched you?"

"None. I liked it that way."

"And when you finished just now, how many gathered for a peek?"

"Eh, maybe twenty?"

"Thirty-two."

"But they all laughed."

"You entertained them. That's the point, Stuart. Think of how fun it is to witness legends like Brannon, Cody, Earp, as well as stage stars, out there on the links."

"I told you, Harriet, I came here to find Tom

Wiseman. I will not let this golf event interfere with that. Besides, we three are past our prime. I'm bent over, Cody's broke, and Earp can't stay out of the poker parlor."

"Fair enough about looking for the U.S. Marshal. But the public doesn't see their heroes that way. Now I need to get back to Edwin and send his guests home."

And I'm going to go dive into a pool of sharks.

Before Lady Fletcher and Ted Fleming strolled back to the hotel, Fleming tendered a warning, "Don't overdo swinging the club too much as a beginner. You can wear a lot of blisters on your hands."

"Not with all these calluses," Brannon replied.

"But you'll rub a different kind of way," was Fleming's parting retort.

Brannon contemplated whether to take his clubs to his room or practice some more.

He pulled a mashie and swiped the air a few times.

Watch foot movement and arm swing.
Keep the head down.
Don't follow the ball.
Replace the divots.
Stay out of trees, water and sand traps.
Not so hard. I can remember all of that.

The Indian youth approached him, timid and hunched at first, then by some hidden, inner cue, raised to full stature. He held a wooden club in his hand. "I can help you aim your shots better," he said. "Even your putts."

Brannon looked him over. Strong body. Almost the same height. The lighter skin made him think of his own son, L.F. *But I can't tell what tribe.* "You've played the game before?" Brannon wondered about protocol at the course for Indians, but also was surprised that the game interested him.

"Not in a tournament, not even when someone's watching. I play at night. I have for years."

"At night? How can you see where your ball goes?"

"I listen, like a blind man. And you play like a crippled man. Think about how you reset the sight of your rifle. You in much pain?"

Brannon snorted. "I've had every bone, muscle and extremity of my body beat, shot and broken. I don't know what it's like to live a day without pain. Not one appendage on me is in its original condition."

"Yes, I can see that. You also walk with a limp. My grandfather told me that a brave warrior can separate pain in his body from the thoughts of his mind. Grandfather practiced doing that all his life. Instead of tormenting himself over the fire in his feet, he meditated on the fresh taste of the sweet, high mountain or ocean breeze."

"What's your name, son?"

"Keaton Tanglewood. My grandmother is the

last full-blooded Clatsop Indian. As she often told me, she lived in the seasons before the earth lay pocked by the urgency of men with picks and gold pans, when the great buffalo still swarmed the tall grass plains."

Brannon studied the young man, looking through him to his past, his heritage, his proud culture. He wished his adopted son, Littlefoot, could exchange stories with this young man. Littlefoot's late mother, Elizabeth, would call him "another brave warrior."

"And you are The-One-Who-Does-Not-Turn-Back," Tanglewood stated.

Brannon shook himself to the present. "I haven't heard that name in a long time. Glad to meet you." Brannon reached out to shake the young man's hand and received a bear hug.

"You looking for the U.S. Marshal who disappeared?" Tanglewood blurted out.

"Why, yes, I am. Do you know where he is?"

"No, but I can take you to the man who dressed Indian for his last meeting." He picked up one of the golf clubs. "But not until I give you a few more lessons . . . and later I must finish my mowing job. Mr. Fleming is a good teacher, but you noticed that he is left-handed."

"What difference does that make?"

"The warriors of my tribe say a mystery surrounds those who shoot from the left side. Some say they learn that trick from the angels of heaven. Others say, 'The demons of hell teach such things.' In your case, you have taken on his stance, an awkward one for you."

Brannon stared at the young Indian as he swung at a dozen balls and each sailed straight and smooth and far down the slope.

"You must learn a lot in a short space," Tanglewood continued. "But I can tell you a couple secrets that will speed up the process."

"And what is that?"

"The first I will make a present for you of this club. Some call it a baffing spoon. See the special curve. It will do two things. One, it will give you a high loft. The other, it will be good for getting out of tough situations when you still have a long way to the cup. Get in the longer grass? Use the spoon. Need to get over some trees? Use the spoon."

Brannon studied the smooth surface. "Nice work."

"There is more. My grandfather was one of the best archers of our tribe and he told me what to do when competing with body pain or a troubled heart. When that happened, he would miss his target one thumb to the left. So, he learned in those times to aim his arrow one thumb to the right."

"Your grandfather sounds like a wise man, but I'm not sure what that has to do with a golf club."

"It is the same with a club or bow or rifle. Find

your normal shot. Determine when it veers wrong and by how much. Then, adjust your aim."

"I'm not sure in my case it will make any difference, but I appreciate the advice all the same."

Tanglewood pushed off with his mower and Brannon picked up his newly acquired baffing spoon club and tried to copy Tanglewood's swing.

There was no one else on the practice range now and no spectators. Brannon set his grip, widened his stance a couple inches, and took a practice swing to check the squareness of the clubface.

His wrists cocked on the back swing. He concentrated on pulling down with his left arm. The clubface struck the grass about an inch behind the ball and bounced along about thirty yards. Frustrated, he rolled another ball towards him and swung harder. This time, he topped the ball so bad it hopped up and rolled behind him.

Okay, Brannon, remember what you've learned. Slow, steady swings.

This time the ball cracked off the clubface and soared maybe ninety yards.

Not far, but straight.

He pulled another ball towards him and hit a duplicate shot.

Yeah, Brannon, now you're getting the rhythm.

He counted aloud every swing.

"One."

"Two."

"Three."

When he got to twelve, he sauntered back to the bag Ted Fleming had loaned him.

Not all of them straight. Not all of them far. But consistent. Felt good. Maybe I won't make a fool of myself. If only I could hit like that in front of other people. Somehow I can't concentrate the same. I've got to think that the club is my rifle.

He yanked out another wood club and returned to the overturned bucket of balls. This time the ball shot off the club's head, slicing sharply to the right.

What did Fleming say about fixing that? Too much. I'm starting to enjoy this game, but I don't understand why I should even bother. It's not my thing. I'll never play golf in Arizona.

The next shot hooked a little to the left. *No . . .*

Keep your eye on the ball and your eye on the prize . . . money for the orphans.

Another shot straightened and rolled well past the one hundred fifty yard marker. *That's better. But I shouldn't spend all this time trying to learn this game. I've got to find Tom.*

He again shot straight, but with a little less roll. *If I hit a shot like that on a short hole, I could be putting for an eagle.* He stopped, pleased with himself. *I even picked up some of the lingo already.*

The next shot came up no more than thirty feet off the ground.

Another shot blasted high and long. It hung in the air, then descended like a diving gull. *If I could hit every one like that, I could be an equal partner with guys like Ted Fleming.*

He allowed himself a sheepish smile. In the middle of his next back swing he heard a woman call his name. He chugged the ball short and right, then scurried to his golf bag. He tried to make a quick exit through the trees.

CHAPTER EIGHT

His attempted clean escape did not succeed. A young woman stood in his path. "Mr. Brannon, where have you been? Surely not on the golf course."

He pulled a wry face.

"I need your help. Aren't you a cowboy?"

"I make my living on a ranch. Is that what you mean?"

"No, I meant your attire. It seems strange to see you carrying a golf bag."

"Well, ma'am," Brannon glanced over at the empty ninth green, then back at the lady. "You might say it's a new hobby."

Her smile was wide and she seemed to know its charms. He studied her straight, white teeth. He decided she was in her late teens. Something about the dark hair and pixie face stirred a memory. "Have we met?"

She stuck out her small hand. He was surprised at the strength of her grip. "I don't think so, not properly anyway. My name's Darcy. I need your assessment of my animal."

"Your horse?"

"No."

"Your cow?"

Her blue eyes narrowed. "My llama. And she is in great distress. Please, could you help?"

"I'm not sure." *I don't have time for this, but something about this girl seems familiar. She reminds me of someone.* Brannon grabbed up his bag and followed her several blocks away to a large spruce forest park of several hundred acres.

Tents were scattered everywhere, as well as elegant homes, cottages and log cabins. There seemed to be no restrictions on the types of structures that could be built.

"We live here," she said, "at least for now. There's entertainment almost every night . . . musical soirees, dance concerts and lots of famous speakers do events here. Some of it's good. Lots of it's boring, but my mother and aunt like it."

They passed an imposing building that appeared to be an auditorium, with arched entrance, belfry and double roof design. Windows provided opportunity for light, in spite of the shade of the surrounding trees.

"My mother would love to meet you. Let me introduce you to her first."

He walked around the flap of the tent and dropped into blackness as a heavy thud pounded his skull.

Brannon peered out at a blurred scene and almost drowned in a sweet, sickly scent. He felt like he'd been drug through a meadow of lupine and skunk cabbage. Though he couldn't view the women in front of him, the girl at a distance looked double, then focused clear. He studied the face.

I've heard those voices before, but where and when?

"You hit him too hard."

He heard a male voice. "No, not for a grown man. Besides, he has an exceptionally tough skull. Many have butted heads with Stuart Brannon and he never lost." *Sounds like Hawthorne H. Miller. But he's in Portland.*

"But he's an old man now. Look at all that gray hair. You could have killed him. Why did you hit him at all? Get out of here, you big ape."

It sounded like the man brushed through the tent flap.

"Mama Darrlyn, now Mr. Brannon won't hear us out or do anything for us."

"So sorry, but he would not have stayed otherwise. You've got to let him know you mean business."

Brannon tried to pry open a slit of one eye. He was in a large tent full of flowers and a few pieces of furniture . . . several small chairs and a rack that held a number of dresses.

"Aunt Dee, you'd better think of something quick. We don't have much time."

"Water. I'll get a pail of water."

Darrlyn. Dee. Deedra! Surely not the Lazzard twins. Brannon strained to see, with eyelids barely apart. *Hair still blonde, but not matted or dirty, like the last time he saw them in a Paradise Meadow jail cell.*

"You got any knives on you?" Brannon tried to rise, although he felt as dizzy as a mouse that got churned in the butter.

One of the twins spoke. "Brannon, you're awake."

"And we take it you recognize us," the other twin said.

Brannon still couldn't tell them apart even with the maturing years. He knew them in their early twenties. Now, they looked in their forties, but they must be pushing fifty. The years had been kind to them. Was it money? He guessed there must be some rich, big-city San Francisco men in their story.

"Stuart, we're sorry about the hit on the head. That was not our original intent. We've got some important requests of you. We weren't sure you'd give us time to explain."

Brannon's vision and head were clearing. "Who hit me?"

"None of us. We'll deal with that man later."

Brannon sat up. "Well, ladies, how can I be of assistance?"

"You've got to help Darcy with her llama. She's over there." She pointed to somewhere

83

outside the tent. "And get us an invite to Lady Fletcher's soiree tomorrow."

"What?" The demanding tone irked him, especially after being knocked unconscious. But the voice had a tinge of southern drawl, full of practiced charm.

"We traveled here all the way from San Francisco to go to the Exposition and attend all the parties we can. A woman we met in Portland told us about Lady Fletcher and we figured out she was married to the Fletcher we knew in Paradise Meadow. We owe him a lot, you know, and we aim to pay. And you promised us a meal with you."

Her twin interrupted. "Yeah, but we're more than willing to let you off the hook . . . if . . ."

Darcy finished. "If you'll put in a good word to Lady Fletcher, so all three of us can enter her circle."

"Her circle?"

"Go to her events. Be part of high society. Wear these expensive dresses we drug all these miles in our trunks."

"And maybe get us out of this tent."

"What is this place?" Brannon rose to his feet and staggered towards what he assumed was the tent opening. He pulled back a flap. Landscaped lawns and gardens stretched as far as he could follow, with scattered tents, buggies, a few motor cars.

"The Gearhart Park. We've got permission to camp here until one of the hotel rooms become available."

He started to say, "You can use mine," but stayed silent. He wanted more information before he volunteered away his freedom and comfort.

Darcy twisted around, reached under a bedroll, pulled out a long, curly black wig and tossed it on her short hair.

A quick look at the girl in her disguise and Brannon's neck muscles tightened. His mind snapped into sharp recall. "At the Louis XIV Drawing Room . . . on the chandelier . . . you pushed me on the bed."

"What?" one of the women spat out. He figured that to be Mama Darrlyn. He made a note of the sapphire rings she wore. The other twin preferred rubies.

"Oh, you know, that job Daniel and I got to play-act at the Exposition. We tried to talk with Mr. Brannon then about helping us and every-thing got crazy." Darcy attempted a cautious smile for his angry eyes.

"Where is it?" he growled.

She went back to the bedroll and slid out a pair of glasses, broken. "Sorry," she said. "Daniel sat on them." She tossed some coins on a tiny table. Brannon grabbed her wrist. She winced and the two older women tried to pull him back.

"She must be very important to you." Her smile was nervous, tentative. "You can have it if you talk nice to Lady Fletcher for us. Otherwise, it's gone. Forever."

Brannon yanked up the bedroll. A number of items scattered around. None of them the locket.

"It's not in the tent," Darcy said. "I've got to trade it back, to the man who gave me the llama. The picture reminded him of his daughter."

"You had no right." Brannon for the first time in his life considered whipping a girl. In a flash, he wondered if his father would approve, under these circumstances. "Trade it back. I want that locket. Now."

"Help me with the llama. She'll need to be returned in good condition."

Brannon followed the girl and the two women to a thicket where a llama lay, panting and eyes dazed. "Did I hear you right? Are you telling me you traded my locket for a llama?"

"Sort of," Darcy said. "Plus all the money I earned at the Exposition."

"Stole, you mean." Brannon leaned down to the unsheared, gray llama. He figured her to be about three hundred pounds and two years old. "Why did you want a llama?"

"Lots of reasons." Darcy spouted her list. "Clean. Don't cost much to feed. They stay calm, even around kids. Their hair makes good sweaters and blankets. And they don't bite or bark."

Brannon wondered why her mother and aunt didn't protest his accusation. Or scold the girl for her actions. As Darcy touted the benefits of a llama for a pet, Brannon determined from his experience with calves that the birth date was a few days away. But he wanted that locket. And he had to find Tom Wiseman. Why was life so complicated out here away from the simplicity of home sweet home?

"I don't know how you're going to do it," Brannon proclaimed, "but you're going to get that locket and bring it to me at the hotel as soon as possible. Or Lady Fletcher will hear an earful and not the sort of recommendation you wanted."

He raised up, took some deep breaths to clear his brain of the overload of emotions and thoughts, then started to head for the hotel. He turned back around instead. "Where's my clubs? Surely you haven't sold them too."

The Lazzard twins pulled him aside.

"It's hard raising kids these days," Mama Darrlyn stated. "We brought her here to get her away from her friends and influences in San Francisco. Her last friend committed suicide by drinking vials of carbolic acid. Darcy was devastated."

"Over an infatuation with a married man," Aunt Deedra added. "Who happened to be Darcy's father . . . and never married to Darcy's mother."

Mama Darrlyn shot her sister a fierce look.

"Please be patient. Darcy's developed a few habits, but we're trying to break her."

"A stint in jail might help," Brannon offered. *For all of you.* Aunt Deedra walked behind a nearby tree and dragged his bag and clubs. Brannon looked them over. "The putter's not here."

"Is that what this stick is?" Aunt Deedra raced over to a hole in the grass and pulled up a long pole. "We tried to discourage a bushy animal that keeps climbing up our tent and poking holes."

Brannon grabbed the putter and swung the bag over his shoulders. He rejected the girl's plea to stay and help with the llama and the women's offer of strong coffee and cookies.

As he marched down a path between other tents and wagons spread out on the acreage, he noticed a handwritten sign at the gazebo that advertised several speakers that day, one from the Women's Christian Temperance Union and the other from the Waitresses Union. A small crowd gathered, mostly women. He couldn't detect if the men in attendance were sincere listeners or collared by their wives.

"You give even your horses one day's rest in seven," he heard the fervent appeal. "We do not want sweatshops nor tenement districts. Now is the time to make laws to prevent such conditions, not wait until these conditions exist and then bring reforms."

A steady rain began to pour, then a cloudburst, which gave him an excuse to keep his head bowed. He didn't wave or greet anyone or say a word until he reached the hotel lobby. He tossed the bag into his room, grabbed up his duffles, and remembered what a miserable night he endured on that bed. He had fully meant to camp on the beach that night . . . and every night.

He gritted his teeth and stomped back out to the Gearhart Park, and told the women in the leaking tent they were welcome to stay in his room that night.

CHAPTER NINE

After Brannon dressed in the only other suit he brought, he packed up his belongings and tucked them in a hotel storage closet that the manager showed him. He sauntered to the lobby, lowering his head when anyone came into view. Recognition or conversation didn't appeal to him at the moment. He pulled on his tight collar and wiped his face with a handkerchief.

An idea hit him as he walked near the library.

I need to do some research on the Indians in this part of the country, to see if that might relate to Tom.

He opened the door and almost collided into Tally Rebozo, dressed in tuxedo, tails and a top hat. This disturbed him more than he wanted to admit.

This guy is going to be very difficult to evade. It's like he knows what I'm going to do, before I do it.

"She is a writer." Rebozo pulled out a copy of *The Yavapai County War*, by Lady Harriet Reed-Fletcher. "That explains her imagination."

Brannon offered a curt nod, then browsed through the books. *The Pilgrim's Progress*, by John Bunyon. *White Fang*, by Jack London. Four volumes of *The Winning of the West*, by Theodore Roosevelt.

Beside *How to Play Golf*, by Harry Vardon, he discovered a linen handkerchief. He tugged it out. Stitched on one quadrant in an array of multi-colors was the U. S. Government Building at the Lewis and Clark Exposition with flag flying. The personalized name of "Sharon" and "1905" in pink thread was embroidered in another corner.

"Sorry." Rebozo reached for the cloth. "That's for me."

Brannon handed it over and Rebozo tucked it with tight folds in his breast pocket. Brannon started to pull out a pamphlet entitled "A Survey of Indians in Washington and Oregon" by Charles McChesney, then slid it back.

Instead, he tried to get Rebozo to talk about himself. "I've been wonderin'. Why were you overdressed out on the beach this morning?"

He affected a grin. "These are all I have. I plan to go shopping later in Seaside. Want to join me?"

"Surely you jest."

"Later I've got some more Exposition duty too. The Centennial is as much political as it is a celebration. Points are being made, contacts scheduled, world business conducted. This Tom Wiseman business is extra. So, will you tell me what you know so far?"

"Nope."

"I didn't think so. Do you know Wax Lanigan?"

"Stood him down years ago after a stagecoach robbery at Globe, Arizona."

"He moved up the line since then. Now he's a union organizer. Moves in high society circles. He could be valuable in this case."

"We must not be talking about the same guy, unless he's taken to working both sides of the law."

"Lanigan also has the sweets for Sylvia Wiseman, Tom's daughter, who is head book-keeper for Consolidated Mining out of Goldfield, Nevada. She's also a part owner. As you may know, Goldfield's the main gold rush region in the country right now, maybe the last. Lanigan spent some time there trying to encourage the mine workers to go union."

"I know . . . that is, I knew Sylvia, when she was younger. She's the middle daughter, somewhat a rebel. Not home much. Travels a lot. The other two daughters and their husbands work the home ranch near Prescott."

Rebozo nodded. "Her mining company is helping to sponsor one of the exhibit buildings at the Exposition. Sylvia was last seen at the Portland depot. She had scheduled a meeting that day with one of her partners and didn't show up."

Brannon paid closer attention. "Perhaps Tom took off to find her."

"Could be, but why didn't he inform the President?"

The door burst open and a woman rushed over to Rebozo, spreading the delicate scent of mint and aromatic sachets. The sprinkle of perfume invaded the room with the promise of spring blooms and general feminine wiles. She planted a tender kiss on both his cheeks.

"Andale! I'm so sorry to be late," she said.

Andale? Brannon averted his gaze, snatched a random book from a high shelf and shuffled through pages about the flora and fauna of New Zealand.

So, he wasn't here expecting to see me, after all.

"Oh," she exclaimed, "I see you have company. Do come see me later." She scurried out as quickly as she ushered herself in.

"Andale?" Brannon repeated. "Is that what she called you?"

Rebozo exhaled and rubbed his forehead as though he hoped to erase some thought or scene from the past. Or perhaps to draw it out. "I met her on another case. I prefer to change my name on occasion."

"So, what's your real name?"

"The President knows." He inferred by his tone that ended the matter.

"And was that Sharon?"

"She also tends to bandy about various names, when it suits her."

"We were discussing Lanigan. Why did you ask about him?"

Rebozo peeked through a slit opening of the

door, then stepped back closer to Brannon. "On opening day of the Exposition, the Vice-President spoke and afterward I was introduced to Lanigan by members of the Centennial board. While we chatted, he suddenly pushed through the crowd, grabbed a Latin American man by the collar, yelled in his face, and shoved him away from the spectators."

"The shoving and yelling part sounds true to character."

"He said the man had been ranting at the Vice-President and threatened to do him harm. I ran after the accused, but lost him. You can imagine my chagrin and embarrassment, as one of the backups for the secret service. Can't be too cautious since the President McKinley assassination at the New York Exposition."

"Are you sure Lanigan wasn't putting on some kind of show for you?"

"Why would he do that?"

"Because it is so like him."

"I think you've got the man pegged wrong."

"I hope so. It would renew my hopes for humankind." Brannon pulled up his hat, swiped his hair down, and tucked his hat back on. "Why don't you follow Sylvia's trail? I'll find Tom my way."

Rebozo plucked out the McChesney pamphlet on Indians in Washington and Oregon, winked at Brannon, then handed it to him. "I think you wanted this. The only real lead I have is to look up someone called Sully. I believe that's one of the other partners. I understand he supervises the Consolidated Pavilion and is looking for new investors for their mining operation."

"No last name?"

Rebozo shook his head and drew out another volume: *The Clatsop and Lower Columbia Indians.* He thumbed through it.

"What I cannot understand," Brannon said, "is why you and me got roped into this duty. The President's got federal Marshals, secret service guys and the U.S. Army at his disposal. But he's going with Serbian spy Rebozo and an Arizona rancher?"

Rebozo affected a smile, as though they shared a secret joke. "You mean, the Brannon of Hawthorne H. Miller dime novel fame. I hear they're a bunch of windies, colorful tales for an eager public hungry for daring adventures. Mysterious drifters. Handsome gunslingers." He handed the book he held to Brannon. "I think you'll be interested in this."

Who is this man? And what does he want?

"Maybe there is someone in his loop he doesn't trust," Rebozo remarked.

"In fact, I've got no reason to trust you," Brannon shot back.

"Understandable, I suppose. Perhaps I can change your mind."

"In addition, I don't have a clue who or what T.R.'s loop includes."

"Sure you do. What is the big news out of Washington these days?"

Brannon tried to keep his gaze steady, not to reveal how dense he felt.

Rebozo answered for him. "The big ditch. Panama. Lots of politics and intrigue. The French still smarting from the scandals. The Nicaraguans bidding for a channel through their country. And the Colombians not too happy with the President about his chess game takeover."

"What does a U.S. Marshal like Tom Wiseman have to do with that?"

"It's up to us to find out. I also happen to know there's gold in that country. But that's not the only crosscurrent of controversy T.R. faces. Among others, there's the railroad mess. Fraud with public land grants, that sort of thing. The Oregonian newspaper broke the scandal last year when they discovered a large percentage of land sales violated federal law."

"That sounds familiar. I believe Tom was called upon to help with evictions."

"There are lots of politicians, businessmen and railroad executives involved. T.R. has vowed to clean it all up."

"I'm not much of a political person, unless it gets personal. Maybe it's about to get personal now with Tom."

"First thing tomorrow, I go hunt for this guy Sully. Or we could both check on him tonight."

"Harriet has my evening planned."

"And an assignment from the President of the United States can't alter those plans?"

"Not a chance."

Brannon gazed at the covers of the books he held, volumes he hoped would help him understand the region's tribes and perhaps provide a trace that would lead to Tom Wiseman. Or not. But he had to start somewhere. And he had to stay alert in regard to one mystery man, Tally Rebozo.

Before he left, Brannon removed the Harry Vardon golf book.

CHAPTER TEN

A coat too tight at the shoulders. Limp tie. Unmatched studs. A yellowed-with-age cummerbund. Old and used, that's what he looked like. That's what he felt like.

Brannon peered into the hotel ballroom filled with young, fresh faces and knew he did not belong here. Even Lady Harriet Reed-Fletcher seemed his junior in age. However, it wasn't the first time he loomed out-of-place. Every wedding he ever attended, including his own, for instance.

Brannon watched the guests saunter the wood plank sidewalk to come to Lady Fletcher's benefit party. The north and south Ridge Path with flat terrain, less than a mile long, tucked in the woods, showed hikers the way down to the estuary at Little Beach. It wound among hemlocks, spruce and shore pine and offered shelter from the stronger winds and salty sprays. Another way to experience Gearhart.

Several couples lingered under the maplewoods and exchanged whispered conversations. He thought of those long ago days with Lisa . . . and more recently with Victoria. "I've known love like that," he muttered to himself, then quietly addressed the far-away lovers. "It's a wonderful experience. Enjoy it while you can."

Self-consciousness washed over him when Lady Fletcher tucked her arm in his. Her jade dress had a graceful poof in front and tucked over her slim waist with a matching sash. "It's the *grande promenade*. They say it follows an ancient Indian trail known as the Ridge Path."

They side-stepped through waves of trailing skirts and broad-brimmed hats with dangled ribbons and masses of feathers. Brannon spied a stuffed hummingbird on top of one.

Harriet introduced him to a number of the men first. One man wore a kilt with his bowler hat. One fellow ran a dairy. The one with top hat and formal evening coat was known as the "Salmon King." Any of these men appeared to be gentlemen who would rather smoke cigars on the veranda, or be on a hunting trip in the desert, or ride some high rocky trail. But they all put on their manners and a bit of pride to huff about the stuffy room, to try to entertain Lady Fletcher's guests.

"What do you think about charging registration for auto cars?" the Salmon King asked them all.

"How far west should the United States go?" pondered the man named Gearhart.

"Do you think the Panama Canal will become Roosevelt's folly?" inquired the man in a kilt, an elderly, dapper gentleman.

Before the conversation got heated, a young

man rushed in to report that a pregnant llama had fallen into the Neacoxie Creek. Brannon stepped up to follow several hardy fellows who ran out the door. But Lady Fletcher grabbed him and insisted he come meet her daughter, whom he hadn't seen since she was a baby.

"The locals are quite capable of handling such emergencies," she said. "You can't save every creature in trouble, Stuart."

But you don't realize what I have invested in that particular creature.

Laira Ashley Fletcher shined with her mother's gentility but with the blush of apple blossom, silky white youth, all firm softness and innocence. Her hair flowed with white flowers and a few white bows and framed a heart-shaped face, pug nose and almond eyes.

"Hi, Uncle Stuart," she greeted. "Oh, twee! I really wanted to go watch the llama get free or have her baby. What do they call baby llamas anyway? Llamettes?"

Brannon tried not to laugh out loud.

"Do stay away from that pernickety scallywag in the kilts. His speciality is to drone on about bumper spoons and sand traps and such as that. What a bore."

"He seemed like a decent chap to me," Brannon responded. "What are you doing for entertainment, besides going to your mother's events?"

"I am not going barefoot on the beach anymore, to dabble my toes in the foamy waves. There's hidden pinchers in crab holes, splinters in the planked boardwalk, nettles in the beach grass. The water is freezing and the sand burns me. Oh, but I do venture to Seaside on the ferry boat to go shopping. And I play cribbage with my nurse." She yawned with a dainty pat of her hand. "Mum insisted she come along, even though I am quite grown now, as you can see."

"How old are you? Thirteen? Fourteen?"

"Oh, twee! Uncle Stuart, I'm so disappointed. You have made it to my list of men-who-lack-sense. I am seventeen . . . almost."

"I do apologize. Time passes like a fog for elderly men like me. So, that means your brother, Stuart, must be . . ."

"Twenty-one. And if he knew you were going to be here, he would have made Oregon his holiday destination, instead of that old musty country he went to. Really, you are greater in his esteem than any other hero, more than Robert Livingstone, even higher than Papa, I think."

"What musty country are you referring to?"

"It sounds like turkey, but Papa says it has nothing to do with turkey."

"Is it Turkestan?"

"Yes, that's it. He's digging in the ground to

101

study their culture. Very boring, but it worries my parents so."

"Are you Stuart Brannon?" A woman in lavender who exuded the scent of lilacs breezed near him. Her golden-brown coiffure hinted of soft hay on a barn floor. Or honey in a bees nest. Her eyes curved like crescents, as though she'd laugh at the merest suggestion of humor.

The woman in the library. And the lady on the beach? "Yes, ma'am. Or is it Sharon?"

"You may call me Sharon, if you like. When I'm not meeting handsome men in libraries, I'm addressed as Mrs. Gillespie."

He tried not to drink in her scent too deeply, too fully. *A woman like that could intoxicate a man.* "Mrs. Gillespie," he acknowledged.

"I can't believe it. Here I am talking to the hero of *Slaughter on the Pampas*."

Ah, another Hawthorne Miller novel, I presume.

Laira Ashley Fletcher slipped away to chat with some young ladies who giggled behind two boys who looked stifled in their suits and starched collars.

Mrs. Gillespie must have mistaken his silence as a sign of assent. She exuded confidence as well as a full chest and hips that swayed. "I've been to Argentina several times. I keep looking for the *El Presidente* Hotel. It must be well hidden from the general *touriste*. And yet, so many of your adventures take place there."

She waited as though expecting a response, then forged on. "Sancho Maleta is found dead in the aviary. Romal Vug hides his plans for the overthrow of Paraguay. Bluff Tarrabee . . . well, I won't repeat what happens between him and that young singer, Louisa. When those two meet in that narrow passageway to the hidden chamber . . . " She blushed. "Of course, you know all about it. I simply must find that hotel and investigate for myself."

"I'm afraid I can't be of much help."

"I understand. Confidentiality is important. But if I could find the hotel, I would do all the rest."

"But, ma'am." He stopped. "Mrs. Gillespie . . . Mr. Miller's novels are pure fiction. There is little or no truth. . . ."

A booming female voice interrupted from behind. "Mr. Brannon, how good to see you again."

As he turned to face her, he wracked his memory for a name from both the auditory and visual clues. Something about her sallow, yellowish skin. Madam Cob? Her nut-brown eyes regaled his. Grateful for the diversion, he said, "Yes, ma'am."

"How are Littlefoot and the family?"

Brannon felt his whole frame relax. He rubbed the wrinkles in his forehead. He had a flash of an image of this woman with Scottish terriers in tow. "Fine, just fine."

"What a busy tribe for L.F.'s wife, Jannette.

Aren't they?" The woman grabbed him with her fleshy hand. "And you, Grandpa. You must be missing them."

"They are a blessing."

"And L.F. isn't here with you?"

"Not on this trip."

Mrs. Gillespie interrupted. "We were talking about South America and the accounts of Hawthorne Miller. By the way, Mr. Brannon, did you know he is in town? And he's got quite a display of your books and photographs and such set up at the golf course booth."

Brannon snapped around as if Miller would sneak up behind him. *I'm sure that was him in the tent. Just what I need.* "He is the one you should talk to about the *El Presidente* Hotel."

He watched Tally Rebozo stalk towards him. Brannon excused himself and tried to steer Rebozo away from the crowd, then reminded himself the man was most likely headed for Sharon Gillespie.

"Did you know that Mrs. Gillespie has received stage and elocutionary education in the East?" Rebozo began.

"Nope."

"She's a fine stage figure with that exquisite soprano. She's been much applauded, encored and called before the curtain."

"That's nice. What are you up to, Rebozo?"

"You packin' your .44?"

"Do I look armed and dangerous?"

"I need an answer."

"Didn't know if you wanted support or confrontation."

"I hear Sully is at the Black Duck Saloon in Seaside right now. Maybe we should take a walk."

"Harriet wants me back at the hotel soon."

"Won't take us more than an hour or two to check this guy out."

CHAPTER ELEVEN

They hiked on an old wagon path, an ancient foredune ridge where railroad track was laid, then past a wooden boardwalk at the Promenade, homes on the oceanfront, some shacks and an octagon-shaped dance hall in West Seaside where they could hear refrains of Scott Joplin ragtime music. They crossed a bridge over the Necanicum River, about six blocks from the Pacific beach.

Brannon counted at least four hotels, numerous stores, a savings bank and a Western Union telegraph office. He followed Rebozo through the village streets and to the other side of the business district. "We are both overdressed."

"What's so strange about a tux at a waterfront town?"

They heard some scratching sounds, like something metal scraped against wood. Rebozo raised his voice. "Anywhere Stuart Brannon goes formal will seem out of place."

The scraping stopped and a ghostly figure lunged out at them. "Did you say you were Stuart Brannon, the one from Arizona?"

Brannon rubbed the outline of his revolver. "That's me. We met somewhere?"

"In the *Sangre De Christos* and you had a knife pressed against my belly."

Rebozo hollered a warning. The arm struck like a venomous snake. Brannon spotted the blade just as he lurched and clubbed the man's chin. Then a volley like a roof collapse followed. Fists flew from every direction. Yells and grunts. Groans and curses from every corner of the boardwalk. Brannon staggered and fell as a fiery slash cut across his thigh. Someone tugged at his leg. A big man with heavy jowls yanked him towards the opening of an empty side room.

Rebozo scooted in behind them. "Brannon, you're so popular wherever you go," he wheezed.

Brannon stared at his ripped tuxedo coat and imagined Lady Fletcher's ire. "Who are you?" he said to their deliverer.

"I'm Sully." The big man led them out another dark street by a back door and into a shadowy room. Wooden boxes were piled everywhere and they had to feel their way to not bump into them. He opened another door and they slipped through.

Brannon tried to talk quickly as they followed. "We're looking for Tom Wiseman."

"Never heard of him," the big man spit out as he reached for and half-dragged Brannon down an alley.

"How about Sylvia Wiseman?" Rebozo pressed, as he ran behind them.

Sully stopped, pushed Brannon against a brick wall and grabbed Rebozo by the shirt collar. "You lay a hand on little Sylvia and I'll bust your guts."

"Whoa." Brannon attempted to shove the man away from Rebozo and got boxed in the ears. "I believe we're on the same side. Have you seen Sylvia?"

"Maybe." He clammed up. This was a man not to be pushed around, but he had his limits. He reclined on a stack of pallets and breathed hard. "She got on the train in Ogden and at least one witness believes they saw her get off the train in Portland. She hasn't been heard from since. She's Tom Wiseman's daughter. We figure if we can find her, we'll find him."

"She's hiding." Sully clutched his hands by the wrists over his stomach, then scratched his arms with an incessant movement as though he had a rash or bedbugs.

"From whom? You?" Rebozo inquired.

Sully looked on the verge of picking Rebozo up and tossing him clear to the ocean. "Nah, she's staying low generally because of this guy Wax Lanigan. She tried to shoot him in Goldfield and he's been chasing her ever since."

Brannon faced off with Sully. "What are you claiming? Wax Lanigan is attracted to Sylvia because she tried to kill him?"

"Yep. Goldfield is a close community. We

either marry them or bury them. Those are your choices."

"But when the gold plays out, the town's gone," Brannon mused. "Hardly seems an important enough event to attract the intervention of the President of the United States."

Sully's raised eyebrows implied interest. "That is where you underestimate the value of the gold being mined in Goldfield."

"But I'll wager it's political clout that's at stake, not dollars and cents," Rebozo commented.

"Sylvia's somewhere by the Lewis and Clark Salt Works, south of here," Sully revealed. "She's also got a secret meeting for a newspaper assignment. We've got a newspaper now, the *Seaside Signal*, and the editor, a guy named Watson, is looking for any and all news fit to print. Sylvia's been here on personal matters and had nothin' else to do, so he hired her."

"I figured she'd be at the Grimes Hotel," Rebozo said.

"Nope. That burned down last year. She told me she was supposed to go to places where people talk, tell what's happening. She hangs out in hair salons, barber shops, saloons . . . and prayer meetings. Then she finds a discreet place to meet for further interviews. Tonight was the Salt Works."

"Is the Salt Works a hotel?" Brannon asked.

"It's a salt cairn, a kind of memorial to signify

where they believe Lewis and Clark camped to make salt for their long journey home."

They treaded after Sully's massive heels as the big man talked the whole time. "It's about as bad as Goldfield here. There's a rabble rouser from Uniontown trying to get the saloons closed, since they had success up there. There's a bunch of guys who are frequently arrested for participating in midnight brawls. And a gang of young ruffians have robbed, plundered and been a growing nuisance around town. It's gotten worse lately, houses broken into and upstanding citizens getting blackmailed."

In the distance, Tillamook Head beachhead protruded like an enormous whale sculpture off the coastline. Further west, the caution beam of Tillamook Lighthouse blinked its warning of rocky dangers to passing ships far offshore, headed to and from the Columbia River.

"Isn't that a police matter?"

"Yes, but Sylvia's gotten involved. A friend of hers has a special interest in the case and the newspaper wants a scoop. She was meeting with a gang representative at the Salt Works."

They reached a long, low stone edifice with pails that lined the top. Firewood crammed the oval opening.

"Sylvia." Sully's harsh, throaty voice penetrated the misty air.

A woman appeared from behind some bushes

that surrounded the Salt Works, a rock pile and stones structure. A sturdy, athletic woman with an ankle-length tweed suit, large brown eyes and full mouth stalked forward. She had a fox fur, but no hat. Even with an unbending frown her face shone with natural beauty, the sort that ages well, that needs little or no cosmetics. Wisps of mostly upswept brunette hair fluttered out of combs, her clothes not quite all tucked in.

"What do you men want?"

"Sylvia, it's Stuart Brannon. We're looking for Tom, your father. No one's seen him for a week and he had been reporting daily to the President."

She sprang forward, knife in hand, fully alert. But the suspicious frown had eased. "Why did you come here?"

"We hoped you might know where he is."

"I haven't seen him since Mama's funeral. What do you know about his disappearance?"

Rebozo volunteered the reply. "Last seen in Gearhart. I just learned that, among others, he was with a Nicaraguan named Chuy Carbón and Bois DeVache, a Frenchman. Do you know either of them?"

"No, I don't, but Papa told me he was asked by the President to assist with some special duties that dealt with important people either connected to or attending the Lewis and Clark Exposition."

"This was his last assignment?" Brannon asked.

"As a favor to the President. He planned to retire after that." She fixed a firm look at Rebozo. "I've seen you before."

"Perhaps. I've been all over the world."

Then she added, "I'm coming with you."

"To where?"

"To wherever you're going to look for Papa."

"You'll have to be on the alert. Wax Lanigan is in Gearhart and I understand you'd prefer to avoid him," Brannon informed her.

"Then I'll get extra bullets. Be right back."

She returned a few minutes later with a leather bag over her shoulder, leading a chestnut mare with a flaxen mane. She introduced the horse as Geode, the color of tea with milk stirred in. She pranced as though ready for a race. "This one can be flighty, but only around men. Don't take it personal."

Sylvia didn't carry a carbine or rifle for the "extra bullets," so Brannon presumed she had a sneak gun tucked in her clothes somewhere . . . and certainly her knife, too. She looked the type . . . steady gaze, muscular arms, firm step. He never blamed any woman for providing her own protection.

She handed a note to Sully. "Give this to Cordelle."

"What shall I tell Editor Watson?"

"That maybe I'll bring him a bigger story."

A shot rang out and a bullet passed over their heads, narrowly missing Sylvia.

"Go, go," Sully told her. He bent low beside the Salt Works while they rushed away.

On the way back to Gearhart they took a different route suggested by Sully. Sylvia took the lead through a dense forest of fir, pine and spruce. Several condors flapped their wings in flight then glided over the treetops. A doe and fawn scooted out of the trail.

Too thick for fast walking, they hunkered down underneath low boughs as they tromped over wild clover leaves and skunk cabbage, which almost overwhelmed Brannon with its carrion-like rank odor. He made a mental note to try to avoid the massive-leafed, yellow-bloomed, poker-like stemmed plant.

A huge branch whacked Sylvia in the head and almost knocked her over. "Watch out back there," she hollered.

"Someone's following us," Rebozo reported.

A crash through the trees followed.

They hurried past a ravine filled with rocks brought by floods or from tumbling down the hillside. A sign cautioned trespassers of traps at one section.

"Traps for what?" Rebozo questioned.

"I don't know," Brannon replied, "and don't want to find out."

"I'm sorry," Sylvia shouted. "Not much of a shortcut."

Rocks whizzed by them.

"We're either being chased out or attacked. Are you sure you can trust this Sully guy?" Brannon asked.

"With my life," Sylvia said.

Brannon and Rebozo doubled back, careful to stay on the path and almost collided into a young boy. "Hey, I'm the one being chased. It wasn't me who shot at you." The boy tried to speak tough, a swagger in his voice.

"Who's chasing you?"

"That big man Sully. The guy who did the shooting went back to Seaside. But he's not chasing me. I just don't want to talk to him."

They waited for Sully to catch up. "Thanks for catching this bully. He's been hanging around with those rowdies."

"What's your name?" Sylvia asked.

"What's it to ya?" he snarled as Sully grabbed him by the nape of the neck and hauled him back to town.

"What's *his* name, besides Sully?" Brannon asked.

"He signs papers with 'Q. Sully.' Don't know anymore than that and he doesn't seem to appreciate it if you ask."

Brannon scratched his neck. "Q? What would that stand for? Quentin? Quigley? Quincy?"

Rebozo pulled on some black gloves and wriggled his fingers. "It's Quintus. His mother was Spanish and he was her fifth child." He looked up at their questioning stares. "I make it my priority to find out these things."

"Why's he in Seaside?" Brannon asked.

Sylvia replied. "He has a temporary office in Portland, at the Exposition, but also rented an office in Seaside . . . for business, of course, but has some pleasure on the side going on there."

"You mean, besides taking in the sights, sunbathing on the beach?" Rebozo ribbed.

Sylvia frowned in a "none of your concern" way. "He's watching after me too. He's a very protective kind of guy."

"I'm surprised he let us walk off with you, without coming along," Brannon commented.

"I'm sure the name Stuart Brannon helped."

CHAPTER TWELVE

When they reached an opening of sand dunes
with a plank road made from salvaged wood
from a shipwreck, Brannon risked an inquiry,
loud enough to be heard over the clomp of
Geode's hooves and their boot heels on the
wooden surface. "What's the beef between you
and Lanigan?"

"The last time I saw him in Goldfield was at a
fancy dress ball. I managed to dance with every
man in the room except Lanigan. I do believe he
noticed."

"Sometimes a man surmises a woman is playing hard to get," Rebozo remarked.

"I don't want him anywhere near me," Sylvia
spouted. "Somehow he landed at the Portland
depot before me, like he waited for me. He was
attired in top hat and tails and wanted to take
me out. I declined and he took it calmly enough.
That surprised me. But I had my mind on other
pursuits this time."

"Such as?" Brannon prompted.

She kept on with her spiel about Lanigan. "He
seemed nice enough at first, there in Goldfield, but
because of his union rants, and me with the mine
owners, I decided to cool things down between

us. He got obstinate. Now I never know when he'll show up to follow me around. Sometimes I think he's a stalker. He makes me real nervous."

"So the guy won't give up the pursuit. He wants to know how serious you are about your 'no.' "

"I'm very serious. He has major character issues. One time he got upset with a telephone in his Goldfield office. He ripped the instrument off the wall and smashed it to smithers."

Brannon shoved on his black hat. " 'Never till this day saw I him touch'd with anger so distemper'd.' " *He's got as bad or worse a problem as mine.*

"Ah, a quote from *The Tempest*," Rebozo remarked.

Sylvia continued as she hiked the uneven trail. "He's not afraid to spar with anyone, even Sully . . . except a couple friends of yours who ran him out of Goldfield."

"Who was that?"

"The Earp brothers . . . Virgil and Wyatt. Virgil's the deputy sheriff there. Wyatt's the resident gambler."

"Yep, I've had occasion to bump into them doing business in Yavapai County, Arizona."

"I hear Wyatt's going to be in Gearhart later this week," Rebozo said.

"Why were you in Seaside?" Brannon asked.

"Because of Cordelle Plew. Met him on the train. Followed him here."

"Are you gunning for him like you did with Lanigan?" Rebozo added.

She whirled around and swiped Geode's reins in their direction. "It shouldn't be a crime for a woman to shoot a man who needs shooting. I don't let any man treat me like that."

"Okay, but tell us about Cordelle. We really want to know," Brannon pressed.

"I'm convinced that Cordelle's a good man, engaged in a good work. He's a Western Placement Agent, a social worker from New York City. He's here to check on some orphans he placed from the orphan train. He saves perishing, neglected children. There's no higher calling."

"But is he your sweetheart?" Rebozo pried.

"None of your business." She strutted forward as they neared the outskirts of Gearhart. Stars glistened above. Lanterns and electric lights glinted through the trees. "Love will grow, if I let it," she muttered as though only to herself.

"Now, we've got to get this guy," Rebozo waved at Brannon, "to a formal shindig and look decent enough for Lady Harriet Reed-Fletcher."

Brannon tried to muster confidence as he looked down at his attire. "She'll understand."

Rebozo huffed as he tried to sprint to keep up with Brannon. "The Frenchman interests me. He should be suspect."

"Bois DeVache did you say?"

"Yes, he was heavily involved the last fifteen

years with the work at Panama while France was involved. Quite a scandal for the French. All the money spent, the loss of life, the years with nothing to show for it. Big-time engineer. Bad ethics. Trying to hold on to his status. I heard a lot about him . . . from other agents."

"Like who?"

"Can't say, but I've heard he's a man of force, as well as vision. He's also desperate to redeem his name and the honor of his country, and make some profit in the bargain."

"Those can be conflicting goals."

"Yes, that's true." Rebozo fingered back a straggle of his dark hair.

"Did you say he's a man of force? You mean, he might resort to violence?"

"That I don't know. But he is used to getting his way, of being in charge. I know he was to meet with some U.S. engineers here at Gearhart, out of the more public view of Portland. The engineers were here on the coast with their families to attend the Exposition. He was to give them advice on malaria and yellow fever, which are so epidemic for any workers in that Panama region."

"In exchange for what?"

"Don't know that either. But it's a distance to travel to do it for nothing, don't you think?"

Brannon considered what would urge him to journey a long way from hearth and home. *A favor for friends. Very special friends.*

CHAPTER THIRTEEN

Lady Fletcher met Brannon at the hotel lobby. "How can any grown man get that messed up in such a short time?"

"It does take a certain flair," Brannon bantered back.

"There's a basin in the ladies' dressing room. Wash your face. Comb your hair. Try to pin the rip in your tuxedo. Oh, and bandage up that wound and hurry back."

"One thing before I go. I have a favor to ask of you."

"What would that be?"

"Could you find a place for Tom Wiseman's daughter to stay . . . and . . . and fix her up a bit. She's outside with a chestnut horse. She doesn't have to come to the party. Not sure she even wants to."

She broke into a gracious smile. "I'll take care of her. You take care of you."

Brannon caused a stir in the ladies' room, but received lots of offers of help. Then he borrowed an evening jacket from Lord Fletcher, very fashionable, but short in the arms and length. "I'm not trying to impress anyone, but I must pass Harriet's inspection," he told Edwin.

"All for King and country."

Lady Fletcher critiqued his appearance and signaled approval, but not without a sigh. "A young woman's been waiting for you."

She steered him to a dark-skinned Mexican woman, thick black braids rolled on the top of her head, in a long, plain yellow dress. She curtsied before him. "This is my husband, Peter Miller Lowery . . . and I'm Angelita." A huge grin followed. Brannon sorted through a mass of graying memories as to why he should know this couple.

"I'm Tap and Pepper Andrews' foster daughter."

A rush of scenes and stories made him check his pockets, reach for his gun. Angelita, the huckster. But he'd already been the victim of a pickpocket. *Nothing left to take.*

Angelita chuckled. "You're safe, Mr. Brannon. Peter and I now own Stack Lowery's Sphinx Gold Mine, by inheritance. I have no reason to sell Stuart Brannon souvenirs any more at train depots and street corners."

"How are Tap and Pepper doing?"

"Fine, I think. We're going to visit them and the kids as soon as we leave here."

Someone let out a loud yelp. The man in a kilt ran for a large glass of water, gulped it down, then dabbed his face with a wet linen handkerchief.

"You must try the cheese ball appetizers," Angelita said. "I made them myself. Very sharp and zesty."

The mingling of small groups of people pulled together to join in a rousing rendition of *The Band Played On.* Angelita's voice croaked with her husband's as they sang along. "Casey would waltz with a strawberry blonde . . ."

Even Brannon joined in.

Brannon surrendered to a playful social lightness he hadn't experienced in years. Only the presence of his grandchildren could duplicate it. After a few more rounds of the song, the band began to play the Blue Danube Waltz.

"How about a dance?" Angelita offered. "My Peter's got a bum leg after a big black gelding out in the hotel barn kicked him."

Brannon looked over the slim, serious, clean-shaven face of Peter Lowery, hair parted straight down the middle. "I'm not sure I could keep up with your youth and vigor."

"Sure you could. Besides, if you dance with me, you won't have to be bothered by those other silly ladies, those widows who think you're such a catch."

She raised her arms in dance mode and Brannon made an awkward attempt to connect. Angelita proved to be a capable partner and they soon waltzed among several other couples on the dance floor. *I miss Victoria, her sunshine smile, her closeness. Maybe it's because of Angelita being Mexican.*

But also a stab of familiar guilt hit him.

Lisa's locket. I shouldn't have lost it. I couldn't save her life, but I must at least preserve her memory.

When the music stopped, Angelita's eyes sparkled. "Mr. Brannon, you've added so many stories to my repertoire. I shall regale many friends and strangers with our night of magic, our dance in the moonlight, our parting at Sunrise Hill."

He offered a grin. "You can get all of that from a stumble with me around the floor?"

"Ah, the imagination is a fertile field from which to draw the staff of life."

Brannon escorted Angelita back to her husband. Peter Lowery slumped on a cushioned chair, his leg raised on a booster. Brannon felt honorbound to address the subject. "Mr. Lowery, I'm afraid I need to apologize."

"Oh, not necessary," the man jumped in. "I'm always glad to keep Angelita entertained, by whatever means."

Yes, I'm sure she's a high-maintenance wife, but I was referring to that black horse in the barn. I suspect that Tres Vientos may have been the villain.

Brannon's attention followed the sounds of a now-recognizable giggle. Laira Ashley Fletcher was choosing appetizers for a suave man with a thin, curved mustache, blunt sideburns and dark, wavy hair.

Rebozo had sauntered up to Laira Fletcher, a drink of fruit punch for her in his hand. "What do you think of the bridesmaids chosen? Are Princess Victoria, Princess Beatrice, and Princess Patricia worthy?" he began.

"Why, Mr. Rebozo, are you keeping up with the London wedding news?"

"I'd better or there's no one to talk to here tonight."

"Oh, twee. They're all pernickety." She waved her hand around the room. "I'd rather discuss whether or not this romance between Prince Gustaf and Princess Margaret has a chance to last."

"What odds do you give them?"

"It's forever, I'm sure of it. They fell in love at first sight, you know." Laira waved a fan and flickered her eyelashes. "Mr. Rebozo, have you ever fallen in love at first sight?"

He better not let Edwin catch him near his daughter.

Too late.

Brannon got close enough to hear the conversation as Lord Fletcher barreled towards the couple. He could hear the insistent *click, click* of the walking stick.

"I say, sir, we hold the Serbians in ill repute

these days. In fact, we're not on speaking terms, as you know," Lord Fletcher began.

Rebozo was quick with a repartee. "Yet so many Roman emperors have hailed from there. It cannot be all bad."

"Out of many revolutions, the blood does cry," Fletcher stated.

"Out of many foreign rulers, the blood does boil," Rebozo replied.

Fletcher shook his stick at Rebozo. "Ah, well taught, but is it well learned? That whole nasty assassination business of the king and queen. . . ."

Laira stamped her foot. "Oh, twee, Papa, Mr. Rebozo was going to tell me about the rides and amusements at the Exposition. When are we going?"

"After the golf tournament. Won't be long . . . and then we'll return to London." He fixed a gaze on Rebozo.

After Rebozo left to whisper something in the ear of Mrs. Gillespie, Lord Fletcher turned to Brannon. "The man's not a native Serbian, but he may have visited there long enough to know the culture."

"Why do you say that?"

"Not barbarian enough."

Lady Fletcher swooped over with Willamette Orphan Farm Director Sam Smythe, his wife, Eloise Smythe, a pleasant woman with a kind smile and masses of hair beneath her flowered hat, and two pretty, young staffers, Penelope Tagg and Henrietta Ober. A dozen children lined a table, hands in laps, stair-stepped in head height. Six girls under large hats. Five boys in knickerbockers, plus another in a sailor suit.

Sam Smythe showed Brannon a small plaque. "We'd be honored to have you present this to one of our orphans, Bueno, the ten-year-old in the sailor suit. He saved an older boy, Hack Howard, from drowning. We want to reward his courage. The presentation will immediately follow the speech by Wax Lanigan, the President of our board."

Brannon aimed a sharp look at the director, then at Lady Fletcher.

"It's because of Lanigan that we're here," Lady Fletcher explained. "He proposed the idea of the golf tournament after he convinced us of the value of the Orphan Farm."

"Yes," continued the director, "although Mr. Lanigan has only been in the area for a few months, he has raised a tremendous amount of money from donors for both the orphans and the Lewis and Clark Exposition. He himself was an orphan and has quite a story to tell. I believe he'll share it tonight."

Brannon tried to assimilate this information while Lady Fletcher led him to a table at the side of a small stage. His mind whirred in several directions at once. He had always tried to convince the wayward to repent, to choose a different path. Some did. Many did not. He regretted those he had sent to their eternal reward with curses still on their lips and in their hearts. He aimed to be ready to forgive, if not forget.

So, had Wax Lanigan switched moral and legal sides? Had he turned to fine, upstanding citizenry as his life's new goal? If so, it had been very recent. However, he did recall that the man had ingratiated himself into the graces of the local society before the stagecoach robbery.

Brannon disclosed the question to Lady Fletcher uppermost in his mind. "Why would Lanigan contact you way over there in London? How did he even think to do so?"

"He explained that he was given a list of officials and dignitaries who would be part of the Exposition. He chose a sampling who might be interested in his cause. He was right about us."

At first Brannon didn't recognize the woman at his table. She squirmed in a lacy, bouffant dress of peach and cream, her hair in a very neat, dainty and loose full roll around her face. A light make-up completed the polished effect. *Sylvia!*

CHAPTER FOURTEEN

"Hi, Stuart. Your Harriet can work wonders."

"I agree." Brannon admired Sylvia's transformation from head to toe.

Lady Fletcher beamed her full approval. "You didn't mention that your lady friend likes to ride her horse English style."

"What do you mean riding English? We walked from Seaside."

"Like a man. The British women do that all the time. When I lived here in the States, I rode buggy, buckboard or wagon whenever I could because of the discomfort of the sidesaddle."

Director Sam Smythe took charge of the program after a supper of duck à l'orange, herb-crusted salmon, wild rice and onions, asparagus au gratin, and blackberry pie. Brannon was not impressed. He cheered up when a waiter brought a bowl of mashed potatoes with fresh mounds of melting butter that formed pools across the top. While he dug in for seconds, he searched in vain for more steak, with or without mushrooms. He settled for two helpings of frozen sherbet.

Then Director Smythe introduced Wax Lanigan.

Brannon had to admit that Lanigan looked the

part in his black double-breasted suit, black tie and polished black Oxford shoes. His neat, close-cut mustache and beard, and swivel of hair on top, emphasized his ears that jutted an inch from his head. He looked humble at all the right times, but his speech seemed to Brannon to be given by rote.

Why am I so suspicious? Can't I give the man a break? It's not unusual to memorize a speech. Lord, I'm sure glad you're more gracious to us.

Lanigan concluded with, "I was born a pauper and lost my mother at birth. My father died by violence before I was born. An aunt tried to raise me, but she fell into ill health. I scrounged in the streets for food and shelter for myself and my two siblings." He paused to wipe his forehead. "But if there had been a place like Willamette Orphan Farm, I would have received good care."

Then it was time for the award for Bueno Diaz. Brannon said a few words about the boy's bravery, as it had been related to him. The boy took the plaque, thanked Brannon in a quiet, stilted voice, then sat down next to a taller boy, the one he had rescued. Bueno seemed more than shy, almost petrified. *Stage fright. I know the feeling.*

Brannon started to hand out the small packages of candy to each of the orphans that Lady Fletcher had prepared for them. "Wait until after the pageant," she prompted.

The orphans acted out some scenes from Charles Dickens' *Oliver Twist*, then all the orphans and the staff were called on the stage for a final bow. Wax Lanigan took their picture with a folding Kodak Brownie camera.

Brannon and a crowd of others admired it.

"They'll make improvements. The larger cameras still take better, more permanent photographs." Lanigan aimed the camera at Brannon.

He turned away. "I've had enough for a lifetime."

Laira rushed up to her mother after the event. "Can we keep one of the orphans for a few days?"

"What on earth for?"

"How about Bueno, the hero? He could stay with me in my room. I have a partition. We can take him back Saturday, after the golf tournament."

"Laira, these kids aren't like pets for your diversion."

"Oh, please, Mum. I want to do something good for someone."

Lady Fletcher checked with Director Sam Smythe. He gave permission for Bueno to stay over Wax Lanigan's objections. "The Fletchers are quite capable," Smythe said.

"To be sure," then Lanigan offered Lady Fletcher a profuse apology. "I didn't want you to be ill-disposed in any way by the boy. They can be quite a challenge."

Lady Fletcher patted Lanigan's shoulder in appreciation. "Perhaps he can room with you, Brannon. You don't have to care for him. Laira will do that. It shouldn't intrude with your search for Tom Wiseman."

Brannon hesitated. "There's no place for him. You see, I invited some ladies to stay in my room."

Lady Fletcher turned crimson. "Oh, Stuart, I had no idea."

"No, it's not like that. They were in a tent out in the park and it was raining and the tent had holes."

"Ah, the compassionate Brannon."

"I believe that Edwin will remember them. They are the Lazzard twins from Paradise Meadow."

"Oh?" The way Lady Fletcher crooked her head indicated an imminent inquisition. Brannon made a mental note to warn Edwin.

"In fact, they wanted me to ask you to invite them to a party or two of yours. They're from San Francisco now and want to get acquainted."

"My, Stuart, we've got our hands full with your bevy of women."

Brannon blew out a breath and scratched his head. "It's not what you think. I know it sounds . . ."

Lady Fletcher lightly touched his arm. "I'll stop by your room and investigate them myself."

CHAPTER FIFTEEN

Brannon noticed Lanigan and Rebozo engaged in deep conversation by the stage. When Rebozo walked by, Brannon asked him about their relationship.

"Well, we've got the same vice: poker," Rebozo explained.

"I hear gambling debts can corral mighty poor company."

"I play smart and prefer partners who do too."

"Got a game going around here?"

"At Seaside. This town's as dry as a sunstruck cactus. And Lanigan's a calculating player. I like the challenge. Never seen him lose a big hand yet of any significant money. Very cautious. If he's not absolutely sure he has the best cards, he's out. Me, on the other hand . . ."

Madam Cob, whom he heard addressed in his presence several times as Mrs. Jedediah Acorn, *widowed,* cozied up to him like a lifelong friend. "Mr. Brannon, we heard about your attack in the streets by some Serbian diamond smugglers. Do tell us about it."

"Serbian?" Mrs. Gillespie had sidled up to Rebozo without Brannon's notice even though she had added purple feathers to her already large hat. "No, no, no. I was told he got throttled by Romanian acrobats."

Mrs. Acorn gently tucked her arm through his one decent sleeve. "Will this be in your next book? You know, my name is Patricia, but I have always wanted my name to be spelled P a t r e s h. When you write the Serbian or Romanian chapter about my eyebrow signal that saved your life, could you spell it that way?"

The slightest swish of a lavender dress and a whiff of perfume closed in as Mrs. Gillespie took up residence on Brannon's other arm. "Don't be silly, Patricia. You'll need to discuss that with his editor, Mr. Hawthorne Miller."

"Or to a real Serbian," Rebozo interjected.

The two women flashed him adoring smiles, then turned back to Brannon.

Brannon took a deep breath and both enjoyed and regretted it as the ladies' competing perfumes filled his lungs. "Mr. Miller is the actual writer. I have nothing to do with his books, especially the royalties."

Patricia Acorn brushed his shoulder with a yellow silk handkerchief. "And so modest too."

"But a bit scruffy, don't you think?" Rebozo pulled at his arm as he winced.

"It wouldn't be right somehow if Stuart Brannon didn't look a bit bashed," Mrs. Acorn huffed. "That's the excitement of sharing the same room with him. One never knows when one could get robbed or clobbered, even shot."

Lord Fletcher rescued him, but it was to a storm brewing and it wasn't long until Brannon fumed with himself about his generosity to the Lazzard twins.

Sorry, Edwin.

"I knew about the Lady McNeil stories, but hadn't heard about these women," Lady Fletcher remarked.

"But we only knew them for a day or two," Edwin tried to explain. "I got rid of them as quick as possible. Sent them to San Francisco."

"Hmmm . . . sent them. So, you paid their way?"

"It appeared to be the best way to handle the situation. Tell her, Stuart."

"I wasn't there at the time exactly. I freed them from jail and told Edwin to take care of them and he did." Brannon knew he wasn't helping much. Edwin's look of defeat confirmed it.

As rumors of the Lazzard twins circulated the party, Brannon realized it was now public knowledge that he would be sleeping out on the beach. He had no reason to skulk out with his gear. He marched in plain view towards the final rays of sunset over the ocean, streaks of red-orange, peach, and deep purple reflected in the wide swath of sea. A gold-yellow cloud halo hung over Tillamook Head.

As the waves tumbled in the distance, Brannon

stretched his bedroll on a flattened place of the tall dune grass. A bright, almost full moon glowed through. Puffy clouds, a mixture of charcoal and marshmallow, chugged across the darkened azure sky. He reflected on what he had learned about Tom Wiseman and what he should do next to find him.

Brannon knew Wiseman had many Indian friends through his duties as a U.S. Marshal and contacts with the Bureau of Indian Affairs. Many Indians were scattered throughout this area and signs indicated recent fires on the beach. Maybe he should contact the nearby tribes or clans. He would search for the Nicaraguan and Frenchman too.

He tried to relax every muscle and almost drifted to sleep when he jumped up and slapped his arms and legs and face. Tiny pricks all over. Stings up and down his arms. He grabbed up his bedroll and shook it out as hard as he could as his legs threatened to turn to jelly.

Mosquitoes? Sand fleas?

With great reluctance, Brannon abandoned his grassy hideaway and ventured out onto the open beach. He gathered driftwood and bits of bark to start a fire, in hopes of warding off the insects. He drank his coffee straight off the campfire from a chipped blue enamel tin cup. "Well, world," he muttered. "Here I am for all to see. One easy target."

He searched the horizons that had turned

indigo after the iridescent sunset for any movement of suspicious shadows. Satisfied that he was alone on this piece of beach, he settled down for another try at sleep. As he dozed on and off, he surrendered to a strange dream.

A beach stretched with pebbles, not sand, for miles. As he walked along barefoot, he faced a fork forced by a stream. He didn't know which way to go, but he felt certain the choice was important.

He decided to try a couple miles on each side and started to the right. He stumbled on tree roots, then tripped over a man's body half-buried in a strip of sand. The man raised an arm in greeting. He resembled Tally Rebozo.

"Are you a Serbian spy? Are you a Serbian spy?" Brannon goaded him over and over.

Finally, the man spit out a spray of sand to reply. "Doesn't matter. Serbians don't care about your country or the Panama Canal or Tom Wiseman. Remember that. And they don't give a hoot about you."

Brannon pounded stakes to mark the path back to the man. Along the way, he passed several abandoned campsites he hadn't noticed before. A huge wave swelled over him. Trout and salmon flopped around on the shore.

Fish. What did this have to do with fish?

Brannon woke to pungent, salty sea smells, a clap like thunder, and a man towering over him. He aimed his Colt through the thin blanket.

"You always sleep with a cocked revolver?" Rebozo said.

"A habit from the old days."

"I'll bet it has stunted your social life."

What social life? Point taken. "Funny, I was just dreaming about you."

Brannon tried to shake off the dream when about ten horses splashed the surf and roared past them. Although he hadn't noticed a rider, a spear soared a few feet away, missing them both. After the rumble faded, Brannon stretched out to pull up the spear. Hand carved. Rough wood. No markings. A threat or a warning? Or a simple greeting?

They both studied the six-foot long spear.

"Someone trying to stick you?" Rebozo asked.

"If so, not a great aim."

Brannon gathered his gear and they shuffled along the beach. The sky was scattered with gray clouds and streaked with light, as though uncertain what kind of day to be. "What are you doing here anyway?"

"Checking up on my assignment. So, what was your dream? Did we do something exciting, like find Tom Wiseman? Was Lady Fletcher chasing us?"

"No women, not even Sharon Gillespie."

"Pay attention to your dreams. They can conceal messages. Someone could be trying to tell you something." He aimed a finger above.

CHAPTER SIXTEEN

Tuesday, June 13

Sylvia Wiseman accosted him before he reached the hotel café. She wore the same tweed suit as the previous day, but had added a fur hat without the wrap. They passed a sign that said: "Good meals: fifteen cents and up. Fine meals served at all hours."

The two of them sat down at a table for four and the waitress slid off two sets of silverware.

"My name's Katie and I am your server." She had a friendly, open face. She gave the impression that if she heard restaurant gossip she'd put a positive outcome to it.

"How are you today, Katie?" Brannon noticed bear meat as a menu item. *Maybe another time.*

"Fine as long as I don't have to work fifteen hour days."

Sylvia ordered a boiled egg and toast. Brannon wanted the special: ham, omelet, hashed potatoes and a stack of pancakes with blackberry syrup.

"I've been on the telephone already this morning," she announced. "Sully grabbed two of those ruffians who shot at us last night. And Cordelle's still working hard to follow up on his orphans. One he fears is involved with that young gang. He's real concerned about a seventeen-year-old named Mort. He ran away from his foster home in Portland after some friends influenced him to do some petty theft. Made major problems for his assigned family."

"So, the boy's roaming the streets of Seaside?"

"Yes, Cordelle told him that at the least he could be arrested for vagrancy. And with the mood of the Seaside citizens right now, he could be implicated in much worse. He's too old to go to the orphan farm, so Cordelle's making arrangements for him to live with a farmer in the area."

"Why shoot at us?" Brannon asked as Katie poured each of them steaming cups of coffee.

"That's just it. They don't seem to have any motive. Sully thinks maybe the new members of the gang are trying to prove they're tough enough to join by random acts of mayhem."

Maybe the orphans do need more help around here. "Is that all you talked about?"

She blushed. "There were other items. Which reminds me, I asked Lady Fletcher to find out if any of Papa's belongings had been saved from his room."

"What did you find?"

She read from a handwritten note. "A Remington bolt-action rifle, a duffle with clothes and personal items, pair of shoes, extradition papers for Chuy Carbón, information on the backgrounds of half a dozen engineers that included the Frenchman, Bois DeVache, and a list of telephone numbers that I was surprised had the name of Geoff Wiseman beside one."

"Geoff Wiseman? A relative?"

"Papa's brother. They have been estranged for years, all my life at least."

"I didn't know he had a brother. What was the rift?"

"They both dated my mother. Papa talked her into an elopement the very night he knew Uncle Geoff wanted to ask her to marry him. Uncle Geoff left the family and the state after that. I know my father wrote to him at least once a year, but we hadn't heard from him since."

"Maybe Tom was going to contact him, try to reconcile."

"I called that number. Talked to Uncle Geoff's wife. Papa did attempt a contact. Uncle Geoff died last year. His wife said the official cause was listed as epilepsy. But she confessed later in our talk that he drank himself to death. She sounded like a nice woman. I'll go see her sometime."

Brannon sat down at a table and looked at the day's menu. "That must have been so tough on Tom. . . ."

Sylvia looked at her ringless hands. "On a happier note, there's more. In Papa's goods, I found a gift wrapped in white lawn material with my name attached."

"Did you open it?"

"No, my birthday isn't until Sunday."

"Oh! Well, maybe we'll find Tom and he can present it to you himself."

"That would be more than delightful. Meanwhile, I'm going to check the rest of the phone numbers and talk to Mr. Carbón myself . . . right after I phone Seaside again."

"And I've got to contact Tally Rebozo, at least to know where he is and to see what he's up to."

Sylvia gave him a quizzical look. "You his brother's keeper?"

Brannon searched for Lady Fletcher and found her in the kitchen giving orders to the hotel staff.

She read another postcard to him from granddaughter, Elizabeth, written by her mother: "Porky the bull got loose out of the fence. Papa fell off his horse trying to rope Porky. Got him back through the gate. Papa has a broken arm and sore ribs. We miss you, Grandpa."

After inquiries about Tally Rebozo produced no results, Brannon hiked to the hotel barn to saddle up Tres Vientos. He planned to investigate the beach, hills, and forest areas for signs or clues of the whereabouts of Tom Wiseman. *But I'll start with a ride through town. Sure won't take long.*

He counted about forty stalls and found the big black gelding in #35. He called to the horse.

No movement. Brannon nudged him. He wouldn't come. As hard as he coaxed, Tres Vientos refused to leave the barn.

I guess I finally found a bronc I can't ride . . . my own.

"I will help you, Mr. Brannon." Bueno, the orphan, rushed to stall #34. He led out a well-groomed, well-fed, probably never overworked white Arabian mare. "This is Amble, Lady Laira's horse. She wants me to take special care of her."

"*Lady* Laira? Is she considered a Lady?"

"I do not know. That is what she told me to call her. Now, watch."

Bueno led Amble out of the barn and Tres Vientos followed as calm as can be. "I will go with you as far as the beach, but then I must get back. Lady Laira has errands for me."

"You seem to know a thing or two about horses."

"I can tell which is a dun and what's a buckskin and that paint and pinto are colors not breeds. I learned that from Miss Tagg. She knows lots about horses."

"What else did you learn?"

"Every horse is different, so you gotta figure out its likes and dislikes, treat 'em like people."

Brannon held the reins as the horses shuffled down a trail and out to the sand. But as soon as Bueno and Amble turned back towards the barn,

Tres Vientos flipped around and headed that way too.

Brannon tried to talk to him. "Come on, boy, we've got work to do. You'll like it out here with the sand, wind and water . . . once you get used to it. Stick with me, you'll be safe and secure." Tres Vientos balked and would not budge.

Brannon finally gave up, but he couldn't help grumble. "I don't have time for this. He's fearful of this new environment. I guess I better bring some apples or carrots with me next time, like I did when he was young and ornery. Meanwhile, I need transportation. How can a horse that helps me drive cattle and ride miles of fence in the desert be so useless here?"

I guess I should have considered that before I drug him out here to a strange land.

"I could ask Lady Laira if you can borrow her horse, you know, as a companion?" Bueno suggested.

"No, definitely not."

"Well, there is a bicycle shop right down the street."

"Bicycle!" Brannon hooted.

"Or you could rent a motor car?" The boy's forehead furrowed in concentration.

"You don't have to worry about it. Sounds like you've got your time spoken for with Madam Laira. You get along."

"No, sir, I won't worry about it because you're

Stuart Brannon. You'll think of something. You always do." The boy made a kind of salute, then ran into the barn.

Brannon stalled Tres Vientos in #35 and stomped out. *Now what?*

He charged forward again for the seashore and stopped. "Now, which way is that bike shop Bueno mentioned?"

He moseyed by Gearhart Park with the auditorium and gazebo and past the cribbed, wooden bridge of the Neacoxie Creek where several boaters rowed. More tents and unprotected bedding filled the outlying grassy areas. Both poor and rich enjoyed the scenic playground. Some of the tents were being used for a daily summer Episcopal camp for local and visiting children.

Neat, manicured yards and mansion-like homes formed this part of the residential area, which included the Marshall Kinney place with numerous gables and a two-storey turret. He passed the Latourette House with lap siding and tongue and groove construction, the Frank Smith and Shaw houses, the Taft home and one called the Honeymoon House. All the citizens subsisted on well water which had to be dug for the owners, then bought, borrowed and carried by less fortunate neighbors. He had heard no complaints on that score.

This is a beautiful place, I have to admit, for city living, that is.

At the center of town, he stopped to gaze at a storefront with men's and boy's clothing displayed in the two side windows. Signs indicated that bicycles, bags and trunks were also part of the merchandise. Inside, he noticed they offered some furnishings and Goodyear Rubber Company clothing, such as shoes and "snag-proof, crack-proof" fishing boots.

At the back, wheels, rims and parts of bicycles hung on the walls and from the rafters. He saw three locked bicycles leaned in a rack.

Like those bicycles that Victoria bought from a peddler to have at the hacienda. Everyone stood in line to get a chance to ride them . . . with varying success. Some got balanced and pedaled right away. Others never did. I was somewhere in the middle, but if I can manage some traction, I'll get in some miles.

"Can I help you, sir?"

"I need one of those . . . for a few hours. Can I rent one?"

"No, sir, I'm sorry."

"Are they spoken for?"

"No, sir, I am very sorry."

"Well, what do you do with them?"

"We sell them. No rentals, as of last week. We've had three bicycles taken out and not returned."

"What if I leave you the full price, then when I bring it back, I'll get a partial refund?"

"Sorry, sir, I cannot do that."

"How come?"

"Well, two of those are ladies' bikes. And the other one is a recumbent with a faulty wheel."

"Well, can't you replace the wheel with one of those?" Brannon pointed to the dozens scattered around.

"Yes, sir, I can, but it will cost you extry, plus some time."

"How much and how long?"

"Ten dollars total and an hour. I've got other customers to wait on."

"But that's highway robbery."

"Yes, sir, I know."

"I'll be back in an hour."

CHAPTER SEVENTEEN

Brannon squeezed through the narrow aisles of the store and scooted past several women with children in tow, merchandise in hand. He gazed around the few businesses in the town proper of Gearhart, besides the mercantile . . . grocery store, bakery, Hoefler's confectioner, blacksmith shop.

He decided to take a stroll towards the depot where the "Daddy Train" would arrive on Friday with the weekend fathers from Portland coming to stay with their vacationing families. Women and children constituted the major population in Gearhart right now. They rented cabins, took up residence in summer homes, or camped out in tents on the beautiful grounds of the Gearhart Park.

He noticed the men in brown lurking at the bakery shop window. A coincidence? Or something to do with Brannon? He decided to find out.

Passing the small depot station, he turned a sharp left down a wooded pathway. After he stepped off thirty feet, he reached down as though pulling something from his boot and looked back. Two men stopped to chat in the middle of the trail. "Let's find out what's on their minds," Brannon muttered.

He marched in their direction, arm out, as if to shake hands. "Imagine meeting up with you boys. What a pleasure."

"County Sheriff Linville knows you're here. You're being watched," the heftier one said.

"And yet with all this attention, I still haven't been properly introduced. You know my name, but I don't yours."

"It don't matter."

"Why, sure it does. I might want to check out your criminal records."

"That's ridiculous." Hefty and his partner began to back away, hands stuck in their pockets.

"I wouldn't go for any weapon, boys. I can out-shoot the two of you put together."

"That's one of the reasons you need to be off Clatsop County streets," said Hefty.

"And our trains." His friend's voice was higher, whinier. "We'll make an example of you . . . if you don't mind your own business." The man pulled up his shirtsleeves for emphasis.

"What's the matter, boys? Did I step in the way of some operation of yours?"

The men looked at each other, then Hefty glared at Brannon with an alligator smirk, broad and menacing. "You wouldn't talk like that if you knew who was right behind you."

Brannon dropped to the ground, then spun and jerked both legs. A man wearing a buttoned black duster toppled but still managed to smack

Brannon hard on his left shoulder with the backside of an axe. Brannon and the man exchanged punches and elbowed each other. The two brown suited men got in the melee but Brannon couldn't tell if they tried to help or hurt him. Finally, he reached for his Colt revolver.

"Okay, guys, the charade is over. Who are you?"

"I'm the shootist, Argentiferous Jones," said the man with the axe. His swollen, crooked nose had been broken before, like a boxer's. He hovered over Brannon. "I'm deadly as a steely-eyed viper, dangerous as a wounded wolf, and a faster draw than a snake's tongue."

"Is that right? At the moment, you look like an amateur axe carrier to me."

"I left my gun and holster in the privy."

"Aren't you the guy that's supposed to have gunned me down?"

"Yep, that's me," the man beamed. "I'm famous now. But think of how much more famous I'll become if I actually do get Stuart Brannon."

Brannon raised his hands in disgust, then holstered his revolver. "I'll tell you one thing, I don't like your name and I don't like your face. Can't do anything about the face, except maybe beat it up some more. But I'll never call you Argentiferous. Maybe Tiff or Russ or Jones. Which will it be?"

"Hey, you can call me Tiff." He raised his axe in a hurrah gesture. "I favor that. Yes, I sure do favor that. Never liked my name before. Kinda had a grudge against my mama about that."

"Okay, Tiff, if you'll stop trying to kill me, we'll get along a whole lot better. And now you can make peace with your mama. Deal?"

Argentiferous Jones pondered that a minute. "Deal." He shook Brannon's hand and walked away muttering, "Tiff . . . Tiff Jones . . . Good evenin', Ma'am, my name is Tiff Jones."

Brannon turned to the men in brown suits. "I don't know why you're following me, but it comes real close to harassment. Either you've got a legal charge against me that is brought to the authorities . . . wherever they are . . . or leave me alone."

Brannon marched back to the mercantile. None of the men followed.

"You got that bicycle ready?"

"No, sir, I am sorry," said the owner.

"Yes, I know, you're very sorry, truly sorry." Brannon slammed the door shut behind him. With the heavy bang of boot heels and the jab of spur jingles on the wooden street, he tramped back to the hotel.

My horse won't cooperate. I can't even rent myself a bicycle. And fictional characters are tryin' to bushwhack me. Tom, I hope you're not in too deep a hole out there somewhere 'cause this old buddy of yours can't seem to get on the trail, much less find the trail.

Brannon entered the large hotel lobby and tipped his hat at Laira Ashley Fletcher playing the piano with Bueno standing beside her turning the pages of the music. He inquired at the hotel desk for Lord Fletcher. *Maybe he'll drive me around with his Buick.*

"He's at a meeting. Shall I tell him you're asking for him, Mr. Brannon?"

"No, I'll check with him later."

"There you are, Stuart." He recognized the voice of Lady Fletcher. "Any leads on Tom Wiseman?"

He shook his head. "What is Edwin up to?"

"He's trying to keep Europe from starting another war."

"Is it really that serious?"

"It is to Edwin and those around him."

"I wonder if that is T.R.'s concern too. This deal with my friend, Tom, does not seem crucial to anyone but those who know him. He may be in danger, but it seems so . . . so . . ."

"Domestic?"

"Yep, that's the word. I think I'll take a walk out on the Ridge Path and down to the golf course. I've got a commitment to keep."

"I'll walk with you partway." Lady Fletcher strolled with an ebony and silk umbrella, wearing a dainty organdy frock scattered with pink roses. "This is one of the loveliest promenades along the Pacific Coast."

Brannon cast a casual glance at trees, flowering bushes and some houses that looked like mansions to him. In comparison to the Ridge Path and Mrs. Kinney's park on the south end of town, Mr. Kinney's golf course on the north side seemed scrubby, dry, almost barren. A few trees dotted the course, none of the trunks straight, all crooked and as bent as old men weary from burdens.

I wonder which enterprise will endure the longest?

Keaton Tanglewood scurried towards them at the golf course, then waved goodbye to Lady Fletcher.

"I saw some wild horses on the beach this morning," Brannon greeted. "The lead horse had a rider, though I didn't see him. I got a spear thrown at me. What do you know about them?"

"At dawn?" Tanglewood hit a long, sweeping shot, then handed the club to Brannon.

"Yes it was."

"Catcher-Of-The-Sun. He's a very old man in our tribe. Rides the mares to spite the stallions, but doesn't keep them. Lets them roam free. He claims a cougar in the area riles the wild horses and chases them on midnight runs."

"Why did he throw the spear?"

"I do not know. He is the ancient one. Perhaps he meant to show you honor. Maybe a warning. Some say his mind has gone crazy. If he meant to harm you, he wouldn't have missed."

"Is he the same Catcher-Of-The-Sun I saw in a painting at the Exposition in Portland? This one ran along the top of a mountain cliff and carried a torch. There was a war scene below him."

"Yes, that's him. My grandfather told me many stories. He is a hero to our people."

"That's not why I wanted to see you. Do you know a man named Chuy Carbón?"

"Yes, I know him. He is not a nice man. He lives not far from here."

"After I practice a while, is it possible for you to take me to see him? I'd be glad to help you finish your job duties afterward."

No matter how structured, how cared-for, how many civic-minded folks bring culture and education to a city, there exists a part of town that insists on being the run-down side. Keaton Tanglewood wound through the streets that Brannon had hiked that morning and several blocks over to a few shacks and cabins with weathered wood siding and roofs of rusty metal.

Tanglewood knocked at the door of the only dwelling with visible curtains. Landscaping consisted of a tall, lush spray of pampas grass in the front, with long, white, tufted and feathery blooms that swayed in the breeze.

A pleasingly-plump, swarthy-skinned woman peered out. "Chuy's not here," she said, door half-closed.

"Mrs. Carbón, we need to ask a few questions, then we'll leave him alone," Tanglewood said.

"Go away. He will not talk to no one, not even me."

"Tell him that Stuart Brannon wishes to ask a few questions."

Brannon recognized the raw fear in her eyes, like Tres Vientos when he got near a rattler in the desert . . . or the outside entry to the coastal beach barn.

"You are the Brannon?" she whispered.

"I don't mean any harm to your husband. I want him to answer some questions about Tom Wiseman."

"Ohhhh . . ." The facial fear did not ease. She held onto the door as if for support.

"What's going on?" a male voice bellowed behind her. The door swung back, teetering the woman who crashed against the wall, rattling the roof. A man with round, dark falcon eyes swayed in long-johns, a bottled drink in each hand. "Ah, it's you, Tanglewood. Come in, my injun friend. You want your clothes back?"

I thought Narcissa Kinney forced Gearhart to make a law about not selling or buying liquor? It takes a little more effort for a man to get drunk in a dry town.

"No, Mr. Carbón, I brought Stuart Brannon. He is Tom Wiseman's friend."

The man's face glazed like glass, rigid and

154

pale. He flailed at the door and meant to slam it shut, but he stumbled and fell forward instead, crashing into Brannon. "I'm dead," he whimpered.

Brannon pushed the man back inside the cabin and shoved him into the only chair he would fit in. The woman rushed over to a stove with water steaming in a kettle. "I will fix you all hot chocolate," she said. "That's a good thing when friends come to visit." She forced a humming sound, a song with no tune.

"I hear you met with Tom Wiseman the night he went missing," Brannon began.

"I didn't do it. I did nothing."

"You didn't do what? What happened to Tom?"

"I don't know. Maybe the Frenchman knows. He threatened Tom. He told him that . . . that he would not deliver the medicines if . . . if Tom didn't talk the President into hiring more Frenchmen."

"Hiring more Frenchmen? For what?"

"For Panama . . . for that canal they're building. I told them both that I had friends in Nicaragua who knew a better route than Panama, a cheaper and safer one. I would contact them and that would be much, much better."

"Is that why you wanted to shoot the Vice-President?" his wife said.

"Shut up, woman, what do you know? Go do your mending. Go stuff your face."

"You were going to assassinate the Vice-President of Nicaragua?" Brannon prodded.

"No," Mrs. Carbón said, "Mr. Fairbanks, the United States Vice-President. And he would have, at the opening day of the Lewis and Clark Exposition, but his gun jammed. Now, he hears a rumor that President Roosevelt might come to Gearhart."

Chuy Carbón had risen from the chair and was halfway across the cabin, swinging the bottles at his wife. "Shut up, woman. You are digging your grave."

Tanglewood and Brannon rushed over and each grabbed an arm before either bottle struck the woman. They dragged him back and pushed him down into the chair. One of the bottles fell from his hand, cracked him on the forehead with a thud, then fell to the floor and smashed into pieces. The flooring got soaked. He began to cry.

"Carbón, why were you dressed as an Indian, that night you were with Tom Wiseman?" Brannon questioned.

Carbón stopped whimpering and sat up tall. "So no one would recognize me. I was representing my great country. I told the Frenchman and Americans that Nicaragua was the best route for Panama. It was a very secret meeting."

"Ha!" Mrs. Carbón spit the word out. "He cares nothing for Nicaragua. He did everything he could think of to talk Tom Wiseman out of sending him back. He is like a crazy man."

"Why would Tom want to do that?" Brannon asked.

"Because he's a bigamist. I found out from Tom Wiseman that Chuy has four other wives in Nicaragua. He thought he was safe here in Oregon, but an extradition treaty was recently signed . . . and the other women have issued complaints. It's all about the money, his money, which he does not have." She jeered at Carbón who shrugged as he downed the remaining liquid in the other bottle.

Bigamist? I believe the word is polygamist. Brannon studied the unkempt, overweight, sloppy lout of a man that was Chuy Carbón. *He got five different women to marry him? And this marriage does not appear to be happy either.* "So, you had a reason to get rid of Tom Wiseman? What did you do with him?"

"No, please believe me, *el Brannon.* Nina!" He pleaded, "Tell them I am innocent. I did nothing."

"What can you tell me, Mrs. Carbón?" Brannon walked over and picked up one of the mugs of chocolate. He took a slow sip and smiled his thanks.

"You like it?" She seemed pleased. Not as pretty as Victoria, but her smile could draw the right man in . . . and the wrong one. She leaned forward as though she sensed Brannon evaluating her. "He's only mean when he's drunk, but conniving always." She sighed. "But he's so often drunk . . ." She trailed off.

Brannon took another sip of the rich chocolate as Mrs. Carbón refocused. "Chuy did talk about doing harm to Tom Wiseman, but the marshal disappeared before he could try anything. He is nervous that he might show up at any minute."

Brannon drank down the last sludge of chocolate at the bottom.

"The Frenchman did it. It's always the French." Carbón staggered up again, then passed out, half-sprawled on the floor and against the chair.

"Do you know where the Frenchman is?" Brannon asked.

She shook her head and handed Tanglewood a mug of steaming chocolate.

CHAPTER EIGHTEEN

As they left Carbón's place, Brannon sensed someone following them, a half block behind. Keeping with their pace. Stopping when they halted. *If it's those men in the brown suits again, I'm going to hogtie them to the railroad tracks.*

Brannon whirled around, his hand on his Colt.

A gentleman approached them wearing a top hat and a frock coat with long lapel and curved tail and very high, starched collar.

"Monsieur Brannon, I hear you are looking for Bois DeVache."

"Is that you?"

"Oh no, he is no longer in the area, that I know. I certainly have not seen him for more than a week. But I have a message that Monsieur DeVache related to me right before the big engineers' meeting he attended. I thought it might help."

"But who are you?" Brannon insisted.

"Ah, monsieur, I am no one, only his partner."

"Partner for what?"

"In gambling. We both liked to play poker. We had games almost every night that he was here, in Seaside."

"I want to talk to him. Where in Seaside were your games?"

"That I cannot divulge . . . and there is no need. Monsieur DeVache disclosed to me that Monsieur Wiseman was to join with the meeting, but he confided to Monsieur DeVache that he was going home right afterward."

"Home? You mean back to the hotel?"

"No, Monsieur DeVache understood he was returning to his ranch in Arizona. He said his work was done and he was no longer needed."

Brannon watched quirly smoke rise above the man's head. "What was DeVache's business with the marshal?"

"Nothing professional. That is, he was meeting with the U.S. engineers, to offer counsel on how to sanitize the Panama areas, to minimize malaria and yellow fever threats."

"Anything else?"

"Also, to help them deal with the general chaos there, by being in charge of excavation of old French equipment. It is a mess. In addition, to argue the positives and negatives of a lock canal versus a sea-level canal."

"Why was Tom Wiseman part of the meeting?"

"Monsieur Wiseman was the *agent . . . de police*. Like the men around your President . . . the bodyguards."

"You mean, our secret service? But why was he needed?"

"A threat had been made on the lives of those at the meeting, by an anonymous source."

"Do you have any idea who that would be?"

"Perhaps someone who does not want the Panama project to go forward. Or it could have been personal. But DeVache had nothing to do with it. Marshal Wiseman was worth more to him alive. He had a straight line to your President. That meant riches for him."

"What was DeVache selling?"

All pretense of *bonhomie* evaporated. *"C'est tout dire."* The man gave a curt bow and hiked away.

As soon as they returned to the Gearhart Golf Course, Brannon kept his promise to help Tanglewood with his duties. They finished within an hour. But then Brannon decided to find Rebozo. If he was a trusted partner, he should be told about his interview with Carbón. On the other hand, if he was a deceiver or complicit in the disappearance of Tom Wiseman, Brannon needed to discover that fact as soon as possible. He also wanted to ask Sylvia about the Frenchman's claim.

He didn't have far to look. Shouts issued from the direction of the train depot. When he investigated, he found Rebozo and Sylvia sparring with knives. A few citizens had scurried into the ticket master's small building and peered through a window.

"What are you two doing?" Brannon pulled out his Colt.

"He's trying to escape," Sylvia accused.

"I've got a lead on some investigations," Rebozo replied.

"Sylvia, Rebozo is an agent for the government."

She kept her knife in thrust position. "What government?"

"Direct for Theodore Roosevelt, the President of these United States." Rebozo slowly pulled off his coat and rolled up his shirt sleeve. "I think she grazed me."

Sylvia almost whispered, "I knew he seemed familiar. Then I remembered a mob scene at the Consolidated strike in Goldfield, him standing beside Wax Lanigan. I figured he was one of his cronies in disguise."

Brannon kept his Colt out, but dropped it to his side. "He might have been in Goldfield, but he was probably doing some secret government work." *Or so he wants me to presume.*

With lightning speed, Rebozo lunged for the arm in which Sylvia held the knife and twisted. The knife dropped. She wrenched herself free from his grip and stumbled. He reached out and steadied her.

Sylvia rubbed her arm. "So, I've accosted a government agent? Does that mean I get arrested? Go to jail or something?"

"There's no jail in Gearhart," Rebozo said. "We'd have to take you to Town Marshal Charles White in Seaside or County Sheriff Linvall in Astoria."

She winced. "Well, I'm sorry for what I did, accusing you like that . . . so, maybe it doesn't count."

"I'm not sure that makes a difference." Rebozo presented one of his charmer grins.

They heard the *clip, clop* of horse's hooves. Brannon holstered his revolver. They all stood to attention as Deputy Kliever rounded the corner.

"I'm investigating the report of a disturbance. Are these men harassing you, ma'am?" He offered a tip of his hat.

"I'm not pressing charges, if that's what you mean," she snapped.

"*You're* not pressing charges?" Rebozo shot back.

Deputy Kliever focused his attention on Brannon. "Are you sure? I've been looking for a way to get this menace off our streets."

"We're fine, just fine," Sylvia assured him as she grabbed each of the men's arms and strolled them down the wooden boardwalk that stretched from the depot to the ocean.

"Did you know Deputy Kliever is the son of a Missouri preacher?" Rebozo remarked as they marched forward. "He sings in a church choir in Astoria on his Sundays off."

"Then he's a brother in the faith," Brannon replied. "I'll try to go easier on his suspicious nature."

"Why does he hang around Gearhart if he's a county deputy and the county seat is in Astoria?" Sylvia inquired.

Rebozo's eyes almost twinkled. "The sheriff has his own agenda. He doesn't manage that tight a ship, if you get my drift. Meanwhile, I believe the deputy has something almost personal against our friend Brannon here."

"I do seem to acquire an enemy or two wherever I go," Brannon acceded.

Sylvia looked back. "Let's keep walking, out to the beach, if need be. Deputy Kliever's still hovering behind us."

"Might as well make this friendly stroll together useful," Brannon suggested. "A friend of Bois DeVache claims that Tom returned to Arizona right after the rendezvous with the Panama and U.S. engineers."

Sylvia didn't waver a step. "That's impossible. Papa wouldn't do that, except in an emergency. Even then, he would have left a message for me. We agreed at Mama's funeral to meet either in Gearhart or Portland, depending on convenience for both of us, for my birthday on Sunday."

"I do remember a time or two when Tom went undercover. Not even your mother knew where he was. You don't suppose he received some sensitive, secret summons?"

"Then why would the President sound an alarm to go find him?" Sylvia noted.

"The better to keep everyone off track, perhaps?" Brannon stretched his arms, shoulders and legs in the mild coastal breeze and drank in the briny, sea air.

"May I ask which birthday this might be?" Rebozo pried.

"You may ask, but I won't tell you, except to say the obvious, I am beyond an old maid . . . which makes your earlier comments even more insulting."

Brannon flipped around. "What earlier comments?"

"None of your concern. It's between me and Rebozo." Whether said in a pout or temper, Brannon couldn't discern.

She's got to be about forty, since she's the middle of those three girls. "How were you going to know when and where to meet your father?"

She dropped her arms from theirs and sat down on a boulder as they neared the shore. The peninsula of Tillamook Head misted like a hidden mine of jewels in the southern distance. The small-seeming western rock that was home to Tillamook Lighthouse boasted a bright beam in the faraway drape of fog.

Sylvia leaned back as though scouting for signs of the deputy. He wasn't visible.

"When I thought Lanigan was after me in Portland, it made me jumpy. That's why I didn't contact Papa right away. If I mentioned about Lanigan harassing me, I wasn't sure what he'd do. Figured I'd handle the situation myself."

"Lanigan's a moonstruck fool, sounds to me. We've all been there. Nothing to cause alarm." Rebozo rolled down his sleeves, slipped his jacket back on and pulled out a small comb to swipe at his hair.

"You men!" Sylvia spouted. "You have no idea how you torment the female species."

Rebozo yawned. "Why is Sully here?"

"For the Exposition, of course, and other things."

"What other things?" Rebozo prodded.

"A big mining deal. Gold in South America, I believe."

"If you're part owner, shouldn't you be informed too?" Brannon inquired.

She shrugged. "Doesn't have to do with Consolidated, so it's not my affair."

They heard a trio of whistle blasts. Rebozo turned back towards the station.

"I've got to go or I'll miss my train. I'm headed up to Astoria. But it's not vacation. My sources have a tip on some money-laundering shenanigans that might deal with our investigation here.

Fairs and expositions entice sharkers with fraud angles, who are ready and willing to dip into the flow of funds. Such characters emerge from the plaster. Always something happening on the side. My guys can fill me in."

"Guys?" Sylvia nudged as they scurried back with him to the depot.

"My social life's my own," he huffed, more out of breath than having taken offense.

"I thought you were supposed to protect me or something like that," Brannon remarked.

"You seem quite capable of caring for yourself, especially with that knife-wielding bodyguard of yours. Be back soon. Don't miss me."

A crowd had gathered. Most entered the train with Rebozo. He sent a quick wave then engaged a female next to him in very animated conversation. *The woman in lavender.*

CHAPTER NINETEEN

Sylvia grabbed Brannon's arm and pulled him towards the Ridge Path. "The deputy's on our tail again."

"I've got to get back to the golf course, to get some practice in. It will also help me think through what we know about Tom."

"I'll come with you. I've always wanted to swing a club."

They weaved around other hikers on the narrow, wooded path. "Stuart, how do you know Lanigan?"

"First met him on a hot, dry summer's day in '91, in the hills of Gila County at Globe, Arizona."

"Isn't that Apache country, with Geronimo and all those guys? I heard the Apache Kid murdered a sheriff."

"Yep, Sheriff Reynolds. He was carting the Apache Kid with other prisoners in an armored stagecoach. At a steep, uphill climb he let the Kid out to ease the weight. The Kid took full advantage."

"You wonder why the sheriff didn't see that coming."

"Everyone makes mistakes, some of them fatal. I was visiting a friend of my late wife

Lisa's father, as a favor to Lisa's mother, to let him and his family know Mr. Nash had passed on."

"Yes, I remember Papa telling me about the Nash family and about your Lisa. She's still remembered by many. She must have been quite a woman."

Brannon sighed. He fought to keep the flood of memories at bay. "Mr. Booth, the friend, took me out to the copper mines. As we rode back to town, we spied a stagecoach running from a gang of four pursuers. Before we got close enough to prevent it, the passengers got robbed. Mr. Booth headed to town to get the sheriff and posse. I went after the robbers."

"But of course you did."

"I cornered Wax Lanigan after he fell off his horse in a bunch of cactus."

Sylvia bellowed out a laugh. "That had to hurt . . . in more than one way."

"Carted him back to Globe. Trouble is, he claimed he was in on the chase too. Just an innocent bystander going after thieves. He had plenty of friends in town to stand by him, including the local schoolteacher."

They heard the *tap, tap, tap* of a hammer. Sylvia peered through the trees. "It's the deputy," she announced.

They tromped through the bushes and spruce trees, off the Ridge Path, to where Deputy Kliever hung hand-painted posters up and down the street. Sylvia tiptoed to one nailed near them.

"Notice! To thieves, thugs and shootists, among whom are Stuart Brannon and others: If found within the limits of this city after ten o'clock p.m., you will be invited to Astoria to a jail cell until further notice. The expense of which will be borne by certain concerned citizens."

"What?" Brannon leaned forward for a closer look, but had to back away to read it.

They studied the sign together as the deputy strolled out of sight. "He's got a one-man crusade against you."

"He's got to have a legal reason to take me in, something besides curfew."

They found Keaton Tanglewood at the golf course. "You like golf pretty good now?"

"Just the repetition of learning the game helps me clear my mind. Especially if I can come out and practice at times away from onlookers or other players crowding me from behind."

"I hope I don't bother you," Sylvia said.

Brannon risked a gaze at her fly-away hair and the roses that sprinkled her cotton dress. As always, except when Lady Fletcher arranged her boudoir, neither neat nor tidy. *She's stout, but attractive, the opposite of Harriet in many ways. Yet she has her charms.*

"Keaton, can you help the lady with her swing?"

"I could, but you know enough to give her some advice."

Brannon felt an alarm bell ding from some distant past recollection of male and female decorum, but he pushed it aside. *Surely at my age I can play the gentleman.*

He started towards Sylvia, to help with her grip, when Tanglewood interrupted. "I'm sorry you have not found the U.S. Marshal yet."

"It is perplexing," Sylvia said. "Why don't you both hit a ball and I'll watch? I'll learn by example."

Tanglewood pulled out one of the clubs he'd brought over for Brannon. He swung it across a wide swath of grass. "What do you think? Should I like a white girl or an Indian girl?"

Brannon, startled by the question, reached for a club and was greatly relieved when Sylvia gave a response.

"Which do you prefer?"

"I don't think about that, until I get questions or stares from others. There's a girl from my tribe who has pretty eyes and laughs at my jokes. Her name is Esther. I feel almost dizzy in her presence, but when I am away from her, I hardly think of her at all."

"That doesn't sound like a serious romance to me," Sylvia remarked and picked out a club for herself.

"And then there's girls like Laira Fletcher,"

Tanglewood continued, "who can be very friendly with me when we're alone, but acts like I am her slave when we're around her friends or family. All of this confuses me."

"You're still young. Play it out the next year or two and see where it leads," Sylvia advised.

"What do you think, Mr. Brannon?"

"Oh, I certainly agree with Miss Wiseman. Good advice."

"I am surprised. I thought you would tell me to ask God."

"Okay, then why didn't you do that anyway?"

"Because I wanted the counsel of both of you."

"Me and Miss Wiseman?"

"No, you and God. Then I would know for sure I was doing the right thing."

After the golfing session, Brannon and Sylvia returned to the hotel.

"I've got phone calls to make," Sylvia announced.

Brannon had been invited to one of Lady Fletcher's parties, but he had declined. This was one not on her "must attend" list and he took full advantage of that.

Instead, he coaxed Tres Vientos with him out on the beach. He hoped to acclimate him more to the night smells and sounds and feel of the coast. They watched seagulls with pink legs, white breasts and dark feathers play rugby. One would

172

get the fish, the others tried to take it away. Some of them remained most of the night, trying to out-screech each other.

Seabirds with long, narrow wings floated high above without effort for hours. Several sandpipers with short legs set in the middle of their bodies waded like sprinters through the shallows. The stars plunged into rolling clouds. The wind laden with salt and sand seemed to test its lungs.

As the darkness deepened to full night, Brannon tied up Tres Vientos near his campsite and laid out on his bedroll. *Tom, what's going on? Are you hurt or hiding? And if you're hiding, do you want me to find you?*

Questions invaded him like incessant waves lapping the beach.

Finally, Brannon fell asleep and dreamed that he was on a ship that lurched through the air when a whale struck the side with its tail. Then darkness. He slipped and slid on a smooth surface. He reached to grab some support and a slimy substance shrank from his touch. He couldn't breathe. It was so hot he thought he was in a cave or mine.

He woke up just before morning's full light. Tres Viento was agitated. He snorted and pawed at someone or something looking at them. He heard a low-pitched hiss, then a growl and purr.

Across from them, crouched low on the dunes, a creature prowled. A large, heavy, tawny cat.

Round head, erect ears. It let out a chilling scream. *A cougar?* When Brannon reached for his rifle and revolver, the cat turned and raced with great agility over the hill towards the trees and brush.

If Brannon had not held tight to Tres Vientos, fed him some treats and talked calmly to him, he would have galloped clear to Astoria.

CHAPTER TWENTY

Wednesday, June 14

That morning Lady Fletcher insisted that Brannon follow her out to the beach. She carried a narrow-bladed shovel and pail. "Stuart, I was digging for clams this morning. This local razor variety is like scallops, a delicacy of texture and they're larger than most clams."

"Ah, so this is a food to live for."

"And to die for. Isn't it interesting how those two phrases mean the same?" Lady Fletcher slowed down to keep from stumbling on a rocky patch. "When I saw these." She pointed to some tracks in the sand.

Brannon studied the baby-like footprints of raccoons who also dig up clams, some gelled blobs that he presumed to be jelly fish, and some large claw prints. "I think it's a cougar."

"Oh dear, how distressing. So much to think about and now this. Do you think it has anything to do with Tom Wiseman?"

"Don't know. Your pail's not very full. Can I help?"

"I find the dimple in the sand and then scoop, but the clams rebury themselves so fast. Zip, they're in their burrow. Somebody told me they're slower at low temperatures. Maybe it's too warm. I'm confused now. Where was I digging?"

Brannon pointed to some holes and broken shells.

Lady Fletcher dropped her pail and shovel. "Stuart, another thing. There are rumors flying about. They say that you, in a drunken, violent escapade terrorized the visitors at the Lewis and Clark Exposition. Some say you should have been arrested and incarcerated."

"Tres Vientos did get out of control, but I wasn't drunk nor violent."

"Are you blaming it on your horse? Oh look, here's another one."

"I really don't know what I'm doing."

"Just keep digging and don't damage the clam." She stretched her arms behind her back. "And I saw Mrs. Acorn earlier walking her basset hound. I think she could use your help."

"Mrs. Acorn could use a lot of help that I'm not prepared to give."

"Did you know Mrs. Acorn's brother-in-law was once married to her sister? And then Tally Rebozo married that same sister, except his name was Warren Andale then. Does that seem strange to you?"

"I suppose that's no stranger than humans eating rubbery, muddy mollusks."

"You're not making sense. Don't you think you should talk to Mrs. Acorn to find out what she knows?"

"Okay, I'll have tea with her, if you come along."

"Oh, Stuart, that will mess up the atmosphere. She won't want a chaperone."

"But I do."

"Then I'll have to invent a reason to tag along."

"Tell her I do odd things when I eat clams and you have to keep me from one of my spells." Brannon dug quickly with a sudden motion. He sifted through the sand for the clam, which he dropped in the bucket.

"I most certainly will not. Have you ever even eaten a clam?"

"Never."

"I will try to keep tea time to a half hour. How's that?"

"Is Tally Rebozo still married to her sister?"

"I know nothing about Tally Rebozo's personal affairs."

Wet sand oozed into Brannon's duckings as he speared his way across the beach hunting for buried mollusks.

"Stuart, I suppose you'd prefer the sort of wilderness supper that Lewis and Clark partook of . . . deer cured over a firepit, whale blubber, boiled elk, marrowbone, roots of all sorts, that sort of thing."

"Why, yes. They'd get up in the morning and order one of their best hunters to kill something for breakfast. *Pow! Pow!* They'd come back with big ducks." He poked a stick at a troublesome crab while Harriet washed sand from some shells. Gulls cried protest overhead, speaking up for their rights on this piece of beach. A lone heron watched it all from the loft of his spindly legs.

"Why can't we eat what we want to eat? Wouldn't that make everyone happy?"

"To become a social being, you must, at times, do an activity that pleases another, not yourself."

"I did something that really pleased me. I punched Hawthorne H. Miller in the nose," Brannon blurted out.

"Did he deserve it?"

"I regretted it soon after."

"Why?"

"Because he claimed to know something about Tom's disappearance, but wouldn't divulge it to a person who punched him."

"But he did deserve it?"

"It seemed so at the moment."

Lady Fletcher sighed. "You must admit, you do have a tendency to violence."

But Miller got his revenge . . . I think.

When they returned to the hotel Brannon spied a familiar form. A flow of gray beard. Fly-away gray hair. Eyes that darted everywhere at once, but shifted to no one particular.

He tried to avoid Hawthorne H. Miller by stepping past the library, his hat in front of his face.

"Hi, Brannon." The voice was much slower, deeper than Miller's.

He looked in the direction of the speaker. Burly build. Lop-sided grin. Brown hair streaked with something dull, yet sticky. "Hi, Tiff. See you later."

He quickened his pace but Argentiferous Jones blocked his path.

"We're setting up your books here," Jones informed him. "Mr. Miller's going to let me sign the stories that have me in them. He's payin' me a nickel for every dozen books that get bought."

Brannon kept his back to Miller. "That's real funny. He's never offered to pay for my signature. Why, I could be a rich man by now, retire and go buy me a ranch in Arizona."

"Is that right? Hey, maybe I'll do the same. This fame and fortune ain't so bad."

"Perhaps you'll be tempted to go straight and leave your life of crime."

"Yeah." His eyes were ringed with doubt.

Brannon caught up with Lady Fletcher as she handed the razor clams to the kitchen staff. Heading back to the benches in front of the hotel, she pulled out and read a postcard from Brannon's

Triple B Ranch: "Baby Jenner has a rash all over. Edwin does too, even on his neck. Everett's is even worse, even in his ears. We had fried chicken, mashed potatoes and corn pudding for supper. What did you eat? Love, Elizabeth."

Brannon enjoyed the vision of his Arizona family.

"Tonight you'll have quite the meal to tell Elizabeth about, won't you?"

"Do you remember that time that you, Edwin and I got caught in the Yavapai Desert with no water and supplies? I fear that was only slightly more treacherous than what I'm about to face tonight."

"Stuart, you only promised to eat one clam."

"What I do to please a woman."

Harriet put on her serious face. "You should have married Victoria Pacifica."

"What does that have to do with anything?"

"You need a purpose in life, out of the same old routine existence of ridding the world of its evils."

"I have a purpose . . . my ranch, Littlefoot and his family."

"You need another goal and someone to push you to achieve it." Her intent stare forced him to let that sink in. "By the way, your Victoria called and wanted to talk to you. I told her you were sleeping on the beach. I did not inform her you had three women in your hotel room."

"Is anything wrong?"

"She is at the ranch helping Jannette with the sick kids."

"That's great to know. Makes me feel everything's all right there, like bein' in two places at once."

"Exactly. You need to make that a permanent situation. How is Victoria?"

Brannon looked over in surprise. "Didn't you ask her? She was fine, as of the last time I saw her."

"Which was when?"

"She had a hard winter. Got sick and couldn't take care of her families on the hacienda in Magdalena. She called me to come. I spent a few weeks helping out. She was very tired and required rest. Then, L.F. needed me back at the ranch."

"Ah," she said. "Well, in the absence of any other women around here to push you to try new things, I will take on that role. You promised me to try a clam."

"You mean, if I eat one clam, I could be immortalized in Lady Harriet Reed-Fletcher's mind forever?"

"Maybe."

"I can't take that risky a chance. The odds are against me."

"But here's your goal. Eat a clam. Support an orphan. Solve a mystery for the President of the United States. Then go home and sit the rest of your days on the front porch of your Arizona ranch."

Lord Fletcher arrived with a brisk smile and

hearty mood. "Ah, I smell clams in the place. What a feast awaits us, eh, Stuart? Quite jolly."

Brannon didn't need to answer because Keaton Tanglewood rode up with a gray mustang.

"I bet you caught and trained that one yourself," Brannon said of the horse.

Tanglewood patted the horse's head. "We might have found your friend."

"Where?"

"On the beach, a couple miles south. Come on, jump up."

Brannon straddled behind Tanglewood as they galloped across the sand, over the twists of driftwood and sprawls of jelly-like seaweed. Seagulls sailed up and squawked as they tore through their landing.

Tanglewood tried to converse as the horse scattered sand. He pointed to the lighthouse. "A legend tells of an underwater tunnel from Tillamook Head underneath the ocean to inside Tillamook Rock, where only supernatural beings can go."

I wonder from what true event that story evolved?

On the beach front of Seaside, in the shadow of Tillamook Head, a monster fish slumped in silence.

"It's a whale," Brannon hollered, trying to catch his breath. "A dead one," he surmised as he got closer.

CHAPTER TWENTY ONE

"Perhaps someone dumped your friend in the ocean, to let the big fish take care of him," Tanglewood said.

An excited crowd gathered around. Tanglewood introduced his Uncle Grant to Brannon, a man with deep-set eyes and prominent forehead ridged with thick, dark eyebrows, the one in charge of the team of family and friends. A brisk wind wailed against the gawkers, making it difficult for them to look or Brannon to investigate. Brannon guessed the beached gray whale to be about twenty-five or thirty feet long, part of it stretched in the ocean. Swimmers stood in waist-deep water near the tail.

"It was alive for about an hour, but they couldn't save him. Now they're going to render the blubber and that can't be done in a day, even with the crew that volunteered."

"Why did it come up here?"

"Maybe a stomach ache," Tanglewood suggested. "Like what happened to Jonah's big fish."

Hope the ladies don't hear that.

"It won't be eaten. It can make you sick. It's for oil. But my Uncle Grant, Uncle Miles, Uncle Stirling and their helpers will take care of it the old way. Get the leather gloves. Use the fish forks and big knives. While it's still fresh, they'll cut off tons of blubber in huge chunks and render it by placing it in large wooden bowls or troughs and piling hot stones on top. Or they could boil the blubber in kettles over a fire. It will stink out here something awful."

"It already does."

"You just wait. Clothes, the air, everything, for days, even longer."

Brannon studied the huge mammal, the eyes, dorsal and hump. "I still can't figure the why of stranding itself. There's the whole ocean to live in."

"Perhaps something scared him. Or sickness. Maybe he hunted too close to shore or got his directions wrong. He could have crashed into something, against the rocks or a ship. I like to think of it as a gift from the creator, to provide us oil."

"Hmmm . . . I guess we'll never know."

"My uncles will tell you what they discover."

"What do you mean?"

"In his stomach . . . if there is a man's body inside . . . before the seagulls get to it. Or he could still be alive."

"Has that ever happened? I mean, besides Jonah."

"Sure. One time men in a harpoon boat speared a whale. The boat capsized and dumped the men in the ocean. One of them drowned. The other couldn't be found. When they carved up the whale, they got to the stomach and noticed something large. Inside they found a man, alive, but unconscious. After a few weeks he recuperated enough to work again. It is well known."

Brannon was glad to twist away from the sight of the beached whale when someone yelled his name. When Brannon turned, Wax Lanigan snapped a picture with his portable Kodak Brownie. He spotted Hawthorne Miller a few yards away wearing a Spanish cloak and Panama hat and his huge tripod spread out on the sand.

"That's incredible," Miller said. "Let me look at that." Lanigan handed the camera to him.

Laira Ashley Fletcher rode up in a charcoal sidesaddle frock with Amble the white Arabian, Darcy close behind in a butternut gray dress trimmed with gold braid.

Amble kicked sand high as Laira reined her near Brannon, causing him to rub his eyes and spit out grit. "That's my first time to try the American way . . . sidesaddle. So novel. Liberating. But it does take practice to keep control of the horse."

Tanglewood's uncles were already stripping the dark skin with large knives, revealing white and pink flesh underneath.

"Oh, twee, I thought it was alive," Laira Fletcher complained. "I want to see a whale that's going back in the ocean to swim and jump and shoot water out his blowhole."

Darcy Lazzard rode in behind her on a dun mare, flopping around the back with a grimace. She reached her foot out to regain the stirrup and tried to get down. The mare swung around and tossed her into some seaweed. Brannon reached to help her up as he heard Laira Fletcher chat with Tanglewood.

"Don't you have a kayak or canoe that could take us out into the sea to watch the whales?" she begged.

"I have one, but it must be the right timing . . . and safe."

Brannon didn't hear the rest of Tanglewood's reply because his Uncle Grant nudged Brannon's arm and whispered, "Do you think maybe your friend is in the whale's belly?" He jumped back up on top of the whale.

"Did you find some trace of him in the whale?" Brannon hollered.

Uncle Grant pounded his chest and laughed. "Keaton will show you what we did find," Uncle Grant yelled down.

The wave of odors began to sicken Brannon. He ran back to Tanglewood with a bandana over his nose.

"Uncle Stuart, there you are," Laira called out. "You must come see the baby when you're through looking at this old, smelly dead whale.

It's a *cria*. That's what a baby llama is called, Darcy told me."

"Thanks for the information and invite. Will you please remind Darcy that she has something of mine to return?"

"Remind her yourself. She's right over . . . oh, she's gone. There she is, way down the beach with those fellows who helped keep her llama from drowning. I like being her friend. She knows lots of boys."

Brannon meant to go speak to Hawthorne Miller, maybe to apologize for his earlier behavior, mostly to ask him about Tom Wiseman. However, by now the man, his wagon and equipment were gone.

"We don't really expect to find a body in the whale. I've got something else to show you," Tanglewood said. "Down the beach." He pointed south towards Tillamook Head and led the horse about a half mile further.

Brannon shouted when he spied a large gray wolf that looked ready to pounce on the horse or them. Tanglewood caught the wolf in his arms to pet him. When Brannon got close, the beast growled and gnashed his teeth.

"Quiet, Pooch," Tanglewood commanded. "He's part-dog, but still pretty wild. We think he's been guarding his master."

"He should be tethered," Brannon cautioned. The horse whinnied in agreement. He now recognized a canoe braced on top of four upright split timbers sunk a few feet in the ground.

"We often bury our dead in their canoes with the personal belongings they might need in the next life. This capsized canoe washed up with a body this morning, about the time of the beached whale."

Tanglewood picked up some pieces of drift-wood. "Could be parts of a ship."

Brannon turned the rough, spiky wood and tried to imagine the origin.

"There were lots of survivors of shipwrecks who made it to these shores," Tanglewood explained. "As did my own father. This coast can be treacherous for ships. The rocks and waves can beat them to slivers. It's hard to imagine the powerful push of large amounts of water, whether in a river or an ocean. That's why the lighthouse is so needed, although it's treacherous to navigate and expensive to maintain."

Brannon imagined the ghosts of sailors and ship skeletons up and down the Pacific coast, each with their tales of adventure and horror.

Tanglewood pulled away the canoe. "Too light. Big hole ripped in the bottom. It sank." Underneath was a corpse, a torso that had been in water a long time. "We could not move it nor report it. We are blamed for many things."

Brannon turned the body over. He didn't recognize the man. The main thing, it wasn't Tom. "It's not the man I'm looking for. Take me to Seaside. I'll report this to the authorities for you."

The guests that evening arrived by carriage, boat, motor car and horse and buggy for Lady Fletcher's dress up affair. Brannon found Lady Fletcher and Wax Lanigan in a deep discussion about employee wages.

Lanigan plied his best smile, which seemed on the wiley side to Brannon. "One of the reasons I came to Portland was to help protest that Portland contractors hired out-of-state workers to build the Lewis and Clark Exposition. We talked about a labor boycott of the event. We did do some strikes. We won a summer wage increase of two dollars, from eight dollars to ten dollars a week during the Exposition."

Lanigan sent Brannon a half-hearted greeting, which he ignored.

"When they refused point blank to carry out an order during the busiest time of day," Lady Fletcher observed.

"The proprietor graciously complied."

"I'm not sure I'm inclined to be that gracious, but I might have to. The waiters and other help insist that since so many celebrities are coming to town, they deserve to be paid more. It's kind of a reverse snobbism, don't you think?"

"Perhaps they presume that celebrities can pay more." Lanigan peered over at Brannon.

"I'd have to rob a stagecoach to afford everyone's salary," Brannon interjected.

"But it's not the celebrities who are paying them. The hotel management and I are."

"Ah, the trials of management." Lanigan strolled away.

"You and Wax Lanigan seem friendly enough," Brannon observed.

"It started with me looking at the wares that a traveling salesman displayed. I'm a sucker for new gadgets. Lanigan passed by and offered some advice on a coffee grinder and the plusses and minuses of various apple and potato peelers. Very good suggestions, I might say."

"I'm surprised. Doesn't sound like the Lanigan I knew."

"He even gave suggestions for the best ice machines and refrigerating machines. In addition, he has played the gentleman for me by partnering with ladies who come alone to my events. I've never had a complaint of his deportment."

"But you'd better watch your silver," Brannon teased.

"Stuart! Wax Lanigan comes with the highest of recommendations . . . from his union bosses, from the Lewis and Clark Exposition Board of Directors, and from the Willamette Orphan Farm. And something else . . ."

"What's that?"

"He's a very temperate man. He told me his

guiding principle is 'eat not to dullness, drink not to elevation.' "

"Maybe he *has* changed." *Or he's throwing sand in your eyes.*

"And here comes the appetizer tray I ordered just for you. An introduction to razor clams, some teasers. There's a plain clam dip, a smoked clam dip, a clam cake and also a special razor clam spread with a touch of hot sauce. Also, a taste of chowder. You may try any or all of them and it will satisfy your promise to me."

Brannon studied the clam samples with care. "You're trying your best to make sure I don't eat to dullness."

He took a small bite of the clam cake. *Not bad.*

He swiped up a scoop of the smoked clam dip with a piece of hard bread. *Okay, that's palatable.*

He passed up the plain clam dip that swirled with large pieces of the fishy substance and used a butter knife for the clam spread on a cracker. *Not that hot. Didn't choke or beg for water.*

"Stuart, I'm so proud of you. Now, here's a whole fried clam in a special garlic sauce. You will love it." She handed him a fork.

"I thought you told me if I did this taste test, I was through."

"Posh, you'll always regret not biting into one of these delicacies. Just one bite."

Even fried, it was slick. It was rubbery. The sauce barely gave it a flavor. He felt sick to his

191

stomach. "How delightful." He clenched his teeth. "But too rich for my tastes. Please, Harriet, no more."

Later that evening, Brannon knocked at the door of his former hotel room. One of the Lazzard twins, the one with the sapphire ring, opened it and swung back to let him in.

The folded-up tent was in one corner. They had hauled in several chairs, a couple cots and the dress rack. He gazed at bouquets of daffodils, poppies and tulips. Pots of rhododendrons and hydrangeas lined one wall.

"Say, are you gals florists?" he jibed.

Mama Darrlyn twirled the rings on her fingers. "We're blessed or cursed with many suitors."

"And we got invited to Lady Fletcher's party. Lots of men there, even though she called it afternoon tea," said Aunt Deedra.

"Where's Darcy?"

"She's out with Laira Ashley Fletcher."

"Where's my locket?"

Mama Darrlyn pulled open a small center drawer in a dresser. "Here you go. We had quite a time retrieving it."

He didn't ask for details. He had no interest in hearing about it.

She pulled out the gold chain and then the tiny glass encased image, no bigger than his thumbnail.

He clasped it gently, then hard. The relief stabbed deep. A lost gem found. He had a sudden desire to get away from these ladies.

Brannon had experienced few times of ecstacy in his life. He could count them, one by one. The first glance of a baby's smile, that initial human response that says, "Hey, out there, I see you." He felt it with Littlefoot. Then, with each of L.F.'s own children. Now he grasped another pure moment of joy with the return of this one earthly material treasure.

The preacher was wrong years ago when he said,
"It'll last 'til death do you part."
It's an Arizona sunrise, my coffee's all gone,
And I still got that gal in my heart.

Brannon rode Tres Vientos out to the beach again that night.

He woke to snorts and hooves eating up the ground. Sprays of water splayed from the ocean shallows. He got up to watch the parade of horses, noses flared, as if catching the scent of battle from afar. White, brown, spotted and a black stallion . . . a nine horse remuda free, flying, wild, kicking up water.

He looked for a rider, but couldn't see one. But now a limber colt joined them. The horses flew almost airborne, manes flowing, necks like thunder, with bulging muscles, sleek coats.

Brannon marveled once again at the beauty, the grace, the prowess of a horse.

A motor car is a poor imitation.

The herd instinct kicked in. Tres Vientos reared and whinnied, wanting to join the ancient race, run with his kind. Brannon tightened his cinch, untied the reins, and leaped into the saddle just as the black horse lunged forward.

Tres Vientos rode hard against the pressure, the perfect storm of a three-winds collision.

At full gallop, Brannon raised high in the saddle. In his younger years, Brannon's back and abdomen could take longer periods of the pounding. But he was relieved when after they sped a mile or two, Tres Vientos became winded. So did the stallion and his harem of wild horses. They stopped and meandered on the beach, then followed the stallion as he grazed up on a hill.

Brannon turned to lead Tres Vientos back to Gearhart, but stopped as he watched a stooped, elderly man stalk a mare, lariat coiled under his arm. He bent the ear, stared her in the eye, then cast the rope over her neck. So quick Brannon couldn't tell how he did it, the man jumped as limber as a boy onto the mare's back, bucked her over the hill and out of sight. The stallion and remuda followed.

Catcher-Of-The-Sun?

CHAPTER TWENTY TWO

Thursday, June 15

As Brannon sauntered into the hotel after his night on the beach, he walked by Sylvia Wiseman who talked low and earnest to someone on the telephone, under dim lamplight. Several auto cars honked outside. "To Seaside." She pointed to the receiver. "I finally got through."

He overheard a reference to motion pictures that apparently Sylvia and Cordelle Plew had seen at the Portland Exposition. End of frontier romance rubbed shoulders with modern marvels.

Lord Fletcher was having breakfast of fried eggs and ham in the hotel café. Brannon plucked Fletcher's cane off the table, balanced it on an extra chair, then asked his friend to read a new postcard from Elizabeth:

"Papa thinks a mama cow and her calf got stolen. We found two mules. Papa says someone made a trade. Everett's pony ran away. Mama chased it and got scratches, bruises and a sunburn. We miss you."

Brannon ordered steak with mushrooms and beans from waitress Katie, reminisced about life full of family and honest work on his Arizona ranch, then turned to his old friend across the table. "I hear you got a letter from your son Stuart."

Lord Fletcher finished a bite of biscuit and blackberry jam and wiped his mouth. "They're studying the glacial and interglacial epochs and they've found a cemetery with wasted, half-buried graves of vanished cities."

"That is so far beyond me to even imagine."

"They're anxious to dig and probe these mounds."

"Who pays for all this travel and work? Is that you footin' the bill?"

"No, they've got a grant through an American institution. I forget which one."

"That's pretty nice. You came out West on your own funds."

"And glad to do it. You made it all worthwhile, Stuart Brannon. Our adventures were better than gold. I shall never forget your many unbounded kindnesses to me. My times with you were, in almost every way . . . jolly, bang on."

"Except that time you got shot in the rump."

"You promised never to reveal that, certainly not to Harriet who may very well do my memoirs when I'm gone."

Brannon's attention turned to several men who entered the café and sat in a far corner, then hunched together in hushed tones. He recognized one of them as Wax Lanigan. The other two wore fitted, heavy, tailored black silk suits and silk hats. He kept the conversation going with Fletcher, but heeded the movements of the three men across the room.

"We did have some good times. The conflicted frontier. Now we've reached the twentieth century, the modern age. Law and order, truth and justice prevail. We ordinary citizens can hang up our guns and be free to enjoy family and pursue peaceful jobs."

Lord Fletcher pushed his plate aside. Waitress Katie scurried over to fetch it and poured more coffee for both of them. "Yes, but my son gets excited over things like pottery, skeletons and fossils. He says you can find the most fascinating facts, evidence of the history of peoples, in otherwise worthless clods."

"Admit it. I'll bet you wish you were over there with him."

"Reminds me of my days riding with the Mongols, drinking fermented horse's milk, living in their yurts."

Brannon noticed that one of the men unrolled a piece of parchment on the table. *A map?*

Lord Fletcher looked away as though reliving those days, then jerked himself to the present. "My son says they're in need of interpreters, as well as surveyors and architects."

"You know several of the languages of that region, don't you?"

"My word, yes. It meant my survival at one time."

"You ought to write your own book, Edwin."

"I'll leave that to my lovely wife. My home library already consists of more than six hundred volumes, covering all the latest information on politics and the sciences. I couldn't imagine adding my drivel to those esteemed works."

"Of making many books, there is no end. That's what the Bible proclaimed centuries ago." Brannon sat up, alert, as Sylvia appeared at the café door. She strolled over to them.

"Men. I can't figure them out. I talk to Cordelle and everything seems peaceful, fine. He's excited about some breakthroughs with that gang of boys. I call Sully and he tells me Cordelle's been seen around Seaside with other women . . . twice with *Miss* Penelope Tagg and *Miss* Henrietta Ober."

"They're probably helping him with the orphan affairs," Brannon suggested.

Sylvia sniffed. "Maybe."

Brannon handed her a linen napkin. She wasn't shy about blowing into it.

"I also made calls to those numbers Papa had written down. Some of them were American engineers assigned to Panama. However, the numbers reached vacation sites. I got hold of family members or managers. Most left the area the morning of Papa's disappearance. Couldn't find anyone who knew anything about it."

She gulped down a glass of water from their table. "This coastal air makes me so thirsty."

"I've got some strong coffee brew left from my campsite you're welcome to," Brannon offered.

She snickered. "Thanks, I think I will. And don't look surprised. Papa got me hooked on the thick stuff at an early age. The stronger, the better."

"You're my kind of girl," Brannon said, then turned away in embarrassment when Sylvia's eyebrows raised. Whether in amusement or disdain, Brannon couldn't tell.

"One of the numbers," she continued, "reached a Northern Pacific Railroad office. Didn't know what that meant. The other . . . well, I got the shock of my life when President Roosevelt's personal secretary answered."

They offered her a seat, but as she started to sit, she spotted the three men in the far corner. She slipped a hand to the inside of a skirt pocket. *Her sneak gun.* Brannon braced for action as she approached the other table. Lanigan stood up as though he was introducing her to the other men and offered her the fourth chair.

"Yes, quite," Fletcher was saying. "How are things going with your search for Tom Wiseman?"

"You never knew Tom in Arizona," Brannon stated as he slowly fingered his Colt, not sure what to do next.

"No, but his reputation precedes him. Heard many good words on his behalf. I had hoped to converse with him while he was here in Gearhart." He raised an eyebrow at Brannon and followed his gaze to the confrontation across the room. "That didn't work out. But my sources revealed a few pieces of information about him."

Sylvia spat out a word or two, then whirled around and stomped to the front door. She opened it for a woman holding a baby and leading a toddler, then exited herself.

Brannon chewed on his steak. He waited for the slow-speaking Englishman to continue.

"Your friend Tom was asked by the President to assist with various issues for important people who would be attending the Lewis and Clark Exposition."

"Uh huh," Brannon muttered.

"As you know, he was then sent to Gearhart for the special meetings with civil engineers who will work in Panama. While here, he noticed Wax Lanigan hosting a number of suppers for prominent citizens. Because of his previous dealings with Lanigan, he checked him out. He couldn't figure his angle, since he seemed to be what you would call clean."

"Uh huh," Brannon repeated between chaws on the steak.

"Meanwhile, one of Chuy Carbón's ex-wives in

Nicaragua, the daughter of a powerful drug lord, wants her honor avenged."

Brannon choked on his steak and grabbed for a glass of water.

"Her father threatened a Nicaraguan politician for exposure of his own crimes if he didn't get Carbón back to Nicaragua. Wiseman arrested Carbón. However, in order to prevent extradition, Carbón offers to give Wiseman information on some illegal dealings, including a money-laundering scheme. Whether that was true or not, or whether he finished the investigation, I don't know."

"How do you know all this? Sounds like personal contact accounts to me."

"Your Tom had a lady friend . . . not a paramour, but a confidante." Lord Fletcher wiped his mouth with care, then folded his napkin on the table. "She is a friend . . . both a confidante and paramour . . . of a friend of mine."

Brannon sputtered a cough. "Tom was a lot like Everett Davis to me, except I knew Tom longer. We did exploits that never made it into Hawthorne Miller's dime novels, for which I'm grateful. Somehow we snuck those in without tattletales snooping around."

"I miss that old Everett Davis. A good man. He didn't deserve what he got."

"Nope, he sure didn't. I remember the first time I met Tom. He stood tall and thin with plenty of gray even back then streaked in his neatly-trimmed dark hair. A true westering man he was, who seemed two hundred years old in smarts and vision. He'd be at the right place doing the perfect action when I needed help. Like a big brother. Yep, Tom would do to ride the river with."

Brannon paused as Lanigan got up from the table, offered the two men a tip of his hat, and stalked out of the café.

"My word, Brannon, I've never known you to say so much at one time about anyone or anything before."

"Oh, I could wax eloquent about you too, my English friend."

Brannon stuck the postcard in a pocket, paid his bill, and sped across the deck and down the front hotel stairs. Neither Sylvia nor Lanigan were in sight. He took a quick slog all around the area, but couldn't find either of them.

CHAPTER TWENTY THREE

As soon as Brannon reached the hotel, he went to the lobby and asked to use the phone. He left a long-distance message with Gwendolyn Barton, Lady Fletcher's sister in Prescott, to check whether Tom Wiseman made it home. He wanted another confirmation, an assurance that he wasn't in Arizona all this time.

Then, he asked her to let L.F. and his family know that he arrived in Oregon safely and "tell Elizabeth that the ocean is beautiful."

Lady Fletcher was in the lobby when he hung up. She paced back and forth, her skirt swirling each time she turned. "What do you truly know about Tally Rebozo?"

"The same as you . . . that he's a Serbian spy."

Lady Fletcher gave him her "I am not amused" look. "But he does work for the President?"

"That's what I'm told. Why are you so bothered?"

"Laira seems to be smitten with him . . . and that can't be, for obvious reasons."

"Such as?"

"His age, for one. His . . . experience, for another." Lady Fletcher rubbed her hands together, nervous and a little angry.

"What do you want me to do?"

"Talk with him. See what his intentions are."

"And then, what will you do?"

"I'll protect my daughter. There are many ways."

Sylvia Wiseman rushed into the room. "Stuart, Chuy Carbón wants to talk to you. Now, he says." She stopped to regain her breath. "And he's sober."

"Where is he?"

"I caught him going into the Gearhart clothing store that he claims rents bicycles. His wife told him to go get some exercise. I introduced myself as your friend. He said meet him at the park."

They scurried down the streets and over to a large, open area at the town center park. Carbón lounged on the lawn with a rusty bicycle that sported several bent spokes. "This is all the man had available," he remarked with a grunt. "I think I'm done in."

"You wanted to see me?" Brannon and Sylvia plopped on a nearby bench.

Carbón plucked up some blades of grass and chewed on them. "I see it all clear now. DeVache approached me with an offer. If a Frenchman and Nicaraguan were part of the meetings of U.S. engineers, it could be explained as a Panama Canal international congress or something like that. Should anyone be curious enough to ask."

"Why? I don't get it," Sylvia said.

"I don't know, but they knew I needed money," Carbón continued. "We play poker together."

"Much is wrought at poker games," Brannon commented.

"During these meetings I learned about how they cheat money out of lots of people and organizations."

"Who did?" Brannon prodded. "The engineers?"

"Oh, no. DeVache and his friends."

"What friends?"

"I don't know their names."

"Did Tom attend too?" Brannon asked.

"Only that last one . . . because there had been a threat against the group. That's the only time he sat at the same table with everyone. I dressed as an Indian in the hopes that if anything happened to the rest of them, it might be blamed on someone in the tribe."

"Whose bright idea was that?" Brannon huffed.

"Mine. But before that night, I wondered why they would let me in on their plots. Then it dawned on me . . . I would be expendable to them. So, I devised a plan to make myself more important, so they couldn't get rid of me. I informed them that Marshal Wiseman is onto them and I will divulge further details of what he knows and when he knows it."

"Why are you telling us this?" Sylvia pressed.

He looked over at her, then out across the lawns. "Because I want you to know that Marshal Wiseman trusted me. Imagine that. He thought he had me in the palm of his hand. But

I wiggled right out." He chortled with glee. "I outsmarted a U.S. Marshal." He peered back at Sylvia. "At least, I thought I did."

"Careful, Carbón," Brannon said. "You're talking about this woman's father."

He jumped up and slapped his legs and arms, as though he landed in a pile of red ants. "Eiyiyi . . . why didn't you tell me?"

"Who did you think she was?" Brannon asked.

"Your woman."

"And you just confessed to setting up her father for an ambush."

Carbón's forehead leaked sweat. He pulled off his hat and wiped his face with his shirt sleeve. He stepped closer to the bicycle as though ready to make a quick getaway.

"Why didn't you go with the Frenchman and my father that night?" Sylvia clearly despised the man.

Carbón wiped his mustache and sniffed a couple times. "I had another engagement."

"You were soused," Brannon guessed.

"So sloshed I could pee an ocean," he admitted. "I couldn't help him. But also, I couldn't hurt him. I did nothing." He emphasized that last word. "Nothing."

"Watch out," Sylvia whispered to Brannon. "There's a man sneaking up on you from behind."

Brannon whirled around and grabbed the man's arm. "Slash Barranca, what are you doing here? Why aren't you in jail?"

"The town marshal at Seaside let me go as soon as those men from the train showed up."

"The men in brown suits?"

Barranca pulled off his ten-gallon hat. "Yes, those are the ones. They paid my bail money."

"Who are those guys?"

"That's what I want to talk to you about. If you'll put in a good word for me with Mr. Hawthorne Miller, I will tell you. If he will write my story, I will confess to all my crimes, and they are many and very entertaining."

"What? Do you think he will buy your stories? That you will get rich off your criminal activity?"

"Why not? *You* are doing that."

Brannon raised his fist to slug the man, then lowered it. *I am not a violent man.* "I get no money for those novels and they are greatly exaggerated. They bear little resemblance to the actual events."

"So? You are very famous, no? That is my ambition too."

"I have nothing to do with Hawthorne Miller and his novels."

"But you know who he is and where I can find him?"

"The men in brown suits. Tell me what you know and I'll put in a good word with Miller."

"You can read all about it when my story gets told. I'll even include an episode about the time I got tossed in a loony bin. That should excite extra interest."

Chuy Carbón kicked the bent spokes and straddled the bicycle. "I think I will see this Hawthorne Miller myself. I have many of my own stories." He rode off with a clank, on a crooked course.

Sylvia and Brannon strolled back to the hotel.

Brannon looked behind them a time or two. "Why do you think those men in brown suits keep stalking me?"

"You're a legend. Legends make modern folks nervous. Do you think Carbón is telling the truth?"

"It's devious enough to be honest, especially since he didn't put himself in a very good light."

"Uncle Stuart!" Laira Fletcher came running up to them, her face flushed. Sweat streamed from her brow and neck. "Mr. Brannon, I can't find Bueno anywhere. I think he ran away. Please, will you try to find him?"

"Where have you looked?"

"I've called out to him all over the hotel and out in the barn."

"Did you check your horse?"

"Amble? Why, no."

Sylvia and Brannon followed the girl as she rushed outside and over to the barn and down to stall #34. Amble opened her eyes and offered a sleepy gaze at her owner. But Brannon looked over at stall #35. *Tres Vientos is gone!*

CHAPTER TWENTY FOUR

"Check with your father if we can borrow the Buick," Brannon said.

Laira ran out of the park down the street towards the hotel.

Soon Lady Fletcher drove up in the Touring Car, black seats shining, yellow wheels with black rims gleaming, chrome spotless. "Of course you can use our Buick. Do you have a driver? I'm not too sure of myself with this thing yet."

Sylvia volunteered. "Daddy's friend, Charles Howard, drove one of these to Goldfield, to entice the mine owners into buying one. He let me ride it all over the desert until I thought I had to have it. Then, he told me the price: twelve hundred dollars."

Brannon whistled. *But I'm not surprised. What a vehicle.*

"Are you talking about 'Rough Rider Charley'? The one who charged with Teddy up San Juan Hill?"

"That's him. And now we'll do our own charging. Which way first?"

Lady Fletcher handed Sylvia the keys, then slipped in the back seat with Laira. "I feel very responsible for Bueno," she explained. "Sure do hope and pray he's safe."

Sylvia pulled on a bonnet, big wrap-around coat, gloves and a pair of goggles, all borrowed from Lady Fletcher, who wore the same. Brannon sat in the front with Sylvia.

Sylvia ran her hand over the steering wheel in admiration. "This two-cylinder engine produces twenty-two horsepower at twelve hundred thirty rpm. It can climb hills, if we need to. On a flat desert road this vehicle can do a minute a mile or a little over six minutes in five miles." Sylvia cranked the auto car in quick reverse, then shifted to first and gunned it forward.

Brannon grabbed onto the side of the seat to keep from lunging into the windshield. "We're not in a race."

"How do we know speed doesn't mean Bueno's survival?"

Brannon tried to relax and not mind the bumps. *I'm more comfortable on a horse. A horse provides a bouncy ride, but it's a different kind of bumps. I'm more in control. Most of the time, that is.*

They drove all over town, starting with around the park and asking tenants if they'd seen him, through the small business district and residential areas, alongside the tracks, then headed for the beach.

The wheels of the auto left definite tracks in the sand, both dry and wet. Sylvia drove as close to the edge of the tide as she could for a firmer route. The passengers strained to survey the landscape as far as their sight could stretch, while they called out the boy's name.

"This travel by the beach makes a much better ride," Lady Fletcher commented. "All those roads that wind around bone-jarring tree roots and torture trails are just liver vibrators."

"Oh, Mum, I shouldn't have bossed Bueno around so much," Laira wailed.

"Maybe he ran back to the orphan farm," Lady Fletcher suggested.

"How far north shall we drive this beach?" Sylvia asked.

Oh, Lord, help us find Bueno! Brannon prayed. "Keep going," he instructed.

Brannon spotted Tres Vientos first and the precious cargo on his back, far down the coastline. They trotted south, their way. Sylvia sped the Buick to full throttle with sand shooting out behind them.

Thank you, Lord, for helping us find the boy.

Brannon noted that the black horse didn't rear or run at the sight and sound of the motor car. He hopped out of the auto first. "Bueno, what are you doing?"

"I'm calming your horse." The boy's eyes darted away, then his head lowered.

"You didn't ask me."

"I am sorry, El Brannon. I didn't know what to do."

"Are those bruises on your arm?"

"Oh these? Nothing. I got kicked by a horse. Not yours," he added quickly. "It was . . . uh, Amble. She was upset when I got in her stall."

"Here's Lady Laira. Let her know what her horse did to you."

"Oh, it wasn't her horse. Did I say that? I meant it was another horse."

The boy eased off the gelding and Laira hugged him, but she couldn't resist a scold. "Bueno, you are a bad boy. You scared me and caused me much trouble."

"I am sorry, Lady Laira."

"Oh, twee, what a really pernickety thing to do. You worried me to death."

Brannon studied the boy's nervous search all around and his confused state of mind. "What's the real reason you are out here?" he prodded. "Don't be afraid. Tell me, so we can help you."

The boy's eyes watered. "I mustn't say a word or I will get whipped."

Brannon pulled up one of the boy's arms. "Looks like that already happened. Who did this and why?"

Bueno began to whimper. Brannon slid up on Tres Vientos and motioned for the boy to climb up with him. They rode back to the barn, the Buick trailing behind.

"I came back to get Hack," Bueno said. "I shouldn't have left him. I shouldn't have left the orphan farm without him." The boy collapsed in a fresh vent of tears.

As he calmed down a little bit, Brannon tried to encourage him. "What did you do with Tres Vientos? He seems so much better."

"I followed your example and gave him some apple slices. I also promised him that he can go out next time with Amble."

"But you weren't planning to come back, were you?"

The boy teared up again.

"Who is hurting you? Please tell me. We won't let them do that again."

"That day I helped Hack, so he wouldn't drown, we saw something bad."

"Bueno, what did you see? Tell me everything."

"Some mean men came to Hack's Hideaway, up on the big mountain." He pointed towards Tillamook Head. "We couldn't see them very well. But later, we think we heard a shot."

"Is that why you are being hurt? So you won't tell?"

The boy's body began to shake. They approached the barn and he jumped when a man hailed them. "Brannon, been looking for you."

Rebozo's back. Is he the one who has been threatening Bueno?

"Have you ever been kicked by a mule?" Rebozo asked as he rubbed his leg.

• • •

Brannon kept assuring Bueno that he and Hack would stay safe, but the boy remained adamant in his refusal to divulge a name. He was more forthcoming with Brannon's request, "Tell me where it happened."

Bueno guided Brannon in pencil sketches as to the position of Hack's Hideaway on Tillamook Head, how to get to it, then the overlook where they viewed the big bay and the three men. When Brannon was satisfied he could find the places himself, he asked Lady Fletcher to keep a close watch on the boy. "We still don't know who is threatening him."

"Maybe he'll confide in me."

With Bueno in Lady Fletcher's secure care, Brannon hunted for Tanglewood and found him tending the golf course. "How soon can you take us on a boating excursion to Tillamook Head?"

"Can't you hike on the trail right out of Seaside?" Tanglewood asked.

"I'm following the tracks of two boys who may have seen Tom Wiseman. I'd rather go where they went. One of them found a path up the cliff side at a small bay."

"I will get a canoe. It's a good thing we're in the long days of summer, but we must watch the tide and the weather and be careful of rocks." He searched the sky. "I've done it before, but we must go soon."

Within an hour, Tanglewood garnered a cedar log canoe—huge, heavy, bright red.

Sylvia insisted on going with them, a sweater over her blouse, a shawl tied to her waist. "This is my corps of discovery too."

"A big raft might have been better, but this canoe's fully equipped for emergencies." He didn't elaborate as to what emergencies they might expect, but he did point to a canvas covering the front third of the large canoe where the supplies were stored.

"Where did you get it?" Brannon asked.

"Borrowed it from a family in our tribe. But I had to talk fast. They complained that the last time the white men Lewis and Clark borrowed a canoe, we never got it back."

"Oh," was all that Brannon could think to say.

CHAPTER TWENTY FIVE

Barely offshore, the canvas tarp burst open and two seasick stowaways heaved over the sides of the canoe.

"Laira! Darcy!" Brannon shouted. "What are you doing here?"

Each tried their best to protect their dresses as they upchucked. Both wore shirtwaists with tall, stiff collars and narrow neckties, Laira's in powder blue, Darcy in pea green.

Laira grabbed a picnic basket. "You forgot this . . . from Mum. It's full of cheese, cherries and pemmican. And we won't bother you at all. We only want to look at whales. Live ones." Laira leaned over the canoe again.

"But does *Mum* know you came with us?" Brannon quizzed when she recovered.

"Oh, twee, I sent her a note by way of Bueno."

Because Sylvia refused to sit next to Rebozo, that left Brannon with Sylvia. So, Laira scooted next to Tanglewood. Darcy hunkered over by Rebozo in the crowded canoe. The three males and Sylvia rowed.

"I hope no whales appear," Tanglewood said. "They could capsize us."

Darcy put on a pout. "I can't swim."

"Neither can I," said Rebozo with great cheer. "We'll go down together."

Darcy clutched the side of the canoe. "Does anyone here swim?"

Sylvia and Laira raised their hands. Tanglewood made a face that suggested, "Of course I can." And Brannon gave an "aye."

They had to pass the gory whale carcass being cut up by Tanglewood's family to get to Tillamook Head.

"I found out that there's nothing in the whale's stomach but algae, rope and a swimming suit," Tanglewood explained.

"A swimming suit?" Brannon repeated.

"That's what Uncle Grant told me."

As they passed the whale's body, an overpowering smell made them almost ill. The air reeked with a rancid scent. When they neared the boiling pots, the odor worsened. Both Laira and Darcy leaned over the sides again, but there was nothing left to heave.

The farther south they moved, the fresher the whiffs of air. A bank of low clouds hung over the great rocks and sea, making a mass of pearled mist out of jagged, haunting grayness. Tillamook Head loomed as a brooding backdrop to the lively beach scene below. Soon, sunrays sprayed and shimmered through, what Lisa called a "glory hole." Brannon tore his eyes from the sight to search for the tiny trail up the side of Tillamook

Head, marked by a boy's shirt at the bottom.

"That's where you'll find the easier trail, the one to climb up the cliff side to Hack's Hideaway," Bueno had told him.

Now he was sorry they hadn't brought the boy with them. The bays on the north side were small and rocky, the cliff walls formidable for amateur climbers.

Finally, Brannon spotted the piece of raggedy cloth shirt on a branch. The rowers worked to keep them upright. The tide slammed them into the shore. Brannon and Tanglewood scurried out to pull them in further before the tide sucked them back out to sea.

They all climbed out. The two girls spread a blanket and the basket and themselves on the small bar of beach, then opened two umbrellas, glad to be back on land.

They were greeted by a swarm of orange butterflies who flitted around as though a huge hand had flung them over their heads. A couple seals with a pup studied them from a distance. A bald eagle with a bright white head, rose up from the highest crag, a strong place from which to scout her prey and enemies.

When a huge bee dived at Brannon, he swatted at it a few times. It attacked again. Brannon smashed it with his hands.

Laira gasped. "How did you do that without getting stung?"

"I didn't." He rubbed his hands together with frantic motions. "We need to climb up to the top, to explore where the boys had been."

"But we won't be able to chaperone these two," Rebozo said.

Tanglewood's face twisted with indecision. "I suppose I could stay. This small beach could flood. Or worse."

"I'll guard Darcy and she'll watch over me. We've got it all figured out," Laira announced.

"But who will protect Tanglewood from you two?" Brannon said.

There was no way that Brannon or Sylvia would stay behind. And they couldn't allow Rebozo to be alone with the girls.

"And I have a feeling we're going to need Tanglewood," Brannon remarked.

"Oh, twee, we'll be fine," Laira insisted. "We're going to be looking for whales."

Why did we get saddled with these two? Such a complication. Lord, protect them.

The four tackled the slope of the incline, much easier to ascend than they first imagined. They did tug on a few shrubs and at the top the ground was muddy and slippery.

"Don't step back without looking. You may need a rescue," Tanglewood warned. They trudged through ferns, bushes and decomposing litterfall. Beds of leaves and twigs, needles and the droppings of fir, pine and spruce provided what some called "the poor man's overcoat," layers of canopy.

Deep in the forest at the top of one of the tallest trees, Sylvia spied a huge bald eagle's nest, seven to eight feet across, on a foundation of sticks and softened with a lining of moss, grass, feathers and pine needles. Not far away, in cool and protected, open shade, they saw a spotted owl and nest in a stovepipe-like cavity formed in the top of a large conifer, the top broken off.

At the high promontory's rim, they admired the shoreline vista and noticed where landslides had fallen into the ocean. The Lewis and Clark expedition hiked here one hundred years before to barter with locals on the other side for meat from a beached whale. Now Tillamook Rock Lighthouse flickered its light a little more than a mile away, with a sixty-two-foot tower on a basalt rock islet.

"No way to get there except by crane to lift you up," Tanglewood said as they stopped to catch their breath. "The keeper's marooned." He sent a wave towards the islet.

A raven cawed: *cr-r-uck.* It flew straight overhead, then showed off with an acrobatic soar, tumble and barrel-roll.

"Cr-r-uck," Tanglewood echoed back. "Hate those birds. They're tricksters, sneaky, plenty selfish . . . but plenty smart too."

They scoured for any evidence of Tom Wiseman's presence.

"That's it. Down there. The large bay Bueno described," Brannon said.

After a careful climb down the other side, they rescued floating packages with medicines, bundles of oilskin-wrapped papers, jerky and rotting leather; also assorted arrowheads and fishing barbs. Playful sea lions poked their heads from the water to inspect them as starfish clung to a rock in a tide pool.

A quick look at the papers revealed advice on preventing malaria and yellow fever.

Sylvia reported from them. "This is astounding. It says here that twenty-two thousand workers in Panama died of malaria and yellow fever from 1881 to 1889. There's an article that claims mosquitoes are the cause of malaria. Wear long sleeves and pants. Use nets at night while sleeping. Don't put legs of hospital beds in tins of water. They protect from crawling insects but the stagnant water breeds mosquitoes."

Rebozo grabbed the packet. "I've watched men die of malaria. And one woman of yellow fever. It's not pretty. It can happen anywhere, even Washington D.C. Epidemics scare me. They erupt so sudden. Kills so many, real fast. They are no respecter of persons, by age or gender or social standing. Makes you want to erect a gigantic screen around every city that's vulnerable."

Brannon stared at Rebozo. *The man does have feelings for more than himself.* He debated whether to pry or not, but he wanted to know more about this chameleon man. "The woman? Was she someone close to you?"

"My mother."

"Look here," Sylvia hollered, "a compass buried in the mud." She dug until it broke free.

"Is that your father's?" Rebozo asked.

"No, he never had a compass that I remember. Didn't need one. He had a sixth sense about direction on land and he never contracted sea fever as a disease."

Brannon examined an early 1800s Georgian English compass. *I've seen one like this before.* "Keep this with the other items," he said. *One of his prized possessions. It belonged to his grandfather.*

"Don't turn around, but there's someone watching us," Rebozo said.

"Are they armed?" A spear skid over the rocks and stuck in the sand, six feet from Brannon.

"I believe so," Rebozo said. "Flee to the trees."

After the report of a rifle, a bullet whizzed near Brannon and spewed sand. "Get down." Brannon scanned the tree-lined cliff.

"Someone's running up there along the edge," Rebozo called out.

"Looks to me like the old Indian who rides the stallion's mares," Brannon said.

"Good eyesight," Rebozo commented.

"It's Catcher-Of-The-Sun." Tanglewood started for the trail.

CHAPTER TWENTY SIX

"All of you stay here," Brannon ordered.

"But I know him. He's my grandfather's friend. I can help you," Tanglewood said.

They scaled up the side behind Tanglewood, kneeled behind some bushes, then raised up and scouted for their attacker. Tanglewood took the lead as they climbed over brush, fallen logs and busted through cobwebs.

I can't keep up this pace much more. The guy with the rifle better appear soon.

As if in answer, another shot was fired, but no bullet whizzed by them. "I think he shot in the air," Rebozo said. "Let's get closer to make better contact."

"Be careful. That might have been a trick," Brannon warned. "I'll cover your flank."

"You'll shoot me where?" Rebozo raised his revolver in the air and shot high in the trees.

They waited. No return volley.

"Hey, old man. We don't want to hurt you," Brannon shouted. "What do you want from us?"

The man grunted something, very close to them. They peered around. His face was rough, course, the color of burlap. He sat on a large circle of moss, only yards away, his long, thin legs pulled up in front of him, his rifle crooked between his knees.

"We're looking for a man," Brannon called out to him. "He is a U.S. Marshal. He's been missing more than a week. Did he come here to Tillamook Head?"

The wizened, weathered Indian kept a steady gaze on them, but kept silent. He held the rifle steady, his narrowed eyes intent on Brannon.

"Let me talk to him. He's afraid," Tanglewood said.

Brannon scooted over to give the youth more room. "Afraid of what?"

"Perhaps that the deeds done here will be blamed on him."

Tanglewood approached the old man and they crouched down to talk. Brannon caught some words but couldn't understand. He guessed it was the old Clatsop language. They communicated with both speech and body language, the marvel of one human conveying the contents of one's mind to another. Then they stopped talking and sat in silence.

Why the quietness? To figure out how to tell us what was said? Or an ancient ritual of some sort, to let the words and their meaning settle between them?

Tanglewood scrambled towards them, but the old man stayed put.

"Why did he throw his spear? Why did he shoot at us?" Brannon asked.

"To chase us away? To get our attention?" Tanglewood shrugged. "The old chiefs dream many dreams."

Am I like an old chief? Are we getting so close to the next world that this one and the other start to blur together?

"Catcher-Of-The-Sun says that he did not see what happened," Tanglewood briefed them. "He considers this place his own, even though he doesn't stay here all the time. Our people have lived around here for maybe a thousand years, you know." Tanglewood took a deep breath. "He says more than a week of days ago he arrived to find two bodies . . . one sprawled at the foot of a rock cliff and had been shot, the other trapped in a thicket of fallen trees, like a crevice. That man had tried to get free, but was not able. He died there."

Tanglewood bowed his head, as though in respect for the loss of life, the lifting of spirits from this place.

"Where are they now?" Brannon inquired. "We didn't see any bodies on that bay."

"They must be there. The old man says he tried to protect the bodies for days from the birds and other creatures, but could not keep it up. He did not want to move them, so their story would remain. But no one came." Tanglewood stopped and they all tried to process what he was saying.

No one came.

But we got here as soon as we knew where to find him.

"Finally, he was forced to bury them, without their personal belongings, as would be the old custom. He was concerned that the story be evident in the here and now, rather than they take their possessions into the afterlife."

"Ask him to take us to the graves," Brannon said. "We must know if one of them is Tom Wiseman."

Sylvia gulped a breath, as though preparing for a hard truth.

"Are you all right?" Brannon asked.

She swished out the oxygen. "I knew I must come."

The elderly Indian led them back to the beach-side. At the south side, rocks had been stacked, a makeshift memorial, like Brannon had done for many fallen along numerous trails. He began to roll away the rocks.

"Surely you're not going to dig them up?" Rebozo questioned.

"What are you afraid of?"

"I'm thinking of the dignity of the dead. There won't be much left to distinguish and we can surmise all the evidence we need right here."

"That's convenient."

Rebozo gave him a puzzled look, then studied the ground, the cliff, the distance from the shore. "From what I gather here and the placement of the articles we purloined earlier, this is my assessment." He spun around several times, then raised a licked finger in the air.

Who does this guy think he is kidding?

"One man somehow tripped and rolled down the incline, maybe unconscious or breaks his neck. A third man lunged towards the other, who lost his balance. He fell back into that knot and pit of trunks and branches . . . up there . . . is knocked unconscious or maybe trapped. The third man surveys the scene and rides away."

Brannon picked up a black leather scabbard with a bayonet knife they had missed before, tucked down between the piled rocks. Smooth wood grips. Sixteen inches. It was stamped "artilleria Fca de Toledo." "I do believe this is Tom's."

"Yes, I have seen one like that. It could be my father's," Sylvia said.

Rebozo examined it. "Spanish. Pommel and Cross guard. Could be from the war. Perhaps there was a struggle over this and someone was stabbed."

Rebozo continued to study the terrain. "Maybe the man who fell on the beach was dead or soon would be. The other was trapped. The third man can either shoot them or ride out of here, innocent of all or any charges. Good riddance. A very good day."

Only the man who was here would be able to

relate such a scene. Or he's an imaginative guesser.

Brannon tried to control his rising frustration that edged on anger. "Keaton, ask the old man whether one of the men had thick, gray hair and wore a badge." He studied the knife and a leather case. "And ask about this knife, does it belong to him? Rebozo, you knew the Frenchman. What would identify him?"

"He had very curly hair, quite dark, and a thick, curved mustache that swerved up on both sides." He rubbed his own thin mustache. "Oh, yes, and the few times I saw him he wore a sort of ribbed sweater with rolled neck under his suit jackets. I think the coastal air felt chilly to him."

Tanglewood conversed with the old man and there was much bobbing of the head. He turned back to Brannon and Rebozo. "He affirms the descriptions. He also explains that the knife was on the beach after he found the men. He used it to dig the graves."

"There's a chip on the handle I don't remember," Sylvia said.

"That could have happened with the digging," Rebozo remarked.

When Brannon, Tanglefoot and Rebozo finished clearing the spot of rocks, they looked over at Sylvia. She insisted they dig.

"It won't be a pretty sight," Brannon warned.

"But I must know if that is my father buried there."

"I will do it," Rebozo offered. "I have examined the dead before, but Sylvia must promise not to look. I will do my best to describe in palatable terms what I see."

"Do you not want me to look either?" Brannon's tone was derisive. He tried a different tack. "I've witnessed body decay before too."

"You still don't trust me, do you?"

They dug deep in the sand while Sylvia paced the beach with Catcher-Of-The-Sun. She tossed shells and pebbles over the lapping waves. A majestic osprey soared above the water, spotted a fish near the surface and plummeted to seize the prey with its talons.

Finally, they uncovered two bodies, side by side, wrapped in a buffalo robe. Rebozo carefully lifted up the robe. The odor almost overpowered them. Sylvia ran over before they could object, then wretched until she crumpled.

They studied the bodies, as Rebozo turned them gingerly over. Parts of them revealed only skeleton, the flesh eaten away. "Well, I was wrong on at least one score. DeVache was shot and killed, probably by Wiseman." He held up a Colt revolver with custom pearl handles.

Brannon feared that nausea would overtake him too. "I guess the old man couldn't resist burying them with something."

Both Brannon and Sylvia definitely identified the gun as Tom Wiseman's. Sylvia could hold back no more. She began to sob.

How Brannon longed for this good friend to rise from the dead, greet them with his ever-friendly, "Howdy," and offer them a cup of strong, boiled coffee from his campfire. He fought back the rage that it would not be so.

"Looks like your friend had a broken leg and possibly a few broken ribs. There's also evidence he may have tried to cut off his leg, to free himself from his trap." Rebozo glanced at Sylvia, but she had stumbled away again, too far to pay attention to his assessment, wiping the Colt revolver in her hand with her skirt. "And this is DeVache, as far as I can tell. We'll have to contact his family."

"Do you know any of them or where they live?" Brannon asked.

"I used to. I'll check back at the hotel."

Catcher-Of-The-Sun approached Sylvia and beckoned Tanglewood. "He wants to make sure you put the gun back," the youth said. "So your father will have a weapon to fight the adversaries in the next world."

"No, that's when the battles are finally over." The statement gave her strength to walk over, take the knife and scabbard from Rebozo, and tuck it with the bodies. She kept the revolver.

"The old man says this is not the first time

bodies have been buried here," Tanglewood informed them. "It's been used as a gravesite for others, many times."

"But they're lost and forgotten," Sylvia said. "There's no markings anywhere."

On the way back, Sylvia tried to speak when she wasn't sobbing. "I can't believe he's gone, that I'll never see him again." She wiped her nose and weepy eyes. "Papa didn't deserve to die that way."

Brannon wanted to comfort her, but didn't quite know how.

"There won't be a birthday party, just him and me. It's like reliving the horror of Wills' death again and losing my mother. Does God hate me so much he destroys every person near and dear?"

Brannon couldn't think of a quick or helpful answer.

"I want to scream, 'God, are you really here?' "

I want to say, "God is good and just. He can be trusted. Look at God's story, the whole of it, and you'll know God's heart, that He is here." But it's not the right timing. And . . . how long did it take me to get to that place?

She whirled and stomped and flung out her arms. Brannon feared she'd lose control. "I've got to figure this out," she said. Her cheeks swelled. Her chest heaved. She looked like she'd explode.

Brannon attempted a response. "Life is unpredictable, but not random. God's ways cannot always be explained, because we're part of His story, attached to a bigger drama. In the meantime, sometimes what we care about the most, we lose. But it's temporary. We can have hope that it's all returned, only better."

Her voice got husky. She filled with somber resolve. "I will figure out some honorable way to transport Papa back to the ranch in Arizona."

Brannon hated to intrude on her very private grief, but he felt he must give some fatherly advice. "It might be better to leave his body on this bay with the rocks marking the spot and erect your own special tribute at home, with the rest of your family and friends."

She burst into tears again. When the sobs subsided she declared, "I will kill the one responsible for this atrocity. An eye for an eye. That is justice."

Or is it sometimes revenge?

Brannon attempted an awkward hug. She slung her arms around his chest and squeezed tight.

CHAPTER TWENTY SEVEN

Brannon and Sylvia caught up with Rebozo and Tanglewood who had tromped on ahead.

As the four hiked over fallen logs and roots spread out aboveground and kicked through ferns with their treasures back to the beached canoe, a storm brewed. Foam topped the ocean waves that bubbled towards the shore. Dark clouds gathered overhead, piled in stacks, then collided into a massive rift. Raindrops sprinkled, then pelted into hail. Thunder rumbled and lightning bolts streaked on the horizon. One display of earth as a great coughing, sputtering machine.

Sylvia unfolded the large shawl around her waist to cover her head and the beach items. Brannon tamped down his hat. "Rebozo, about your mother, where did she get yellow fever?"

"Where else? Panama."

"Why was she there?"

"We both were . . . to visit my father, one of the workers for the passageway being dug by the French."

"But you're not French." Brannon meant it as a statement, but immediately considered a doubt. *I don't know all the cultures of France.*

"I'm a mixture, what some in the States call a

breed. I was born in Philadelphia, lived part of my childhood in Colombia. My father's work took him all over the world, and my mother and I with him. The President was impressed with my travel resumé. Also, I have an innate sense of detection. He found that very useful."

"Is your father still in Panama?"

"Yes . . . and no. It wasn't the disease or squalor or sanitation standards that got him. He was eaten by an alligator."

Sylvia glared at Rebozo. "You shouldn't tease about such a thing."

"I'm not joking. That's the most accurate thing I've told you."

"So you confess that everything else is a lie?"

"O, she doth teach the torches to burn bright!"

She glowered at Rebozo again. "Okay, Romeo, I don't think that was a reference to my beauty."

When they slid down Hack Howard's trail and back to the tiny beach, they discovered the waves had beaten the canoe against some rocks and cracked the hull. Plus, the girls were gone.

Brannon found Laira hiking up in the thick forest. He couldn't help notice the initials of Laira and Tanglewood and the date carved in a nearby tree.

"Where's Darcy?" he demanded.

"She stayed on the beach. She didn't want to

miss a whale. She was going to shout at me if she saw something."

By the time they returned, Rebozo and Sylvia had dragged a soaked and limp Darcy near a prepared but not lit bonfire. A lone cottonwood, dead on top, provided wood to burn.

"Is she all right?" Brannon asked.

"She tried to catch the canoe when it began to sink back to sea," Sylvia explained.

"And I almost drowned." Darcy's pale face lacked its usual sparkle. "I was going down for the hundredth time when Mr. Rebozo saved me." She tried to smile at him, then coughed and gagged.

"Oh, you poor thing." Laira tried to comfort her new friend while she avoided Brannon's eyes.

"I am so sorry," Tanglewood said. "I should have stayed here." He touched Darcy's arm, a move that brightened Darcy and brought a frown from Laira. "I am so glad you are okay."

Brannon started the bonfire. The storm eased and passed. Sylvia wrapped the items they found at the big bay in a tarp. Laira passed around cheese, huckleberries, blackberries and pemmican as Darcy sniffed and coughed.

Brannon opened the jar of cherries and pulled out a few pieces of the tart-sweet fruit, recalling a Christmas Day during a hard winter at a place called Broken Arrow Crossing . . . the agony of a mother, Elizabeth, and the birth of a baby, a brave warrior named Littlefoot. *Elizabeth ate all the cherries that night.*

"Are we going to be marooned here?" Laira said. "All day and all night?"

Brannon couldn't tell if the girl considered that a good or bad idea. "We'll leave as soon as the storm dies down and Keaton gets the canoe fixed."

"This is like being shipwrecked." Darcy wrapped the blanket tighter as she scooted close to the fire.

"Keaton's the son of a shipwrecked sailor," Brannon said.

"Oh, twee," said Laira. "That must have been dreadfully pernickety."

Tanglewood hummed as he caulked the seam with pitch and rosin.

"Tell us about it," Laira prodded.

Tanglewood stopped his work. "Not much to tell. My father's ship stalled in a windless pocket, got stranded and drifted into the rocks. The captain of the ship was drunk at the time. I think my father was too. But he turned out to be a good father."

"Where is he now?" Laira asked.

"Out on another ship. I see him about once a year."

On the way back to the mainland, in spite of a violent and fierce current, the canoe stayed on course. It seemed as if even the sky and ocean mourned the loss of at least one good man.

Tanglewood hollered as a gray whale broke the surface beyond them, then disappeared. He surfaced again, jaw wide open. Giant fountains of water ejected from his blowhole.

Laira and Darcy clapped, entranced. The whale sighting accomplished the outing's goal for them.

However, high waves threatened to prevent a safe landing. The temperature dropped and the girls shivered. Sylvia offered to share her fur wrap with them. They huddled next to her. Water sprayed everyone on board.

"It's rougher out here than it looks like from the shore," Laira said.

No one disputed her observation.

Finally, they landed and everyone dispersed back to Gearhart. Brannon determined to figure out something that troubled him. He found Lady Fletcher in the hotel lobby. "I'm looking for Edwin."

"He's up on the roof."

"Why on earth for and at this time of evening?"

"To get his prize golf balls that landed up there. He's been practicing out on the lawn."

Lady Fletcher scurried outside and called to her husband, who peered over the edge and waved. "Oh good, there you are, Stuart. I'll get right down and we can have a chat."

Brannon held the ladder for him as he wobbled down each step.

"I met with several foreign representatives from Italy, Germany and France today. They're here for the Lewis and Clark Exposition."

"What great controversies did you have to solve?" Brannon asked.

"Not much. Some are concerned about vandalism to their exhibits, especially the French Exhibit." Lord Fletcher squinted his eyes at Brannon. "Apparently a marauder broke Louis XIV's bed and shot up his mirrors."

"They should be as concerned about their staff attacking visitors."

"Stuart, why can't you be a normal tourist like everyone else, instead of leaving carnage behind wherever you go?"

Brannon pulled out the compass found on the Tillamook Head beach. "Are you missing this?"

Lord Fletcher took the compass and looked it over. "Very nice, but it's not mine. There are no initials and the one I inherited from my father is in London in a drawer of my drawing room."

"So, I've only got your word that this doesn't belong to you."

Lord Fletcher scratched his cheek. "I say, that's about it. Why do you ask?"

He engaged them both with all earnestness. "We found this compass in the beach near where we found Tom Wiseman's body."

Harriet gasped, her hand over her mouth. "Oh, dear!"

Edwin put his hand on Brannon's shoulder. "So, Wiseman's dead."

"Yep."

"I'm so sorry, Stuart. This compass is your best lead?"

"So far."

"But surely you didn't think I had anything at all to do with that?"

"I had to check it out."

"Yes, quite. But I have seen that compass . . . or one like it. Can't recall where or with whom. It's this aging thing, you know. The mind's a bit bonkers at times. If I recall, I'll let you know, old chap."

Relieved, Brannon searched for Rebozo and found him in the café. He tried to change his attitude from adversary to partner. For now, it was a necessity. "Edwin says the compass doesn't belong to him."

Rebozo lit a Murad. "Do you believe him?"

"Without question."

"I say we stir the stew, confront some other suspects."

"Like wearing the compass around one of our necks and watch the reactions? Or offer it as an auction prize and nab the highest bidder?"

"Or we could narrow the field of contenders and challenge them to a duel or to a game of

some sort . . . such as poker, one of my fortés . . ."
Rebozo fostered a light tone, but then he became serious.

"And pile it in a pot?"

"Actually, it might work. But we've got to corner actual suspects. Can you hazard a guess?"

"Yes, two . . . you and Lanigan. Any on your list?"

"I'm on a hot trail, a paper trail, that is. Should point to a guilty party any day now. Meanwhile, I sure don't mind pulling together a table of players for you, but it will take a little arranging. I'll aim for late tonight. Should be fun."

"And revealing, I hope."

Later, Rebozo announced, "Game's all set. Just have one more player to contact. We're meeting at the Black Duck Saloon at ten o'clock."

CHAPTER TWENTY EIGHT

That evening, Brannon pushed through the partially-open door at the back of the Seaside barroom, the slap of his spurs and boot heels on the wooden floor the only sounds.

As the door swung open, a mix of beer, wine and whiskey fumes with sweaty heat slapped against his face like the tail of an annoyed horse. The small card room held a round table in the center with enough space for seven or eight players. The backs of the chairs, when occupied, crammed against the rough-hewn walls, impossible for anyone to walk behind them without turning sideways.

And the smoke, as thick as tar and twice as toxic, spread like a caked fog from the lit cigars of the men already at the table.

If I had smoke this thick in my eyes at a campfire, I'd move to the other side of the ring. Probably should be grateful for it, though, as it helps to cover the other smells.

As the close quarters exposed the increase of mingled layers of stale and foul breath, Brannon felt as out of place as a milk bucket under a bull. He laid his hat crown down on a tiny table next to the door, then inched into the room as he surveyed the players.

Lanigan, tense and focused on his cards, sat two seats away from Rebozo, who barely glanced in Brannon's direction with his red, glazed eyes and rosy hue in his cheeks.

Stay alert, Rebozo. Keep with the plan.

Next to Lanigan plopped two men. The first was the Frenchman, the friend of DeVache, with his air of aristocracy. At this late hour his tie was unfastened, his collar unbuttoned and his dinner jacket slouched on the back of his chair. Indentations in his graying hair just above his ears indicated a hat had been recently worn, but was not in the room.

The fourth man appeared to be a gentleman, in dapper suit and bowler hat, but the man's eyes had the weary look of someone who spent many hours on the trail, his hands worn from years of hard labor.

Brannon had seen this type before and he let himself conjecture. *Maybe he's come into some money and now trying to break into high society . . . with only mediocre success.*

The last player took Brannon by surprise—a lady! From the back, in the dim haze of the room, Brannon couldn't identify her.

"Room for a sixth?" Brannon bumped and circled his way to the chair between Lanigan and Rebozo, opposite the woman. Burgundy velvet dress, black ribbon and cameo around the neck, burgundy flowers on the tall, narrow hat. Then he noticed the gleam in her eyes. *Sylvia, what are you doing here? How come you look so different with such a little effort?*

All the players ignored him. They gawked at Rebozo instead, who grabbed a stack of chips and shoved them in the middle of the pot, crying "Call!"

The man with the rough hands and new suit slumped in his chair and threw down his cards, face up: a pair of sixes. *Overbet his hand to scare the others out.*

Rebozo broke into a surly grin, leaned back in his chair and slapped his cards down with a thud: tens and threes. He figured two pair took the biggest pot of the night.

Seems like so far the luck's rolling Rebozo's way.

The other players relaxed, lounged in their chairs, sipped their whiskey or drew a long drag on their cigars. Brannon noticed only a few dollars left in front of the losing man, perhaps a long night for him.

A rough night of bad cards and losing hands can make a man desperate. That's a lot of money to bluff.

Brannon recalled his occasional poker games in Arizona, stretched out on the porch with his grandkids, playing for bragging rights in the cool of the evening. *That's the way a game—any game—should be played. With loved ones, in a familiar place, with nothing at stake but the right to say "I won."*

Brannon chuckled to himself as he thought of the exasperated looks on the kids' faces, as each lost, one by one.

"How come you always win, Grandpa?" Everett asked one night. "Can you see our cards?"

"Nope. I just look into your eyes, because a mouth can lie and a face can mislead, but the truth is always in the pupils."

Brannon returned to the present after a remark from Lanigan. "Didn't take you for a card player."

Now everyone's attention was riveted on Brannon. *Now's the time to play the part.* "That would normally be a correct assumption, but tonight I'm feelin' lucky."

"Minimum buy-in's one hundred dollars at this table," the Frenchman said in a gruff voice.

Brannon reached down into his boot, pulled out a couple folded-up bills and laid them on the table. "Any other rules I should know?"

The man picked up the bills, counted them out for all to see, then folded them and reached over to Sylvia. She tucked them in a tin can on the chair next to her and passed a stack of chips to Brannon.

"Dealer's choice, stud or draw. One dollar ante. Table stakes," Sylvia explained.

"And no wild cards or other child's play,"

growled the man who had lost the previous hand. He downed the rest of the whiskey in his glass and latched onto the half-empty bottle. He refilled his glass, scowled as though the action stung him somehow and slung his arm over to Brannon. "My name's Thompson, Stanley Thompson."

"And I'm Yves McKinley." His demeanor softened to a tentative gesture of friendship. "My mother was French. My father was Scots–Irish and English."

"McKinley, like the President?"

McKinley looked down for an instant. "A distant cousin, but a shock to the family, all the same."

Thompson broke in with, "Your deal, Lanigan. Do you know the others, Brannon? Lanigan, Rebozo," he pointed out, "and the lady is Miss Sylvia Wiseman."

"We're acquainted. Thanks." Brannon gave a slight salute to Sylvia. He then turned to Rebozo who wagged his head like a dolt.

He hasn't shown the compass yet.

Lanigan called five-card draw and dealt the cards as everyone anteed. The bets were small as they played cautiously after the previous pot, which Brannon estimated at over two hundred fifty dollars. The tension magnified when McKinley splattered them all with a sneeze, Thompson blew his nose long and noisily, and

Brannon folded. He wanted to concentrate on each player as they studied their cards or made a bet.

The light of the body is the eye. You can tell so much about a person by their gaze, their attention, especially if they don't know you're watching.

The next several hands progressed the same with polite but reserved banter between the players. Brannon perceived a kind of recoil before a strike.

No unbelievers in a foxhole. No friends once the cards get dealt.

Brannon bet small or quickly folded, but never made it to a showdown. Sylvia pivoted towards Lanigan, followed his every move and encouraged with "nice hand" when he won a few dollars. Lanigan flushed with pleasure, pulled at his collar like he needed air and strummed his chips with a nervous *clink, clink, clink.*

Come on, Rebozo, I can't stand much more of this.

CHAPTER TWENTY NINE

Sylvia dealt five-card draw. Rebozo bet hard at twenty-five dollars. Brannon folded his rainbow ten-high hand and Lanigan raised to seventy-five dollars. McKinley gaped at his cards and fingered them one by one several times each, as though he missed an extra ace. Then he slapped them face down on the table with an "Arrrrgh!"

Thompson seemed happy to fold and Sylvia offered no argument or complaint to exiting the hand.

Now all eyes centered on Rebozo, who had played whiskey-loose, though his stack had not suffered.

Lanigan had been the tight player all night and had refused all offers of drinks, although he did challenge Thompson on a large pot at one point. Rebozo's hand shook as he plucked out a stack of chips and shoved them into the pot, an implied call.

There are only a few hands in a night that catch the attention of all the players, and maybe only one that feels destined to be talked about for days to come. This began to feel like one of those hands.

"How many?" Sylvia asked.

Rebozo croaked out, "Two," without looking up. He threw down his pair of cards onto the table.

Sylvia counted out both cards and pushed them towards Rebozo, who glowered over at his competitor. He stuck the deal in his hand with a quick glance, then watched Lanigan as he pulled out one card and flipped it, spinning, onto the table near Sylvia. She reciprocated with a new card flung, spinning in front of Lanigan.

At first, Lanigan registered no reaction as he placed the card in his hand. He gazed at his cards for a moment, then folded them and set them face down in front of him. Rebozo grabbed his glass and drained the contents with a whiplash-quick head bend, as Lanigan turned towards him with a smirk on his face.

Rebozo, less amused, slowly closed his own cards and laid them down in front of him. He let out some whiskey breath, counted out three equal stacks, and pushed the chips towards the center of the table.

"One hundred fifty dollars," Rebozo stated and focused his attention to the center of the table. Though he had won the large pot earlier, his stack had since diminished.

Less than one hundred dollars left, Brannon calculated.

Lanigan snorted, his glassy eyes sparkling as though exuding confidence.

Rebozo's whiskey brimmed to full force, swimming in his head.

Stay in the game, Brannon advised in silence.

"You expect me to believe that?" Lanigan cajoled. "No way you got a fourth. You're sittin' with a small set, and we all know it."

Rebozo ogled the center of the table, a bead of sweat at his temple.

Lanigan tried to stare Rebozo down, but couldn't get him to engage. He squinted his eyes, then widened them trying to read the other player. Rebozo played whiskey dumb.

"Nope," Lanigan confirmed. "All in." He used both hands to shove his chips into the pot.

The other players shifted in their seats, moved closer, intent on the action. Even Brannon leaned forward.

However, Rebozo leaned back and looked down at his stack. Then he raised his head slightly to study Lanigan, who rocked in his seat and folded his hands behind his head.

A clock ticked. Cigars smoldered or died out.

Rebozo's cheeks twitched. He rubbed his eyes, then frowned at Lanigan as he swayed. He reached out to his stack with the inaccuracy of the inebriated. "I can't cover your bet in full, but this should make up the difference."

He pulled out the compass from his pocket and balanced it on his remaining chips, never taking his attention from Lanigan.

McKinley was the first to protest. "Table stakes only. You know the rules, Monsieur Rebozo."

"Yeah, we all agreed," Thompson chimed in.

But Rebozo, Brannon and Sylvia watched Lanigan for any sort of response to the compass. Recognition? Fear? Anger?

Lanigan bent far over as though to peruse the object, squinting, then enlarging his eyes. He then righted himself. "Fine by me."

Before anyone could further protest, Lanigan grabbed his cards, flopped them down, and sprayed them around the table, with two still face down. Sylvia grabbed them one by one and lay them in a neat row next to each other. All black. All clubs.

"Flush," she determined.

The others signaled approval.

Lanigan fixed a look on Rebozo with only the barest hint of doubt, as though his grand reveal hadn't been for naught. "Beat that."

Rebozo, boozy breath in full heave, slowly turned his cards over one at a time. Five of spades. Five of hearts. Five of diamonds. Lanigan crafted a smile as Rebozo turned over the fourth card: two of diamonds.

"I knew it." Lanigan reached for the pot with both arms.

But both Brannon and McKinley held his hands back as they waited for the fifth card. Rebozo flipped it up on its edge so that only he could see it, then let it slowly drop, face up, onto his other cards. Two of spades.

"Full house," cried McKinley and Thompson.

Sylvia slapped the table, which seemed to refocus a befuddled Lanigan, still basking in his win, arms still extended, ready to embrace the pot. As the others murmured among themselves, reality sunk in.

"What?" He exclaimed. Then he got nasty. "What?" he snarled as he pulled his hands back, his fists clenched. He stood with a jolt, bumping the table and slamming his chair against the back wall.

"How in the world?" He glared down at Rebozo.

Brannon rose to defense position as Lanigan swung at the weaving, lunging Rebozo. Brannon reached out to stop Lanigan's fist, but missed. In an instant, Rebozo lost his drunk act and installed his reflexes. Lanigan hit air, then a wall, falling into Brannon. Brannon pushed him back against the wall. Lanigan reached for his revolver. Brannon's Colt was cocked and pointed at the man's heart before Lanigan had cleared leather.

"I think we've all had enough for the night, don't you, Lanigan?" Brannon stood calm, confident, aim steady. *Lord, I've been in this situation so many times before, way too many . . .*

Lanigan let his revolver drop into its holster. He spat on the floor, then pushed his way out.

Brannon replaced his Colt. "That was entertaining, but it's late."

McKinley counted out the chips. Sylvia swapped chips for cash. Brannon looked over at Rebozo and shrugged his shoulders in defeat.

Lanigan did not take the bait. Nor did anyone else. But that does not eliminate Rebozo as the third man.

Rebozo picked up the pot, but Brannon grabbed away the compass. Rebozo whistled a tune from an advertisement, "Come away with me, Lucille, in my merry Oldsmobile," and strolled out the door.

Out on the beach, cozy in his bedroll, Brannon pulled out a tattered, black Bible from his duffle and opened it to Revelation and read as far as he could before he drifted to sleep.

Brannon tossed and turned for more than an hour, then dreamed again, this time of elegant buildings with towers, parapets and sculptured columns that rose above him. One was filled with mounds of multi-colored ice cream. Over the door a sign said, "Prize of Panama." Gallons of Neapolitan scoops spilled out and rolled down a tree-lined cliff. He reached out for a lick when he heard horses at full gallop and saw their silhouettes on the rim at sunrise.

The white horse's rider carried a massive bow

and shot white gleaming arrows into the horizon and across great oceans.

The rider of the red horse swung a sword over countries and continents.

The black horse's rider raised a torch aloft and climbed the highest mountain's peaks to shout, "glory," a word that echoed through hundreds of valleys and canyons.

And a lone pale horse sped through flames and graveyards, never stopping, never looking back.

Brannon woke with his heart beating against his chest and heard the words, "Watch. Be alert. Redemption draweth near."

He tried to remember where he was, see through the dark shadow land, then listened to the rush and lap of the waves. *The beach. I'm in Oregon.*

Why am I dreaming so much? Is it because I'm in unfamiliar territory, away from home? What did those words mean? Are we getting close to an answer about Tom's death?

He tried to focus in the mists that lifted from the rocks and waves, to get back to the real world, the one where a stallion and his mares and ponies appear like an army of warriors at dawn.

But they didn't come.

He rolled over and went back to sleep. No more dreams.

CHAPTER THIRTY

Friday, June 16

Sylvia pulled and pushed at Brannon's bedroll until his eyes opened to a streak of daylight. "What are you doing here?"

Geode stood beside a calm, controlled Tres Vientos, waiting for her call to duty. Sylvia's skirt was swept into a ball of some sort, but was still below her knees. Her hair scattered in whiffs of disarray. Smudges sketched her face and arms and a spot stained her blouse. "Cordelle heard about my being in Seaside till late at the poker game, about my being snug as a rug with Lanigan, and not coming to see him. Also, he's been jealous about Tally Rebozo. He's ready to go back home to New York."

Brannon raised up on an elbow, his head ached like he had a hangover. "Explain it to him. He'll understand."

"You've got to help me. Be my backup. Our romance is being ruled by rumors and innuendoes." She fought to hold back the tears. "I've lost my father. I lost my fiancé. I can't lose this good, decent man too. I want to spend the rest of my life with him." She stopped as she quivered all over. "I need him."

Brannon extended his hand and Sylvia pulled him up. He spread his arms in a wide sweep over the western horizon, down to Tillamook Head, and around to the stretch of cities from Seaside to Gearhart.

"Where is he?"

"I don't know. Somewhere in Seaside, I hope. Please hurry."

Brannon splashed some water he used for coffee on his face and reached for his hat to ply over his unruly hair. "I don't mean to be rude, but it don't matter much what I look like, except not to resemble a bum who hitchhikes the railroad, but bein's you're going to try to convince a fella not to cut out on you . . ."

Sylvia looked down at her unkempt appearance. "Uh, yes . . . well, turn around."

Brannon plodded south down the beach, slapping his cheeks, trying to be fully awake and alert. The lighthouse far out on its rocky perch seemed to blink a "good morning."

How did I get myself mixed up in someone else's love affair? She ought to do her own fence mendin'. On the other hand, if Rebozo and I hadn't engineered that poker game, maybe she and Cordelle would be spendin' the day at a jewelry shop lookin' for a ring.

"Yoohoo, you can come back now," Sylvia hollered.

She appeared neater, tidier, cleaner. She looked

as fresh and pretty as a calf licked by its mama after birthing. Maybe she'd do to test the love of an honest, good man.

They cinched their horses and mounted them, Sylvia on hers English style. They rode to the pearly walls of Seaside and began their search. After a fruitless initial round, Sylvia suggested, "Let's find Sully. Maybe he knows what's going on."

They discovered Quintus Sully eating breakfast with two men, the same ones they had last seen with Lanigan at the hotel café. He introduced them as gold mine owners from Panama.

"Do you know where Cordelle is?" Sylvia quizzed.

Sully sucked in his ample stomach. "On his way to the orphanage to gather his things and say farewell to the inmates there. If you need some help, I'll be glad to come with you."

"Thanks, but I've got Stuart with me."

They made a quick exit and headed southwest for the banks of the Necanicum River. The fifteen acre orphan farm included a two-story building with plenty of windows, though all were barred in criss-cross fashion. They had electric lighting, pumped-in water and a basement furnace for heating.

Outside cement walks and a graveled driveway gave easy access. Rhododendrons and azaleas across the front provided a homey atmosphere. A garden and diverse farm added a variety of fresh vegetables in season. Some horses and dairy cows wandered behind fences.

"They need funding to keep their staff and for over-all operating expenses since the state no longer subsidizes them," Sylvia said.

Miss Penelope Tagg greeted them at the door.

Sylvia hesitated, but Brannon poked her gently in the back. "Is Cordelle here?" she managed.

There. She asserted her claim. Now she must find out how Cordelle stands.

"Mr. Plew is in the boy's dormitory. I'll get him for you."

Inside good light and ventilation gave an airy appearance for the assortment of large rooms, as well as a laundry service and sewing area. A large dining room with hand-carved tables had been set with knives and forks, linen and china, in a cozy, homelike atmosphere.

Cordelle Plew, hat in hand, approached Sylvia with reddened, but kind eyes. A dozen boys, many still in their night clothes, followed at a polite span behind him, peering at Sylvia, then fixed their attention on the revolver in Brannon's holster.

Hack Howard loomed a head taller than the oldest boys.

Miss Tagg started to shoo them away, but Cordelle prevented her. "What we have to say, we can say in front of them. After all, they are a part of my life too."

Sylvia hesitated, as though unsure what to do. Then she weaved back and forth in front of the unexpected audience, wringing her hands, casting side glances at Cordelle.

Brannon was surprised that she didn't commence with explaining the last few days.

"Before we go any farther, I want you to know my whole story." She finally pulled up a high-backed chair and plopped down, her back straight, legs stretched forward.

Plew eased into a chair across from her, set his hat on a table and leaned closer.

"Long before we met recently on the Northern Pacific train, I traveled east for adventure. I met some girls who liked to meet sailors at all the ports. I was attracted to one of them. Wills Bennett was the boy all the gals wanted. I couldn't believe he chose me. We hit it off in every way. But I lost him on February 15, 1898. To be honest, I couldn't help but wonder what my life would have been like if he hadn't died."

She paused and watched for her intended's reaction. He didn't frown or scowl or shy away from this truth.

"I know that date," he said, "the day of the U.S.S. *Maine* explosion."

"Yes, in the Cuban harbor. I was there to be with him, on the mainland. He served his duty on the ship. Later, I stood on a high balcony in Havana to watch the horse-drawn carriage they made into hearses for the lost sailors." She wiped a tear. "Somehow it brought me a little comfort that this horrendous act started a war. Our whole country would try to avenge Wills' death and all the others."

"You feel like you got a bad deal?" Plew said.

"Yes, I do. Because of that, I've had a hard time trusting people or God. But I also have a penchant for wanting to know the truth. It's just so difficult to commit, to tell anyone I love them . . . and I also dread growing old alone. I guess I'm complicated."

Brannon looked around at the boys' faces, as well as Miss Tagg's. They seemed attentive, interested. Henrietta Ober and the Smythes had also gathered nearby. He noticed some solemn and giggly girls sitting and lying on the floor behind them.

Plew didn't pay attention to any of the others in the room. He focused only on Sylvia. "So, you're trying to survive with broken dreams."

"Yes, but I still have those dreams. I thought I was getting close to fulfilling two of them."

"I'd be honored to know what they were."

"Finding a man I truly honor to invest in a lifetime relationship . . . and . . . doing something significant with my life. I'm educated, can sing soprano and am a pianist. I embroider and can broil kidneys. I believe I'd make a good wife. But there's some barriers . . ."

Uh oh. Here's a crucial point. She may be treading delicate ground. I suspect this will be make or break and that this has been totally unrehearsed. Brannon braced himself for the results. As he gazed around again, so did many others.

"Tell me," Plew said. "I really want to know."

"Being assured that a man can trust me and believe me when I tell him the truth . . . and . . ."

"And what?"

She pulled up the hem of her skirt a few inches to reveal a tattoo with a sailor hat and the name "Wills" stitched across. "Any man I marry has to live with that."

In the quiet that followed, Brannon heard only the ever-present ringing in his ears. One of the smaller boys made a sucking sound with his thumb. Miss Tagg stole over to a drawer and slowly opened it to tug out some handkerchiefs.

Plew leaned in closer to Sylvia, stared her in the eyes with confidence. "If you can bear my working with children like these," he waved an arm at the orphans behind him, "I can welcome Wills Bennett as part of who you are."

Everyone released their held breaths. Mrs. Smythe looked like she might even clap. But Cordelle Plew hadn't finished. "However, there is another consideration . . ."

He rolled up his long-sleeved shirt. A colorful tattoo with the name "Susanne" and an anchor was emblazoned on his shoulder.

"Who is Susanne?" Sylvia asked.

"I can't remember. I did that back in my own sailor days and I admit to a few rip-roaring times."

Now they all waited for Sylvia's response. She started with a soft titter and then swelled into a belly laugh. They all joined in, especially the girls hunkered down on the floor.

Cordelle and Sylvia stood up, still laughing, and hugged tightly. Miss Tagg blew her nose again. The children got restless and began to disperse. Brannon turned his head and brushed his sleeve across his cheek.

Before they left, Hack Howard crept over to Brannon and whispered, "Is Bueno all right?"

"Yes. He's safe. Did you recognize any of the men you saw from your hideaway?"

"No. They were too far away and I was too frantic later when the man in the motor boat arrived." He held his head in either shyness or shame. Brannon hoped it wasn't due to telling a falsehood.

Before they left, Brannon carved his initials and '05 onto the largest hemlock on the orphan farm.

On the way back to Gearhart, Geode and Tres Vientos galloped the beach in perfect, harmonious tandem, cream and ebony tails and manes swishing the air.

Brannon said, "See, you didn't need me after all."

"Oh yes, I did. You gave me courage and strength to say what I must."

CHAPTER THIRTY ONE

"Steak and eggs?" Waitress Katie granted him a smile as wide as her hips. Her ebony face offered kindness. "Looks like you've been burning both ends." Her coal eyes darted around as though looking for an errant empty cup or plate.

"I'll have ham and eggs. No, bring me some of that bear meat."

"Sure thing. Hey, I'm so sorry to hear about your friend. He was a gentleman to us all."

Brannon thanked her. *Word gets around fast.*

Steam from the forest-green mug lifted Brannon's mind and elevated his spirit. Sometimes coffee slowed him down. Or sped him up. It accomplished the right thing for the moment. This morning's coffee break stirred him to realize a fact. At least one person somewhere near him knew the why of what happened to Tom Wiseman . . . and by whom.

He didn't mean to eavesdrop, but Lady Fletcher and Rebozo stood at the counter, their backs to him.

Lady Fletcher grabbed Rebozo's good arm. "Here is my Serbian spy. Where were you last night? I expected you to be your congenial self at my party, full of intrigue and inside information and juicy gossip."

"Your friend, Stuart Brannon, keeps me busy, my Lady."

"But not too busy to keep the promises he made to me. He is a man of his word. How about you, Mr. Rebozo?"

"I'm a man of action. I can do more than talk."

Lady Fletcher backed away. "I'm sure you can."

He bowed and left the room.

Brannon tread lightly to her side. "Is he bothering you?"

"Oh, no. It's not his fault . . . this time. I've hatched a plot to find out more details about that man, especially for Laira's sake. But he's a hard one to penetrate. And he has a one-track mind."

"Then you did find out all you needed."

"Yes, I must keep him away from Laira."

"I will try to talk to him." He handed her Elizabeth's most recent postcard. "I sent the President a telegram about Tom."

"Stuart," she admonished, "you really must get those glasses fixed."

"I can see fine at a distance. It's those words up close that blur."

"And I can't tell if you've shaved yet this morning. You do tend to look a little in the beard most of the time."

Brannon rubbed the sparse stubble on his cheeks and chin.

"Looks like more drama at the ranch. 'Yesterday Edwin was missing. We looked and looked. Mama even cried. But we finally found him walking down by the dry creek bed with a wild and dirty cat. Mama said he could keep it.'"

"I'm so thankful little Edwin's found. I would have worried myself to a tizzy if I had been there."

"By the way, there are a number of important people arriving today for the weekend. I do hope there won't be any shooting, or anything of the sort, unless you can make it seem part of the festivities."

After breakfast, Brannon asked about Tally Rebozo. Katie the waitress said she last saw him dawdling in the hotel backyard with Mrs. Gillespie.

He found the woman in lavender pulling weeds out of the hotel landscaping, alone. She was immersed in rhododendron with their large blooms in umbrella-like clusters, ocean sprays of cream-white flowers, bright pink roses and azaleas that proposed hints of skunk scent.

"I absolutely adore gardening," she said. "And I haven't seen Andale in ages, simply ages . . . except about an hour ago." Mrs. Gillespie attacked the weeds with such vigor, Brannon feared she might turn and throw the sharp tool she held at him. "I would look for Mrs. Acorn at the Chautauqua. He won't be far away."

"Thank you, I'll go check it out."

"He's been grilling the poor lady, absolutely grilling her. He imagines that she has access to information about a crime. Such nonsense. He'll use any excuse to play with a woman's affections. But why her, I can't imagine."

"Is there a Mrs. Rebozo? Or a Mrs. Andale? I'm confused about this man's identity."

"I'm not privy to his marital status. The man of many names belongs to everyone . . . and no one."

While Mrs. Gillespie kept mumbling to herself, Brannon hiked over to the park.

Children ran through the trees playing various forms of "hide and seek." A band marched out of the auditorium with a reprise of "The Anvil Chorus" from *Il Trovatore*. Down the trail their instruments blasted, along with four husky tympanists in leather aprons, while dogs barked and trailed behind. The sparse weekday audience dragged out of the doors and arched overhang to disperse to their temporary homes on the grounds or beyond.

The Chautauqua movement, what Theodore Roosevelt called, "The most American thing in America," had become a traveling circuit of culture. Started in New York, over four hundred auditoriums sprang up across the country.

The Gearhart posters and billboards advertised the summer's speakers and programs . . . a magician, Carter the great; William J. Bryan "A Potent Human Factor in Molding the Mind of the Nation"; Kate Douglas Wiggin, author of *Rebecca of Sunnybrook Farm*; and John Philip Sousa and his band . . . "A dollar show for ten cents."

Brannon sauntered under the belfry and arched entrance, took a peek inside the building and was surprised to see Rebozo up on the stage alone, silently acting out some scene or discourse, like a charade or pantomime. When he looked up and viewed Brannon, he ushered him to come forward.

As Brannon scooted down the aisle towards the front row of seats, Rebozo thundered: "Mercy and truth are met together; righteousness and peace have kissed each other. Justice and judgment are the habitation of thy throne: mercy and truth shall go before thy face."

Like a great orator, with an expansive sweep of his arms, he projected to every corner of the auditorium, "Throw the sand against the wind, and the wind blows it back again. Is there justice in God? Can His justice be called truth? Doth God have mercy? Can justice and mercy work together for truth?"

Silence roared through the echoes over the great room. Brannon waited on the edge of his seat to hear what answer this man might give to these critical questions. But they didn't come from Rebozo's lips.

"What's on your mind, Brannon?" Rebozo began to rearrange the stage. He picked up chairs, scooted some over, stacked them, then removed the podiums. "An old habit," he explained. "Used to work the theaters, you know." The words edged with reverberation.

Brannon observed his ritual, then blurted out, "Are you married?"

Rebozo didn't respond except to keep at his volunteer job.

After a decent pause of waiting, Brannon pushed on. "Either way, a young girl like Laira should be off limits." He then opened the canvas case to his Winchester take-down rifle.

"Off limits for what? I'm being friendly to the girl in a brotherly way."

Rebozo kept clearing the stage as Brannon put together his take-down. "Should be fatherly way. How old are you?"

"Not that old. What's eating you, Brannon? The girl's virtue is intact, at least as far as I'm concerned."

Brannon opened the action to his rifle. "Let's start with glib charm."

"Sounds like jealousy on your part to me."

"Playing with the vanities of women is no light manner. They deserve respect and honor."

"All of them?"

"Yep."

"I beg to differ."

Brannon turned the lever on the end of the magazine tube, then began to unscrew it like a handle. When it loosened, he turned the two pieces of the rifle to a ninety degree angle and clamped them together with a twist. "I can't tell . . . do you love 'em or hate 'em?"

"Each woman is her own person. She earns her treatment."

"Hmmm . . . if I hadn't been told that you were a government agent, I'd suspect you of being a woman abuser." He watched Rebozo's face for a response. He seemed amused, in a spirited kind of way that confused Brannon.

"I assure you, I've never laid a hurtful hand on any female, but I have felt a sting or two from them."

Brannon sensed sincerity in that statement. "I'm curious. Why did you take this assignment, to come alongside me?"

"Because I admire a man with brass, because I'm jealous of you, because I want to draw from your glory. In fact, I felt the same about Tom Wiseman."

"Enough to kill him?"

"Apparently, you suspect so."

"But I am surprised."

"About what?"

"Your honesty. Few men would admit to such motives . . . unless you're joking. I guess you could be playing me. Is that your style?"

Rebozo offered a cheerless laugh. "I'll go even further. I love to be part of grandiose schemes that have potential for pomp . . . and especially the receipt of personal praise."

"You won't find any of that around me."

"But I might with Lord and Lady Fletcher. Or Wax Lanigan."

"Lanigan! He's nothing but a dime store thief. A small time guy trying so hard to gain status."

"That's where you and Tom Wiseman are wrong. I think you misjudge the man. He's got a compassionate side that makes him willing to champion causes . . . and want to change. You as a man of God should understand that."

"I'm glad that you could tell I'm a believer. I haven't been the best example lately. I hope more than anything that God is not ashamed to be called my God. But getting back to you, why try to corral ladies you don't want to keep or snare some who are already fettered?"

"Ah, I get it. You want Lady Fletcher for yourself."

Brannon balanced the Winchester over the arms of the seat. "That's an insult to a woman who truly is a lady."

"Brannon, I admire you . . . your values, your courage, your discipline, even your faith. I wish I were more like you. But I am who I am."

"I still don't know who you are."

"But everyone thinks they know Stuart

Brannon. That could be deceiving. Who is the real Stuart Brannon?"

"Sometimes suspicion can save a life."

Rebozo's voice dripped with irony. His eyes twinkled with a store of private jokes. "That's true. Tom Wiseman could have used that to his advantage. But these are modern times. We're civilized now. This is the world your generation of citizen vigilantes fought for. We now have law and order. Civil discourse paves the means to ultimate justice."

A burst of doubt welled up like the first blow of air into a balloon. *Are those telegrams that I and supposedly Rebozo received really from T.R.? Am I being set up for some ambush? If so, by whom? And why? And more puzzling, why here in Oregon? Why not on my own territory in Arizona?*

That I could handle.

Maybe that's the point.

Brannon stood up, raised the Winchester and aimed the barrel at a lone cymbal still at center stage. Pulled the trigger. *Click.*

"You need to load that contraption," Rebozo remarked.

Then both of them turned their attention to the back of the room as applause erupted. An audience had appeared. How long they might have been listening, Brannon didn't know. Mrs. Gillespie, Mrs. Acorn and Lady Harriet Reed-Fletcher sat in the farthest row. Behind them stood the band.

CHAPTER THIRTY TWO

Brannon accompanied Lady Fletcher back to the hotel. She didn't mention the spectacle at the auditorium, so he didn't bring it up either. She invited him to the Fletchers' suite for tea. When he declined, she insisted. "I have another matter of some importance to discuss with you."

Brannon exhaled slowly, took off his hat and tried his best to lounge comfortable in a settee.

"I am not prejudiced against Indians," she began. "I don't mind my daughter having an Indian for a friend. But . . ."

"But you wouldn't want her to marry one," Brannon finished, "even though Tanglewood has a mild disposition, very inquisitive and accomplished in whatever he undertakes to do."

"I know. He's a fine boy."

"I thought you were so concerned about Tally Rebozo. Why the sudden shift?"

"Because I can't keep up with Laira. Why is life so hard sometimes, especially when it comes to our children? I know how I want to be, but certain situations come along and I am the opposite of who I imagine myself to be."

"Maybe life challenges help us recognize who we really are."

"I suppose. We live in a room of mirrors, at least we women do, and we're constantly checking the reflection. Then, a test comes along and all our illusions crash."

Brannon chuckled. "It's not just females. That happened to me only days ago, except I shot my own images into pieces."

They heard a soft cough. A boy stood at the door, hat in hand. White skin, hair short and plastered and combed. "Excuse me, Lady Fletcher. Could you give Laira a message for me?"

Laira's mother offered a warm smile, tugged him into the room. "And your name is?"

"I'm Nicholas Yancy, ma'am. I work at the golf course with Keaton Tanglewood."

"I saw you recently pushing lawn mowers with Keaton," Brannon said.

"Yessir, we traded."

"How's that?"

"I told Keaton I could help you learn to play golf quicker, but he insisted he wanted you himself. So I get William 'Wild Bill' Cody."

"I'm impressed."

"You shouldn't be. When it comes to golfing, you're both a toss."

"So you have a message for Laira," Lady Fletcher prompted.

"Yes, ma'am, I mean, no ma'am. That is, the message is from Keaton. He says that . . ."

"I'll get Laira for you. You can tell her your-self."

Before she turned around, Laira appeared at the door with apple-blushed cheeks and a peach-colored dress. Pigtails hung on each side of her head, making her look almost fifteen.

"Hello, Nicholas," she said with a giggle. "I was expecting Keaton."

"Oh, he's coming, but he'll be a little late. So, I, uh . . . I thought . . . that is, we figured I could fill in for him until he gets here."

Lady Fletcher smiled. Laira clapped her hands. "That's very thoughtful. Where shall we go?"

Nicholas Yancy twisted his hat, then scratched his head. "We thought it would be good to wait here until Keaton arrived."

"Oh, posh and twee. Let's take a walk to the ice cream shop."

"Oh! Well, I'd like to, that is, I enjoy ice cream, and I'd enjoy your company, Laira, but I wasn't expecting . . ."

Brannon tossed him two bits. "Hey, you two go, but hurry back before Keaton gets here."

"Thank you, Mr. Brannon." He beamed with delight.

Laira grabbed his hand and pulled him out the front door.

One romance strained . . . and another begun? Ah, young love.

Within minutes, they heard a knock at the back door of their hotel suite.

Lady Fletcher recoiled. There stood Keaton Tanglewood, a dead doe on his shoulders. Shot in the heart, Brannon surmised. He swung it down and laid the deer at Lady Fletcher's feet. "This is for you . . . and Laira." He offered a merry grin.

"Laira's not here," Lady Fletcher informed him. "And you can't leave that at our step. Pick it up. Get it away. Now."

Confusion played on his face. "But I sent Nicholas ahead . . ."

"Yes, Nicholas came. She's with him. At the ice cream shop. Please go."

"The youth is bringing you a gift," Brannon explained. "It's rude not to accept it."

"But what will I do with it?" Lady Fletcher shot him a desperate glance.

"Get the hotel butcher. He'll prepare it. You'll have a wonderful feast for your guests."

Lady Fletcher studied the slain deer at her feet. She cleared her throat. Not once, but twice. "I see. This will be good for company. Quite a conversation piece, don't you think?" A wan smile paled on her lips. "Thank you, Keaton."

"You're welcome, ma'am. I must go." Tanglewood ran down the street towards town, in the direction of the ice cream shop.

• • •

That evening the banquet table was spread with razor clams and oysters, whole roasted chickens, a fruity punch and a dozen varieties of cake. An orchestra played background music.

Brannon tried to stretch the coat and vest of dark-blue serge, borrowed from Lord Fletcher, to reach his wrists and waist. As he did, he bumped into Rebozo.

"You've been out on your own investigations," Brannon observed.

"One thing I learned . . . Lanigan's orphan background story is true. He lived on the streets and struggled to support himself and two younger siblings. That meant minor crimes. No medical help when they got sick, so both his siblings died. Perhaps he blames himself."

"But where is he from? Where did this happen?"

"A New York City slum. He was transported to the Midwest on one of the orphan trains. On the way, there was a horrendous experience . . . a flood washed out some tracks and a bridge. They were stranded several days near the main torrent. No one knew if they would survive or not. A very traumatic event."

"Perhaps we should combine our information."

"In good time," Rebozo said. "Something stinketh here and it's not the whale blubber and skunk cabbage. I've got a hunch about the third man on Tillamook Head. I'm going to go rough on one of them. Want to come along?"

"You know I promised Harriet I'd stay here. And I want to be close by for Sylvia. Besides, I thought you might be that third man."

"Well, if I am, your problems are solved. And if I'm not, somebody needs to be on this case."

"*I* am on this case."

"I know you don't trust me. But since you found out that compass does not belong to Lord Fletcher or Wax Lanigan, will you please loan it to me again? I think I can fish out who it belongs to."

"Surely you jest."

"I'll bring it back later tonight or in the morning. If I don't, you can load your rifle this time and shoot me. You'll know I'm your culprit."

Rebozo followed Brannon through the hotel to a storage closet where Brannon kept his belongings. He rummaged in his duffle, found the compass and handed it to Rebozo who said a quick "thanks" and rushed out.

Brannon returned to the dining hall just as Sylvia entered. "Where's Rebozo going in such a hurry?"

"Chasing a cloud. He's acting like he's been thrown high off a horse."

"Or maybe he's about to implicate someone. Do you still think he's responsible for what happened to my father?"

Brannon slammed a boot heel against the floor.

"I don't know. I should be following him right now."

"Well, I never made any promises to Lady Fletcher. I can do that."

"Wait. Let's let him play another hand or two. If he's our guy, we'll get our chance."

Brannon sat rigid and awkward next to Sylvia at the head table after they filled their fine bone china plates. The empty places were reserved for the Fletchers, Bill Cody, Wyatt Earp and his wife, Josie, and Sam and Eloise Smythe of the orphan farm.

Hawthorne Miller cozied between the Lazzard twins at the next table. Darcy clustered with Laira and two boys with stiff, starched collars he had seen before. He gazed around to find Wax Lanigan and realized he was at his shoulder.

"Greetings to you and the lovely lady," he said.

Sylvia said nothing. She kept her head down and ate a bite of fried razor clams with nonchalance, no action of delight or disdain.

"Evenin', Lanigan. This table's reserved. I guess they all are. Do you know where you're assigned?"

"Oh, yes. I'm to host the governor, two senators and their wives."

Brannon buttered some sourdough rolls as Lanigan strolled away. "How are you doing?" he asked Sylvia.

"Not well. I fully intended to stay in my room

tonight, but my mind's so busy, I can't rest any-way."

"Are you uncomfortable with Lanigan here?"

"Not really. He's been the perfect gentleman. I can't complain."

Brannon stared at large flower bouquets in tall wicker baskets and tried to avoid a bobbing Adam's apple in the throat of an opera singer. She sang half a dozen aria duets with a tenor who looked like he could be Ted Fleming's twin brother. Burly man with curly, salt and pepper hair, but a sour expression for every precise note. Not a trace of Fleming's infectious grin. He smoked a pipe in between harmonizing, while the female singer ran through her long parts. He appeared anxious for her to get done.

Applause rang out and Brannon relaxed in hopes of a finish to the program. No finale. However, a tumbling act was presented, which he found entertaining. Then, a series of monologues by both men and women in a wide range of pitches. This did not amuse him.

He pulled a watch out of the pocket of the borrowed Lord Fletcher waistcoat. *More than two hours!* He was about to nod off again, when Lady Fletcher approached from behind and grabbed his arm. "There's a frantic woman at the door. She says her name is Nina Carbón and that she must talk to you."

CHAPTER THIRTY THREE

Brannon felt more relieved than alarmed. He met with Mrs. Carbón on the front deck of the hotel. "*Gracias, señor.* I can't find my husband. I'm worried that he will do someone harm or get into trouble. We do not need that."

"Why come to me?"

"A man who said he is Tally Rebozo came to our home. He hounded Chuy with many questions, like you did, but also beat on him. I believe he is an acquaintance of yours."

"What kind of questions?"

"I don't know, lots of things. He wanted to know if Chuy went to Tillamook Head with Tom Wiseman the night he disappeared. Chuy said, 'no,' that he had too much firewater. He had gotten into character with that Indian outfit."

"Ma'am, that's a horrible stereotype. Your husband's a drunk with any kind of clothes."

"Mr. Rebozo kept asking him over and over, but Chuy insisted he did not go."

"If so, maybe it saved his life."

"He told Mr. Rebozo that the Frenchman was very upset that night. He told Chuy how useless he was, that he might be cut off from the rest of the deal."

"What deal?"

"Chuy doesn't exactly remember what they discussed at that meeting or much of anything afterward. So, when he sobered up he figured he better find out what deals had been made. He went to look for the Frenchman and couldn't find him. When he heard that Tom Wiseman was missing, he suspected the Frenchman was responsible."

"That's it? That's all he knows?"

"My Chuy is a loyal kind of guy, in his own way." She paced the deck. "Then Mr. Rebozo showed Chuy a compass. He wanted to know who it belonged to. Chuy said, 'The Frenchman,' but Mr. Rebozo did not believe him. He beat on him some more. Then Chuy said, 'It belongs to Wax Lanigan,' and Mr. Rebozo still did not believe him. 'How do you know Wax Lanigan?' 'He brought the engineers to the meeting,' Chuy answered."

Mrs. Carbón sighed. "I don't think Chuy had ever seen the compass before. He was trying to protect himself. After Mr. Rebozo left, Chuy said he was going to talk to someone who could help him. I told him not to go alone, that I would go with him. He slapped me and shoved me against the wall, then ran out."

Brannon closed his eyes and stretched back his neck. *I cannot abide any man who will hit a woman. Why do that?* "I'm sorry but I can't go looking for your husband right now. Go home.

Lock the door. Don't let that man back in while he's violent."

Nina Carbón wrapped her arms around her chest. Her eyes pleaded with him to understand. "He's all I have," she said. "Both the good and the bad."

Brannon studied the agitated face and pondered the plight of lonely people who make such choices. "I'll ask around about your husband." He turned to leave.

Meanwhile, his suspicions of Rebozo grew. *Was he trying to force that boozed up Nicaraguan to confess to something that would cover up his own involvement?*

He was about to return to Lady Fletcher's party, when he heard a woman shriek. Her screams reached a crescendo as he ran towards the sound that seemed to come from the Neacoxie Creek.

He saw Nina Carbón peering down into the dark waters. He ran to her side. A body floated next to a rusted out bicycle, the spokes bent. Brannon scooted down the ledge and got close enough to identify the bloated face of Chuy Carbón.

Mrs. Carbón ranted, "Chuy, Chuy," as tears rolled down her face.

With some effort, he and Mrs. Carbón pulled him out and Brannon looked all over for gunshot or knife wounds.

He either fell in or was pushed. Where is Rebozo? He's got his own answers to give.

CHAPTER THIRTY FOUR

Rebozo followed Lanigan down the grande promenade and over to his Thomas motor car. Before he got in, Rebozo called out, "Lanigan, hope there's no hard feelings about last night."

"Nah, new night, new game. Going over there now myself."

"Can I catch a ride?"

"Hop in."

Rebozo thought he heard a woman's scream, but he scooted into the Thomas. As they chugged along, Lanigan chattered. "I like it here. It feels good to work with the orphans and there are great folks in this town. It's close enough to Portland that I can hop on the train for a meeting to see my friends from the Exposition, even long after they close the gates and tear it down after October. Think I'll stay in Gearhart, at least for now. Maybe move to Portland in the spring."

Rebozo blew out a puff from his Murad cigarette. "Hey, don't want to put a damper on that, but thought I'd let you know what I've discovered. In helping Brannon in the search for Tom Wiseman, I've happened onto some curious information, some of which affects the orphan farm."

The steady roar of the engine provided the only

response. Lanigan clutched the steering wheel tight. "What do you mean?"

"After some intense encouragement, a Nicaraguan by the name of Chuy Carbón said the compass I had in the pot last night belonged to a Frenchman, Bois DeVache. I think he's lying. It's an English compass." Rebozo pulled it out from his suit pocket.

Lanigan reached out for it, turned it over, and gave it back. "Yes, I noticed it at the poker game, of course. Many folks would use an English compass. Even I, if I had a reason."

"Perhaps. We set it up so that if anyone in the room claimed to own the compass, we'd know whom to question about Tom Wiseman."

"Why is that?" Lanigan stared straight ahead, arms and neck stiff.

"We found it on Tillamook Head . . . near where an old Indian found Tom Wiseman's body and buried him."

The motor car slowed. Lanigan leaned against the driver's side door, as though panting, short of breath. "Do you know for sure it's Marshal Wiseman's body?"

Rebozo sucked again on the cigarette. "Ninety-nine percent certain. We found Bois DeVache's body with his. The Frenchman had been trying to entice investors for a gold mine in Panama. Something doesn't ring right about that guy. Part of the puzzle."

Lanigan heaved a kind of sigh. "Maybe he and Wiseman had a shootout."

"There's something else," Rebozo continued. "Someone's been threatening some of the orphans and there may be some funds missing. As chairman of the board, I thought you should know."

The motor car slunk along, even slower. "Of course I should. Are you sure about that?"

"Those two pretty gals on Sam Smythe's staff gave me some clues. However, I don't know who to finger. Do you know anyone who might be involved? Could be Sam Smythe . . . or his wife . . . or any of the staff or board members. Or perhaps a donor. That happens sometimes in a twisted kind of way."

"Can't imagine anyone involved with the Willamette Orphan Farm doing harm to the children."

"I think Tom Wiseman knew about it too. There could be a connection to his death."

"What does Stuart Brannon think about it?"

"We haven't discussed it yet. It's a growing hunch of mine. I thought I'd run it by you first since you're involved with the orphan farm. Does any of this make sense?"

Lanigan sat very still. His eyes brightened. "Yes, it does. In fact, it's becoming clearer."

"Tell me what you know."

"I'm the connection." He yanked out a Smith

and Wesson revolver and shot Rebozo in the chest.

Rebozo's eyes glazed. His face tightened. Blood spurted through his white shirt. "You! Brannon . . . right . . . again," Rebozo wheezed and slumped forward.

"Brannon right?" Lanigan shrieked. "Brannon's right about what? Rebozo, tell me, what has Brannon told you?" He pounded Rebozo on the back. Rebozo doubled up and collapsed against the dashboard and crumpled onto the floor.

Lanigan braked the Thomas car to a halt. He looked with care all around the dark residential street for a sign of anyone in view. He sprinted around to the passenger side and dragged Rebozo out, careful not to get any blood on him. He dumped Rebozo beside the road and sped away.

CHAPTER THIRTY FIVE

Lady Fletcher made a *clip, clop* sound with her shoes down the long hotel hall from the lobby, her face ashen. "Brannon, Deputy Kliever is here. He has shocking news, says they found another dead man. This time it's Tally Rebozo. Shot in the chest and abandoned by the side of the road, right in the middle of town. He wants to talk to Sylvia Wiseman. To you, too."

Brannon felt a rush of cold, then hot. He tried to assimilate the news. "But that must mean that Rebozo is not the third man." He swallowed and let his scrambled thoughts settle. "When did it happen?"

"Sometime in the last couple hours."

"But Sylvia's been here during that period and so have I."

"Tell it to the deputy." She folded her arms. "And inform him there were others who had cause." She licked her lips. "Including myself."

"I'm willing to bet there's a long line of women that stretches from here to South America."

Brannon headed to the lobby and found Deputy Kliever pacing back and forth. Sylvia was seated in a chair as he interrogated her. He turned to Brannon. "We've got three men dead under very suspicious circumstances since you arrived."

"Three?"

"The body that washed up on the shore too."

"You're blaming me for that? What about Marshal Wiseman and Bois DeVache? That makes five. But I have an alibi for them. I was in Arizona."

The deputy sported a white cowboy hat and spurs so large they scraped the linoleum. "I'll have to take you both to Astoria if you don't give me better answers," he threatened.

"You can't do that," Sylvia protested. "We want to find this killer as much as you do . . . maybe more."

"It might be linked with Tom Wiseman, Bois DeVache and Chuy Carbón," Brannon said.

"Impossible," the deputy stated. "There's no attachment. Each situation is totally different . . . accidental deaths and a cold-blooded killing . . . and you both had a motive in the latter . . . at least, you threatened Rebozo more than once, with witnesses." His gaze was riveted on Sylvia, but she glared right back.

"At least we can rule out Wax Lanigan. He's a coward. He certainly wouldn't shoot a man, especially pointblank," Brannon said.

"He might hire it done," Sylvia suggested.

"I agree with the deputy to a point." He offered Kliever a brief nod. "It could be a series of isolated, random events or . . ." He halted to fully assess the train of ideas forming in his mind. "Or it could be one perpetrator whose acts have gotten out of control."

"Doesn't absolve either of you," the deputy said. "I'm taking you both in. Anytime Stuart Brannon's around, you can be sure people will wind up dead."

"I can't let you do that." Brannon felt for his Colt revolver and plotted a plan of escape that would include Sylvia.

"I'm the law talking. Are you a lawbreaker, Stuart Brannon?"

"No, but if truth is to be discovered, if justice is to be done, I must be free to roam. If you take us in, none of us can follow through on this case while it's fresh."

The deputy rubbed his rowels back and forth. "I've got someone I need to talk to. Until then, I'm locking you both up."

"Where?"

"In a hotel room."

"You better make that two hotel rooms," Sylvia inserted. "I'm not going to have my reputation shattered for the sake of an over-zealous, inexperienced deputy."

Deputy Kliever blushed blood-red. His eyes fired so hot Brannon worried he might explode on the spot. Brannon prepared for defense. None was needed.

An amazing transformation took place. They watched the deputy physically cool down. His body relaxed. His natural color returned. He slipped off his hat and rubbed the inner lining. "You each pay me one hundred cash dollars and I'll call that bail for your release."

"That's highway . . ." Sylvia spurted out.

"I'll pay it," Brannon replied. "For both of us, if necessary."

Sylvia reached into her purse. "You most certainly will not. I can take care of my own fees."

After the deputy left, Sylvia commented, "That was as close to paying a bribe as I've ever come."

"He's got a streak of greed in his gut. Hope he turns around and goes the other way while he can."

An elderly man with a bald head shuffled through the door, a paper flapping in his hand. "I'm from the telegraph office. Anyone here know where Stuart Brannon is?"

A telegram almost always brought anticipation. Either a good report or bad news. The information Brannon received set a mood of contemplation. He and Sylvia moseyed across to where Lord and Lady Fletcher waited for a report about the deputy's visit. "Well, it's official."

"What do you mean 'official'?" snorted Edwin.

"Looks like Tally Rebozo was a foreign spy. A double spy, in fact. Harriet made a lucky guess. But it wasn't Serbia. He helped set the stage for the bloodless coup against Colombia in Panama."

"If he's such an important and smart spy, how come he was fooled so badly he got shot?" Edwin chimed in. "For that matter, I cannot understand how your friend Tom Wiseman got trapped. They were both experienced professionals."

"I can't answer that. For some reason, they let their guard down," Brannon replied. "That's why we've got to stay alert. Suspect everyone until he or she has proven innocence or fostered guilt."

"She?" Lady Fletcher retorted. "Surely you don't think that a woman . . . ?"

"At this point, we don't know anything for sure . . . except that Rebozo discovered something that we haven't yet."

"Or don't realize you know," Fletcher said. "Have you listed all the facts of the case?"

"Ah, Edwin. I sense you getting involved," Brannon said.

"You don't sense anything of the kind," Fletcher responded. "I'm helping you be practical."

"Edwin, you were born for adventure. When we first met, you drug into Everett Davis' cabin at Broken Arrow Crossing, half-frozen and looking for gold at the Little Yellowjacket.

Before that, you told me you'd been in northern India trying to keep the Mongols and Hindus from killing each other."

"Yes, quite right." His eyes misted over in a faraway gaze. "For decency, mankind, King and country."

"And what have you been doing the last ten years?"

"I sit around English gardens sipping tea and managing world affairs. Dreadfully boring. How about you, Brannon?"

"I've been ranching and trying to be a father and grandpa."

"You miss the old times?"

"Not the backbreaking, unrelenting toil of keeping bad guys under control. But I do sometimes yearn for that sense that we lived in a momentous, history-making period."

Lady Fletcher sighed. "Stuart, I feel a lot of remorse over this. I'm serious. You came to town to help the President and Tom Wiseman. I came to town because I didn't have anything else to do this week. It wasn't worth anyone losing their lives. I've been playing a game. No more of that. What can I do to help you?"

"Not sure yet, but I've been contemplating another scheme. Edwin, at the tournament tomorrow, can you offer some sort of posthumous award citation for Tally Rebozo? Can we give such a gaudy, patriotic display by your country and ours that the person or persons responsible who did him in might chafe at the bit and perhaps reveal themselves in some way? Most criminals possess immense egos."

"Bad form, Brannon. I can't go around inventing awards for British royalty to declare. You think they grow on trees like Portland apples?"

"You're right. Forget the whole deal."

Fletcher flinched when a sharp, pointed shoe cranked into his ankle. "Well, I suppose it could be some sort of minor award. But then it has to be important enough to make the setup seem believable. Perhaps we can call him a Commodore or Captain, something like that."

"How about we make him a double captain?" Brannon suggested.

"Double captain? Here's a different tactic." Lord Fletcher was on board now. "Make it sound fishy to everyone. He's going to be a double captain of the Frazier River Exploratory Brigade, awarded for his courage and sacrifice against the Metis Rebellion."

"I've got lots of jewelry," Lady Fletcher chimed in. "I'll make up a medal hanging from a ribbon of some sort."

Brannon scratched his chin. "It's worth a try, until we think of something else. In the meantime, Harriet, you have parties to give and I have exploring to do."

•••

Wax Lanigan leered up into the face of a full moon that glowed in the expanse of starry sky as he staggered over the sand dunes.

The natives will be restless tonight.

After another all-night poker game, the intoxicated Lanigan pulled out a packet of Murad cigarettes, picked out three and stuffed them in his mouth. He lit them one by one, then coughed and gagged until he choked himself into a spasm. He tossed the cigarettes into the tall beach grass.

I forgot. I don't smoke. I don't drink either.

He stumbled down the beach and passed out on a wooden walkway.

And I don't murder people.

CHAPTER THIRTY SIX

Saturday, June 17

Brannon woke in the dark before dawn to what sounded like a firestorm and viewed a mini-inferno. He jumped up and stared at rings of flames lapping at the southern hilly landscape.

A fire? On the sand?

Tres Vientos panicked. He yanked at the bush where he'd been tied until it pulled out from the roots, then ran in wild circles before he dashed down the beach towards Gearhart with the bush trailing.

Brannon jerked out his blanket from the bedroll. He ran until he reached the closest rim. He slapped quick hits against the burning grass. It smoldered and went out. *But I can't stop all of this. It's more than an acre already.*

He heard sharp clangs like hammers up and down the railroad track and a bell. Within minutes, silhouettes of people with searchlights and flashlights rushed to the scene. A fire hose cart appeared, but also a brigade with buckets soon followed and surrounded the fire. Brannon tossed away his blanket and helped throw buckets of water. The organized crew ran back and forth to West Seaside. They stopped the advance of the fire and soon a huge black patch fumed with smoke.

"Thanks for your help, mister," one of the Seaside volunteer firemen said. "Any idea how the fire started?"

"Nope."

"Well, there was no lightning or fireworks this time."

"What was that clanging noise before you got here?"

"We alert the volunteers by our bell for town fires and the special alarm for out of town. We've installed locomotive rims at strategic places and we hit them with sledge hammers. All our equipment's stored under the train station platform."

"Sure works good," Brannon noted.

"At least for now."

"You camping out here? A fire like this could be started by an untended campfire. Or a tossed quirly from a hobo. I heard of a town that got burnt by a passing freight train that threw cinders onto buildings as it passed through. Destroyed two entire blocks. We wouldn't be much of a match against that. We keep thinking we need to reassess our system."

"I saw some nice horse-drawn ladder wagons over in Portland at the Lewis and Clark Exposition."

"Yeah . . . speaking of horses, saw one big black speed down the beach and try to kick the hotel barn door down."

As the early morning twilight streaked shafts of natural light, Brannon trudged to the hotel barn, covered with soot. He noticed one of his boots didn't jingle. *What a way to start the day of the big golf tournament. Even lost a spur. What else can go wrong? Brannon, don't be so pessimistic. It's going to be all uphill from here.*

He found Tres Vientos in his stall with Bueno.

"He wanted in," the boy remarked, "real bad."

"Glad you didn't get kicked." Brannon filled a leather bag with barley and maize.

"He's missing a shoe."

With care and caution, Brannon picked up the right front hoof.

"I will replace it for you," Bueno offered.

Brannon could read the postcard this time because it was printed in large letters: **"PAPA PACKED US ALL IN THE CARRIAGE AND WE WENT TO PRESCOTT TO LOOK AT AUTO CARS. WE LOOKED AT A HUMBER AND A LIMOUSINE. WE DROVE THE HUMBER HOME. NOW I HAVE THE RASH TOO."**

Brannon tucked the postcard in his golf bag and showed up at the golf course for the Willamette Orphan Farm Tournament in the suit that Lady Fletcher requested, plus his cowboy boots and black felt hat. He was glad to note that Wyatt Earp and William Cody dressed in similar style, except that Cody, always the dapper dresser, added a diamond-studded buffalo head stick pin. Earp had on his infamous long coat. Cody still cut a grand figure with his flow of white hair, beard and mustache and was almost as tall as Brannon. He could still end any fracas of rowdies with a scowl.

About the same age, Earp, Cody and Brannon stood apart in this gathered group as the symbol of the Old West. Brannon admired Cody's trick riders and sharp shooters and appreciated his stance on the rights of Indians and women in general. So much controversy swirled around Earp, he didn't know for sure what was true or false, but he liked the man. He reached out a hand to each of them.

"We all three have worn the badge," Earp commented.

"And I'm sure we'd rather do something else than play golf," Brannon said.

Cody bubbled with laughter. "Shooting glass balls from horseback comes to mind."

The lavender lady squeezed in. She touched Cody on the cheek. "My friends dared me to come ask you for your secret," she gushed.

Cody didn't balk, as if he were used to such familiarity. "Which secret did you want to know?"

PROPERTY OF CHESTERFIELD TWP LIBRARY

"Any that you'd be willing to share, but mainly how come you still have your baby skin? What kind of product do you use?"

"I wash my face. That's it. This was what I was born with."

"But, I insist," the lady stood firm in front of him, "on behalf of womankind in the twentieth century. What else do you do to keep your complexion from turning to sandpaper and prickly pebbles?"

"Be born with it. Live outdoors. Don't overeat."

"Oh! I was sure you were going to say use Pears' soap. All the advertisements do."

What have we come to? Truly, the frontier is over.

Brannon grabbed Lady Fletcher's arm and walked away from the spectacle. "I have to admit. No woman's ever asked me that question."

"No woman ever will," Lady Fletcher responded.

Brannon studied the attire of the rest of the participants. They wore laced, polished leather shoes, a variety of full suits, many with vests and loosely knotted cravats or ties.

"I can't play well if there's no comfort," he countered to Lady Fletcher. He had been pleased to discover that he could hang his canvas cover with the take-down rifle on his golf bag with a leather thong tied to the satchel handle.

They decided to give away the phony award at

the end of the tournament. Lord Fletcher took charge by beginning with a story of how the game of golf originated, according to folklore. He swung his walking stick in jabs and circles for emphasis.

"Some Scottish shepherds were hitting round stones with the crooks in their hands. On the bye, one of them happened to get their stone in a rabbit scrape. Of course, he had to try again to see if it were luck or skill. When, after several attempts, the stone glanced into the hole once more, he searched for a witness. For what man wants to accomplish anything without he can brag to a fellow?"

The crowd guffawed and he continued. "The friends tried too and made it after a while. So, they increased the difficulty by backing further away. One invention led to another. Soon they had to 'go off' to get the ball a distance and that's where the word 'golf' came from."

Everyone clapped and Lord Fletcher welcomed the large crowd to the event, thanked them for their sponsorship. Then he introduced Sam Smythe and his wife, Eloise, and their staff and the board members. However, Wax Lanigan didn't appear.

"Mr. Smythe says Mr. Lanigan has been called out on some important union business. He'll return as soon as he can," Lord Fletcher replied to Brannon's query.

Most all the orphans attended too, hauled in by hay wagon and four bay horses. Henrietta Ober stayed at the farm with several sick ones.

Each child had been scrubbed and dressed in the finest of their clothing issues. The girls wore large, droopy hats with their pinafores. The boys had on knickerbockers or sailor suits. Only Bueno and Hack hopped off the hay wagon to hang out close to Brannon. He finally scooted them back to the wagon.

Lord Fletcher presented each of the celebrity participants and their foursome partners, chosen mostly by coin toss. Brannon teamed with Ted Fleming, Willie Anderson, U.S. Open Champion, and William "Buffalo Bill" Cody.

"Do you each have your caddies?" Lord Fletcher asked.

"Caddie? What's that?" Brannon asked Lady Fletcher.

"The one who carries your bag around the course. Didn't Mr. Fleming appoint you one yet?"

"Must I have one?"

"It's customary."

He looked around and noticed Tanglewood peering through from the back of the crowd. Brannon pointed his way.

"I want him."

Lord Fletcher craned his neck around and spotted the tall young man. "The Indian lad, you say?"

"Yes, I want to choose Keaton Tanglewood to carry my bag."

"But he's not on the list. There are plenty of others. You can have Nicholas Yancy, for instance. He'll do quite fine."

"Edwin," Brannon challenged, "are you saying I can't have an Indian for my caddie?"

The crowd rustled with murmurs.

"Not exactly . . . well, yes . . . I mean, no," Lord Fletcher blustered. "It's just that he's not . . . he's not *official*."

"Well, I'm making him official. Any objections?"

After a moment's pause and a poke in the side by Lady Fletcher's parasol, Lord Fletcher cleared his throat, shook his head, and said, "Not from here."

Brannon motioned to Tanglewood and the Indian youth sauntered his way, glancing to the left and to the right with worried eyes.

"It's okay," Brannon assured him. "I'm on your side."

Tanglewood picked up Brannon's bag. "Thank you. I have always wanted to be a caddie and it is the greatest honor that my first time is with Stuart Brannon."

CHAPTER THIRTY SEVEN

Lanigan pushed through the crowd for a front row view. His wardrobe was impeccable, but he looked fatigued and he jerked around in a nervous twitch as though he expected to see someone or something.

The participants were introduced one by one. Brannon shook all their hands, including William Frederick Cody and Wyatt Berry Stapp Earp. He wished them well with their golfing.

They both chortled.

"I hope I can get through without hitting one of the spectators," Cody said.

"I already did that at my last practice," Earp admitted. "A gal behind me. Now I hope I can get some forward motion going."

Mr. Smythe asked the celebrities if they'd take a photograph with the orphans. Buffalo Bill and Brannon jumped up on the wagon with the children, while the others stayed on the ground in a semi-circle. Lord and Lady Fletcher joined them too.

A young vaudeville comedy juggler, named W. C. Fields, refused to be part of the picture. "Any of those urchins get close to me, I'll hit them with a club," he snarled.

Everyone ogled him in disbelief, then a few nervous laughs skittered around the audience. Brannon also did a mental double take. *Surely he jests. What a rude, nasty young man. He won't get far in the entertainment business.*

"Buffalo Bill's only son died at age five from scarlet fever," Lady Fletcher told Brannon. "Kids are important to him. He gave free tickets to his Wild West show for everyone at the orphanage."

The foursome of Wyatt Earp, W. C. Fields, and John Mitchell, state senator, plus Alex Smith, another U.S. Open Champion, approached hole number one.

After a black bird dive-bombed him several times and threatened chaos and disorder to the game of decorum, Fields finally managed a swing that dug a deep divot, ricocheting the ball off a tree and into a water hazard. Fields placed swim fins on his feet and wobbled down to the hazard, to the delight of the audience.

Mitchell hit a solid hundred seventy-five yard shot.

Ted Fleming's blast flew straight down the fairway about two hundred yards.

The crowd roared.

Now, Wyatt Earp approached the tee. His brassie hit the ball in a bounce for about twenty yards, but at least it went in front of him. However, Brannon didn't have his attention on Earp's game. He stared at Earp's golf bag.

Hanging by a leather tag was a compass, the one he had given Rebozo the day before.

Brannon charged up to Earp. "Where did you get that compass?"

Protests rang out from all around.

"At a poker game." Earp's caddie picked up his bag and Earp slung the club into it. Brannon stood toe to toe before him. "If you'd like to know, I also won a brand new pack of Murad Turkish cigarettes. This guy was playing his last dime."

"Who was? Was Tally Rebozo there?" Brannon felt the tug of arms attempting to pull him away. He pushed back.

"No, Rebozo wasn't there. He got himself shot, I heard."

The crowd gathered closer. Several shouted, "Get on with the game."

"Not cricket," he could hear Lord Fletcher say very near. "Not good etiquette at all."

"How did you get the compass?" Brannon pressed. He pushed his hand on his Colt revolver, just in case the fiery gunman took offense at his mode of questioning. Lord Fletcher kept trying to tell him something, but he was beyond paying attention to anyone but Wyatt Earp.

"It was in the last pot of the night . . . or should I say morning? We played until three o'clock."

Brannon spit out each word with force. "Who put it in the pot?"

"Well, there were only four of us left . . . me, Argentiferous Jones, one of the Rincon brothers and . . ." Earp searched the people gathered around the first hole. He reached out his arm and pointed at one of them: Wax Lanigan.

Lanigan blanched almost white. A range of emotions melded his expression from one to another. He made his decision in that one split second.

A shrill cry penetrated the tension as Lanigan jumped up on the hay wagon and shoved a gun against Penelope Tagg's head. "Drop your weapons." He waved the gun over the heads of the orphans. "Don't any of you come close or these kids will get hurt."

"He was the fourth man," Earp said.

"No, he was the third one." Brannon had his Colt .44 revolver cocked and ready.

CHAPTER THIRTY EIGHT

No one moved. In the hush Brannon's mind clicked in rapid fire, sorting the options. *Rush him? Talk to him? Shoot him?* Nothing seemed viable at the moment.

One of the boys close to Lanigan kicked him in the shins. Lanigan swung his Smith and Wesson revolver against the boy's side. He screamed and crumpled down next to Miss Tagg. One of the horses lunged forward. The other three whinnied and shuffled their hooves.

Lanigan grabbed one of the older kids and pushed the revolver into his ear. "Brannon, Earp, Bill Cody . . . that means all of you!" He swung the weeping boy around, gun cocked.

Brannon knelt down and scooted his Colt .44 revolver towards the wagon. Earp followed with his ten-inch-barreled Colt, then Buffalo Bill laid down his Colt .36 pistol. Other revolvers filled the pile. Brannon didn't include his take-down rifle with the leather thong still strapped to his golf bag.

"Bueno! Hack! Grab a blanket. Go get the guns," Lanigan ordered.

The boys hopped from the wagon and tossed the blanket down. Bueno grabbed Brannon's

Colt first, then looked Brannon in the eye, as though to apologize for not fingering Lanigan sooner. Brannon tried to signal him to be careful. *Fear kept him silent. Now I hope guilty fear won't force him to do something stupid.*

Brannon noticed there were no sneak guns in the pile.

The two boys hauled the weapons on board and Lanigan barked demands. "Wrap the guns in that blanket and bring them here. All you kids cram in the center. Bunch together." His head erect, his shoulders back, he commanded like the captain of a war ship, the victor of a sea battle.

"My word, shoot him, Stuart," Lord Fletcher rasped from behind.

"Can't take that chance. Can't even try it, if I wanted to." *And here's where the take-down is mighty unhandy.*

In desperation, Brannon tried to figure out how to storm through Lanigan's effective barricade of human shields.

Lanigan stayed tight with the boy he held and scooted to a makeshift seat for a driver. "We're headed down the road," he announced. "No one is to follow us or I hurt the kids, one by one. Leave me be or the kids suffer."

"You need only one or two," Brannon called out. "Let the rest go."

The crowd muttered affirmation.

Sam Smythe stepped forward. "I'll be a

hostage in the children's place. Take me instead."

Lanigan smirked at the director. "Won't work. Each one of these kiddos provides me a ticket out of here and Brannon instigated it. Remember that, all of you. This wouldn't have happened if it hadn't been for the interference of the one and only, Stuart Brannon."

"Well then, take both of us," Brannon suggested. "Me and the director. You'll have two bargaining chips and we're both unarmed."

"Shut up, Brannon. Shut up, all of you. If I see anyone on the trail, I won't be responsible for what happens."

Lanigan forced the boy into the seat as he bent down in tandem beside him. He untied the reins with one hand and aimed the gun with the other.

"I need volunteers . . . go ahead of us, clear the way of people. I don't want to see anyone, anywhere."

A half dozen men in the tense horde raised their hands, including Deputy Kliever whom he hadn't noticed there before. The deputy hopped on a buckskin dun horse that he had tied to a cottonwood not far away.

Good. At least law enforcement will be part of this crazy operation.

The others climbed into motor cars and a carriage. Another man joined them on foot.

"Go!" Lanigan yelled. "Get moving!"

The volunteer trailblazers zoomed down the street shouting alerts. The man on foot repeated the message and pointed back at the hay wagon. Everyone scurried into houses or cabins.

After a minute, Lanigan shouted and slapped the horses. They moved forward as the children in the wagon whimpered. Penelope Tagg calmly talked to each one, hugging as many as she could.

A crowd of people gathered around Brannon. Earp and Cody lounged on the side as Brannon turned to them. "You got any ideas?"

"This is your fight, not ours," Earp replied, "except that I sure-fire want my gun back."

Cody nodded assent. "This is your story, Brannon. We'll only get in the way, make things more dangerous. However, if you do need our help, send up a smoke signal. We'll come running."

Lady Fletcher scurried over to her husband's side. "Such a desperate move to protect himself for evil deeds. In one flash of a moment he has lost everything he wanted."

"No," Brannon replied. "He's traveled this journey a long time. Many choices. Twisted thinking. Ignoring God." Brannon turned to Fletcher. "Come on, it's your turn to ride." Brannon pulled off his rifle from the golf bag and made a dash towards the barn.

Lord Fletcher clambered behind Brannon, along with Sylvia Wiseman. Brannon rushed to stall #35. Lord Fletcher got Laira's Amble in stall #34. Sylvia grabbed the flaxen Geode.

When Brannon turned to object, Sylvia growled, "There's no way I'm not going."

"Shall I get the auto car instead?" Lord Fletcher hollered.

"No," Brannon ordered. "Let's stay together. Besides, we can't get too close to that wagon until we've got a plan."

They mounted up and galloped out of the barn and almost crashed into Tanglewood, riding up on his mustang.

"Go back," Brannon shouted.

"I know the terrain," Tanglewood yelled.

They spurred their horses forward. As Tres Vientos sped up, Brannon listened to the measured three beats of the hooves, like a drummer's cadence over and over. The horse had conquered his fright, at least for now.

As they followed the wagon, they kept a pace in the tall beach grass that they hoped kept them from the wagon's view. A wind swelled and nudged the rise and fall of the ebbing tide. The waves rose higher. A sudden summer's downpour intervened.

Rain pounded over the roar of swells. Waves broke in every direction. *The tournament would have been rained out anyway . . . at least part of it.*

Brannon trudged ahead clutching Tres Vientos

as waves dashed against the beach and scattered rocks. Whitecaps boiled onto the beach. He took a quick peek behind him. Fletcher, Sylvia and Tanglewood followed by several horse lengths.

Tres Vientos found his beach stride. *When he is good, he is very, very good. But when he is bad . . .*

He spotted the wagon as a moving dot on the beach, far ahead of them, but he realized they couldn't chance that Lanigan could see them. *At this point, he's loco enough to follow through on his threat.*

Brannon got down from Tres Vientos, led him to a thick growth of pine parallel to the beach. Back on horses, they plowed through the trees at a more rapid clip and soon sighted the wagon. Brannon slowed down.

He pulled out the two pieces of his take-down '92, .44 Winchester rifle from the canvas bag. He balanced the barrel on his lap, opened the action on the walnut butt stock with crescent metal plate, turned the lever a half dozen twists, then locked the two pieces together.

"Very nice," Fletcher commented. "I brought my carbine."

"Lanigan got the Colt revolver, but I retrieved Papa's rifle." Sylvia patted a canvas cover behind her. "And of course my sneak gun."

And knife too, I'm sure.

Tanglewood displayed his bow and arrow

and slid out of his scabbard a long bayonet knife.

"Good. But this situation also requires wisdom. The weapons are backups," Brannon said.

He knew they waited on him for a strategy. He was their man to figure a way out. The same gunman who spent years fighting injustice on primitive western trails now faced one more battle. Perhaps his personal finish line. Was he up to the task?

A new and delicate matter forced a dawning truth, one he hated to admit. His mind skipped now and then. His body lagged. Could he lead his troop of followers on this crucial campaign?

He had one hope.

God, give me strength and wisdom.

CHAPTER THIRTY NINE

"Why aren't they moving?" Tanglewood asked.

They had nearly caught up with the wagon. "It's stuck," Brannon said. "The wheels are too deep in the wet sand. The axle's twisted or broken."

Lanigan shouted something as he and several of the boys untied the horses. The children bounded over the sides and underneath the wagon.

"If he would just get away from those kids, we could shoot him down." Sylvia urged Geode nearer an opening in the trees.

"Be careful," Brannon cautioned.

"He's going to ride away with all four horses," Sylvia informed them. "But not alone. He's got two of the boys with him."

"And the guns. The boys look like Bueno and Hack." Brannon slid off his horse. "Let's check on the children when Lanigan gets out of sight."

Lanigan had both boys on one horse, Bueno in front with his hands tied to the saddle. Hack was roped to Bueno. He rode one horse and led the other two, a blanket-bag of guns bundled on a riderless mare.

As they trotted away, Brannon's team could

hear the singing . . . a sweet song of affirmation, of safety, of protection in God's arms. *Jesus loves me, this I know, for the Bible tells me so. Little ones to Him belong. They are weak, but He is strong.*

They waited until the coast cleared of Lanigan and his pair of hostages, then ventured out of the trees and over the grassy dunes. The song reverberated despite the thrust of the waves. Out of possible horror, a holy moment. Though all the danger had not passed, these children knew one important lesson they affirmed for themselves and the departing Bueno and Hack: *Jesus loves me.*

Lanigan kept going. He didn't threaten the singers.

Penelope Tagg rolled out from under the wagon and ran to greet Brannon. "We need a doctor. One of the girls fell out of the wagon. I forced Lanigan to pick her up. She may have a broken leg. The one he hit with the revolver may have a broken rib. Others got scraped and bruised. They're terrified to come out from under the wagon. Lanigan told them to stay there or he'd shoot them dead."

Brannon and his crew helped Miss Tagg coax the children out from under the wagon, then lifted them up on the hay.

"What do we do now, Brannon?" Fletcher inquired. "Do we use our horses to pull them back to Gearhart or do we leave them and race after Lanigan?"

"I'm going after Lanigan," Sylvia asserted.

"We all are," said Brannon. "But look back there."

Lady Fletcher drove the lead in the Buick with passengers Laira and the Smythes. Darcy and the Lazzard twins rode with Hawthorne Miller in his wagon. Behind them, a huge swath of people in motor cars, on horses and runners, as wide as the beach, surged forward, a welcoming committee. Horns blared among the hoots and hollers.

"A scout told us Lanigan left the wagon," Lady Fletcher reported.

Brannon searched the throng for the famed, familiar faces of Wyatt Earp or William Cody.

"They're on the course," Lady Fletcher explained, "betting high stakes on each shot, every hole, with all the winnings going to the orphan farm."

"Where are the other players?" Sylvia asked.

"The politicians are talking to the *Seaside Signal* reporter," Lady Fletcher said, "and that young Vaudeville comedy juggler went down to the Chautauqua to do a show. Sure hope he doesn't snarl at the children."

She opened the Buick door to march over to Lord Fletcher. "Dear, do please be careful. You've got guests waiting." Then she turned to

Brannon. "You simply must save at least one decent jacket for Sunday service or go to the haberdashery. Edwin's out of lenders."

Sylvia's horse twirled around. "We've got to go," she said to Brannon.

"Our prayers are with you," Sam Smythe assured the four.

Darcy got into the Buick with Laira, Eloise Smythe and Lady Fletcher, who drove behind the wagon. Everyone else trailed behind them. Except Hawthorne Miller. His wagon with two teams of mules aimed north, primed and ready for adventure.

"You can't go with us," Brannon asserted.

"I know where he's headed," Miller said.

"How could you possibly know that?" Brannon retorted.

"I have my sources." Miller put on a stovepipe hat, lit a cigar, and leaned back in the buckboard. "A meeting had already been scheduled."

Brannon got up on Tres Vientos, placed his black felt Stetson firm on his head and fumed. *Do I play his game? Do I ignore him once again? Or do I take any available opportunity to make a tough job easier? Oh, Lord, what to do with my pride?*

"Okay, where's he headed?" Brannon asked.

"I'll tell you, if you allow me admittance to record this event for posterity."

"Miller . . ." Stuart began.

"Make up your mind," Sylvia scolded. She spurred Geode and trotted him down the beach.

Brannon judged women in two ways. There were standers and there were runners. They would fight for what was right even with the odds stacked against them. Or they take flight. To save themselves. To avoid the pain of sacrifice.

Sylvia definitely was rated a stander.

And she was right. They must chase down Lanigan. Now. But Brannon must decide. Would he put away his pride this time and depend on the likes of Hawthorne Miller for perhaps crucial information? "Okay, Miller, where's he going?"

Hawthorne Miller tossed his cigar on the beach. He sat straight up, loosened his collar, and grabbed up a whip. "To the abandoned William Smith house. Been there for decades. At the former Fort Clatsop property where Lewis and Clark wintered a hundred years ago." He flicked the whip over his mules' rumps and sped north as the wagon rattled, bounced and squeaked.

CHAPTER FORTY

Brannon caught up with Sylvia. They had to get to Lanigan and stop his madness. As the horses plodded with great labor through the sand, he contemplated the events that led to this chase.

At peace on his thriving ranch in Arizona.

The telegrams from the President.

Tom Wiseman left injured and helpless on a cliffside of Tillamook Head, now buried under a stack of memorial rocks on a secluded beach.

Tally Rebozo's cold-blooded murder.

The kidnapping of the orphans.

Whether he wore a badge or not, this was his duty. Just as it was when he faced the countless series of miscreants and evildoers he'd helped to incarcerate or eliminate over the decades. All of this somehow bundled with the darkest time of his life, when death and tragedy took away everything he held dear.

Lisa. The lovely face. Her gentle disposition. Her graceful manners. *She was my life, my riches, the highest and noblest spirit I have ever known.*

And our baby.

The trek during that hard winter to Broken Arrow Crossing. How painful then the long, relentless hours of stinging, blowing snow as it sliced into his skin.

But have I gotten too fond of dwelling on the past?

For a moment, he forgot about his mission to right the world's wrongs. The memories trapped his mind, misdirected his focus. Yet Brannon realized from the lessons learned and experiences lived that fairness would be served, somehow, some way. The deaths of Tally Rebozo and Tom Wiseman and any others in this case, would be rectified. If not by him and those who came alongside, then in some other time, by some other means.

God's will would prevail.

The world would be saved.

But for now, he and his comrades bowed under another rain shower.

After a brief break to spell the horses, they started at a walk, then a trot. Brannon spurred Tres Vientos to a lope and off to a gallop in the uneven sandy dunescape. Brannon whipped from side to side in the saddle, his hat flapping on his back, held by a stampede string, as he depended on the strength, stamina and speed of the animal beneath him. Hard to imagine this was the same horse who only days before had been so fearful that he would flee from a seagull, balk at the smell of saltwater.

If he kept him at a walk, they'd go about four miles an hour. Tres Vientos moved his head and neck up and down, a steady motion, keeping horse and rider balanced. The rainstorm had left the air so clean-tasting that every gulp seemed to lift Brannon's spirits.

Brannon checked to see that the others kept up. Hawthorne Miller began to lag behind, impeded by some distress with one of his wheels. Brannon didn't stop to offer help. He knew the man would fix the problem and forge on to meet up with them later. Meanwhile, they easily tracked the four horses they followed, even though a few places had been wiped clean by the wind, rains or a purposeful swipe by a tree branch.

Sylvia rode up beside him. "I'm not complaining, just stating a fact. No woman could possibly be more soaked than I am right now." Her hair dripped in ringlets down to her shoulders. The tweed suit clung like a leaky balloon to her body.

"I've been to that place before, where that house is, when I was a child," Tanglewood informed them. "I remember a little river with high, dark woods on one side."

The day had started cloudy, with a high gray bank, but now hung so low that thick fog hid the ocean and most of the sandy beach like a blindfold. The four crossed a small stream and skirted a pond.

The big black horse dropped between beats and bounced up again. Brannon jolted upwards out of the saddle and bumped the horse with force. He finally found the rhythm on the sand dunes to keep going and not be jostled out of the saddle.

Tres Vientos had been a sturdy horse for Brannon. One time Tom Wiseman had helped Brannon round up some stray cows that stampeded in a thunderstorm. He rode Tres Vientos a hundred miles that day. Only a fit horse could complete such a ride. But Tres Vientos, like his owner, had aged. He needed extra care and patience. And Brannon tried to recover from the slap of humiliation that he was unable to control any horse, especially his own.

They halted when they reached the bottom of a hill full of high, course grass and rocks. The tracks ceased.

Brannon hopped off his horse, to give him a rest.

Tanglewood scrambled up beside him. Sylvia's face was set, her body rigid, as she pushed on her flaxen horse. Fletcher wheezed up last. Brannon spied Miller taking a different route around, across the sand in the wagon.

"Shouldn't we follow him?" Sylvia asked.

Tanglewood pointed northeast. "The William Smith House is over there."

"That must be the way Lanigan went,"

Brannon stated. "It's a good thing we know the destination. Otherwise, we'd stay north. Or track him around this hill. We might not have picked up his trail again or wasted a lot of time."

"If he harms those boys, we'd better be hot on his tracks," Sylvia said.

"I hope it wasn't a mistake for you to allow me on this venture. I do seem to be lagging," Fletcher groaned.

Brannon punched his friend's arm gently. "I'm certainly not as hardy as my Kansas cattle drive days."

"Buck up, man. You've got lots of miles in you," Fletcher countered.

"Have I ever told you that survival as a way of life depresses me?" Brannon dragged himself up on Tres Vientos. "But we're of the breed who live adventures until the end. Men like T.R., Tom Wiseman and you, too, Edwin."

"I say, I believe there are lots out there who'd kill, metaphorically, to live like we have."

"That's exactly why we're chasing a madman right now and there's no metaphor about it. Come on, we've got our duty."

Edwin climbed up on his horse, back erect, primed for the ride. "That's the Brannon we know and love."

Yeah, right. All I need is some direction from you, Lord. Any word would help.

They left the beach and plodded over the

grassy dunes, into some woods, and over a bridge that crossed a river. Then it was easy going through pastures sprinkled with lakes. They approached another forest where they spotted a Roosevelt elk, moving very quietly among the trees. Long, dark hair encircled the thick neck above the pale brown body.

Then a gentle descent.

"Not too far from here where Fort Clatsop used to be," Tanglewood announced.

After a mile or so, Tanglewood observed a press of grass down the slope to their left on the rain-wrecked trail. He scrambled down the incline partway. "A horse fell," he reported.

"Do you see anybody or any gear? How about the bagged blanket of guns?" Brannon said.

"No, nothing else, just the horse. I think he broke his back and somebody shot him to put him out of his misery."

Up ahead Brannon isolated a column of smoke. Somewhere on the skyline were signs of fire. Either friendly warmth from a chimney or possible trouble. Tres Vientos reared and Brannon patted his neck down.

"Okay, guys, try not to start anything. No shooting unless you absolutely have to. We want Lanigan, not a gunfight."

They stayed behind some hemlocks and alders.

"There's an old Indian trail, part of an elk trail

that goes to the ocean from here," Tanglewood said.

They rode towards a small clearing. Brannon leaned low in the saddle with his sternum on the horn. His face bounced in the black mane as he peered between the horse's ears. Wind whipped through the treetops and they heard the eerie whine of a dead tree as it screeched and moaned.

The former Fort Clatsop of the Lewis and Clark expedition was now a simple farm of a two-story frame house with shake roof and a scatter of outbuildings behind. A few old cherry and apple trees dropped stony fruit. They passed a slough and a spring with brownish, brackish water that might hold iron deposits. Moss, lichens and ferns filled the area. Peering through the trees they could see a part of Young's Bay in the far distance.

The marsh ground made slow travel for the horses. The woods that surrounded the house included hemlocks with droopy branches and very small cones, the tops of the trees nodding, as though to welcome them. They rode under firs, alders, ash and spruce, whose stiff, sharp needles brushed them. A number of dead trees also stood around.

"This ground is what we call a fen or sump," Fletcher commented.

As they neared one of the outbuildings, Fletcher's horse almost tumbled over what looked like an oval fire pit with red clay in the center, charcoal around the top and edges. It had been used much less than a century ago.

To think, Captains Lewis and Clark had stepped here, had slept here many a winter's night.

Charcoal gray smoke rose from a chimney at the aging house, which was what Brannon called "makeshift." There was a lean-to with sloping roof, an empty water well with sink and pump at the edge of an added wing. A crosswalk stretched from the house to a woodshed in back. A huge spruce tree decorated the front yard.

A half-dozen horses were tied to a deck in front. The windows provided high visibility and little opportunity for any of them to rush the place unnoticed. They slinked back further in the trees and waited.

The branches dripped from the recent rain. No insects buzzed. No birds flew. The forest drank in the nourishment.

"It was such a difficult winter in 1805, even after they built the fort," Brannon mused. "Standing right here in this spot, it's hard not to think of it."

"I've read all about it. Only twelve days without dreary, driving rains. Dismal fog with no letup," Fletcher commented. "Hard winds, violent flood tides, constant high waves."

"I have to agree with Captain Clark. The

Pacific isn't always peaceful. I'm not too fond of the saltwater myself. It gets in your eyes, your ears and parches your joints. Get me back to the . . ."

"Brannon!" Sylvia called out.

The door of the house had opened and three men scooted out on the front porch.

CHAPTER FORTY ONE

"Who are those guys with Lanigan?" Fletcher craned his neck to get a closer look.

"Slash Barranca, the one with round face and greasy, long hair under that ten-gallon hat, is the robber on the train to Portland I took earlier in the week. The short guy with sharp, long nose and beady eyes wearing a black duster is none other than the infamous former Argentiferous Jones, now known as Tiff."

"Never heard of them."

They scooted closer and caught parts of a conversation.

Tiff Jones was speaking. "I don't know. The liquor's wearin' off. I didn't count on involvin' kids. This doesn't sound as good as it did before."

"You're up to your gizzard," Lanigan said. "All of you are. You can't back out now."

"Yes, I can. So can you. We both have weapons, but you will have to draw yours and I will shoot first. You know I'm faster." Brannon examined the man's gaping grin that revealed bad teeth. He even noticed a quiver. *Why can't I see this well when things are up close and personal-like?*

"I recognize my mistake now," Lanigan

replied as Jones whipped out his gun and jabbed him back with the barrel. "Now don't get nasty. I am going to pull out my gun too, real slow. Don't get jumpy on me. We're all friends here. Slash, you get your weapon out too. That way we're all even up."

"I'll watch my back," Jones retorted.

"And I'll watch mine," Lanigan said.

The three walked side by side towards the house. They all turned at the sound of a distant *chug-a-chug* of an engine. Lanigan swung his revolver straight at Barranca.

"Shoot Jones," Lanigan ordered.

Barranca stared down the barrel. "I can't."

"You won't get a dime," Lanigan said.

Barranca raised his gun.

"Put it down, Slash." Jones lowered his weapon. "I got no quarrel with you. You're my friend."

At that instant a gunshot rang out. Jones teetered forward, then tumbled with a *whomp* to the ground. Barranca cursed at Lanigan, whose revolver still smoked, then fell down at his friend's side.

"He was messing up the whole deal." Lanigan tried to drag Jones off the road. "Help me," he yelled at Barranca.

"My word," exclaimed Fletcher. "Now we know what happened to Rebozo."

"Only I don't believe he had even that much of a fighting chance," Brannon commented.

Sylvia clamped both hands over her mouth as she quivered.

Brannon cautioned them to stay put. "Let's see how this plays out."

Two men puttered onto the scene in a Ford Model C, the men in the brown suits.

"That's the Rincon brothers," Sylvia announced. "I don't know which is who, but their first names are Francis and Ditson. They're railroad agents or used to be. They visited Papa at the ranch a few times and were pleasant enough. However, Papa had to evict some farmer families for them. He hated that part of his job."

"We have got to get closer," Brannon said in hushed tones.

"You first," Fletcher urged.

Brannon crouched on his stomach and crawled across the muddy bog ground. Tanglewood, then Fletcher and Sylvia followed.

A man on a horse trotted up the road to the house and passed the motor car.

"It's the deputy from the golf tournament," Fletcher whispered.

"Good. In the old days, we'd take care of the murderer ourselves," Brannon stated. "Now, we wait for the law to show up." He propped himself up on elbows and sank an inch or two in the spongy ground.

"We've got the evidence from the bay. It can

be collected and done right, for a court trial," Fletcher added.

"But there's just one guy. If he tries to take them all in, he's got plenty of guts and pride," Brannon replied. "Or stupidity."

Deputy Kliever greeted the other men, swung out of his saddle and walked over to Lanigan.

"Get ready," Brannon whispered, "to protect this fool of a lawman."

Lanigan reached out and shook the deputy's hand. Then each of the men, including the deputy, handed over to Lanigan either leather valises or canvas bags and they tramped into the house.

"The deuce! It's a payoff," Fletcher exclaimed.

"Well, that's it for waiting on law and order to come to the rescue. I thought you said the deputy was a preacher's son, a brother in the faith," Sylvia said.

"God has no grandchildren. Each man must choose for himself," Brannon said.

Sylvia got up, shook out her soiled suit and stomped over to Geode. She yanked out her father's Remington bolt-action rifle.

"Wait," Brannon cautioned. "It might not be what it seems. Or if it is, we need to know more about what's going on."

Within minutes the clomping sound of hooves and a jingle of bells could be heard down the road. Soon, two teams of gray mules and a wagon came in view. Hawthorne Miller parked behind the Ford Model C, climbed out of the wagon, stepped over Jones' body, hiked around to the side lawn and set up his photography equipment on a leather tarp in the overgrown yard.

"He's going to get himself killed," Fletcher sputtered.

"Nah," Brannon retorted. "You watch. This guy's indestructible."

"Or he's in on the deal," Fletcher replied.

The front door of the house banged open and Lanigan, Jones, Barranca, the deputy and the Rincon brothers marched out. Lanigan waved at the photographer and novel writer. "Any trouble on the way in here?"

"No, the trail was empty the whole way."

Lanigan carried out a bench from inside the house, directed three of the men to sit on it, then the rest to stand behind.

"I can't be pictured with the likes of you," Deputy Kliever protested.

Lanigan pulled him in. "Tell the authorities we forced you or that you didn't know at this point what was going on, that you thought all this crew were upstanding citizens. Either way, you'll be famous like us."

After the poof and flash, Lanigan handed Miller his Kodak. "Take one with my personal camera too," they heard him say.

Miller fussed about that, then gave in. It took him a couple minutes of fiddling to figure out how to use the modern invention.

"C'mon, Miller." Lanigan turned to the others. "We've got to be out of here pretty soon. They're gonna figure out where I went eventually."

"When do we make our grand entrance?" Fletcher said. "This is getting more ridiculous by the minute."

"Our objectives are the safety of those boys and to capture Lanigan so he can pay for his crimes. The other business is for honest lawmen to investigate."

"But we can round up the whole gang right now while the boys are safe in the house," Sylvia suggested.

"That's right," Fletcher remarked. "Why catch one outlaw when you get the entire lot of them?"

"Maybe. But we don't want to shoot them all," Brannon asserted. "Once the first shot's fired, there's no control. And, we're not sure there's not someone left inside guarding the boys."

Tanglewood crept near them. "The back of the house and windows are all boarded up. No way to sneak in, unless we crawl on the roof and try the chimney."

"I know this sounds strange, but wish I'd kept that Spanish War dagger of Papa's," Sylvia remarked. "The one the old Indian forced me to bury. I wanted so bad to volunteer myself, when Papa helped pioneer the Rough Riders in Prescott. Of course he wouldn't let me. I never told Papa about Wills Bennett. It ran too deep."

"One day your father showed me the list from Yavapai County. I noticed Lanigan's name and asked him about it," Brannon said.

Sylvia spit out a gasp. "What? Lanigan a Rough Rider, part of Troop A?"

"Tom claimed he had several high placed references."

"Another reason I wish I had that dagger. It would be sweet justice to confront him with it now."

CHAPTER FORTY TWO

Something popped out in the forest, like a pine cone falling. The men posed in the clearing jumped to attention. "Are you sure it's safe out in the open like this?" one of the Rincon brothers asked.

"No one could track me," Lanigan said. "But what about you?" Lanigan pointed to Miller. "Or any of you? Hurry up, Miller."

Brannon watched a shimmer of light illuminate the trees and around them.

"Do you notice how unnatural the atmosphere seems?" Tanglewood shivered.

"Perhaps there is something awful ahead of us," Sylvia whispered.

"Or something glorious," Brannon remarked.

After the shutter on the camera snapped closed, each of the men scurried around to leave. Barranca and the deputy slung Jones over a blood bay horse. Barranca rose up into the saddle of a sandy bay and led the two horses down the road. Miller got his wagon turned around with some help from the Rincons.

One of the Rincon brothers sat in the Ford Model C and fussed with the controls while the other waited out front. At a signal from the driver, the other man cranked the engine and it roared to life. The second Rincon brother hopped in the Ford and after a few jerky lunges, they putted down the road.

The deputy followed in a gallop on his buckskin dun.

"I'm going to bust in there," Brannon said. "But not shooting. I don't know where the boys are."

"You're crazy, Stuart," Fletcher protested.

"So is Lanigan, but maybe he'll appreciate that I gave him a fighting chance, better than what he's given his victims."

"I don't think he will notice," Fletcher remarked.

"If it will help," Sylvia said, "tell him I've changed my mind, that he's the man for me, that I don't blame him for my father's death. He'll believe you. His ego's that strong and delusional."

"Here I go." Brannon crept forward.

"If you're not out of there in five minutes, I'm coming in," Sylvia called out, "and I'll be shooting."

"Give me ten."

Brannon counted on the presumption that Lanigan hadn't detected their presence nor expected it. He rushed to the south side of the boarded house and crouched low, in case there was a peek hole in any of the windows.

A soft breeze bristled through the pines. In the grasses he rubbed with his boots, a minty scent almost choked him. Brannon scraped his hands across the rough lumber of the old house walls to cling as close as possible.

As he rounded the corner to the front and full window openings, he stopped. The smallest sound might bring Lanigan charging out the door or flinging his gun hand through the window.

He kicked open the door and lunged in. Lanigan spun around and raised his gun. Brannon dove and tackled him to the floor. Lanigan kicked and flailed. Brannon grabbed his arm with the gun. Lanigan landed a punch on Brannon's face. They rolled together. Lanigan's gun shook loose as Brannon got kicked twice in the side. With clenched hands together, Brannon slammed into Lanigan's face. He tried to sit up. He had wrenched his left leg and had trouble standing on it.

Brannon tried to crawl to the gun. Lanigan whipped out a knife from his boot and threw it. Cold steel ripped skin in Brannon's left arm. His shirt sleeve ripped and blood streaked from below the elbow down to his wrist. He gasped for air as Lanigan's knee shoved into his chest. Lanigan locked his hands together and drove them into the wound in Brannon's arm. Brannon kicked hard at Lanigan's shin. Knuckles crashed into his cheekbone like the sound of a bullwhip.

Brannon's eyes met Lanigan's, full of chill hatred. Brannon tried to rise, swung wildly at

Lanigan's bleeding face once more, and passed out.

When Brannon became conscious of sounds and smells, he couldn't move and could barely see.

Bueno and Hack sat hunched in the corner of the room, bound and gagged. Hack's eyes were edged with fear. Bueno looked like he'd been crying.

Brannon suddenly longed to be riding across a desert trail with cactus in bloom, calves all around kicking up their heels.

Nothing wrong with the coast. It just isn't home. And right now it looks a speck like hell.

"Who's out there with you?" Lanigan's face tensed like taut leather.

When Brannon didn't answer right away, Lanigan dragged a shaking Bueno across the loose-board floor, gun shoved in his cheek. "I'll kill this boy, if you don't tell me. Now, who . . . is . . . out . . . there?"

Brannon concentrated in desperation for words to stop the insanity, as he took a quick scan of the layout of the house, to find a possible escape. A partition, a stairway to a landing and perhaps several rooms. He was in a living room with a fireplace. There was a side parlour and bedroom. A hallway led to a long pantry and kitchen. He could see a stove with a pipe outlet to the roof.

He started to list the trio who waited in the

trees, when Lanigan shoved the boy away and suddenly switched to a different train of thought. "Brannon, I am puzzled about one thing. It gnaws at me."

"What's that, Lanigan?"

"How come it was even noticed? And so quickly too. How come you got here so fast?"

"What are you talking about?"

"The disappearance of Tom Wiseman, that's what."

"Tom's got friends who care about him, including the President of the United States." Brannon strained to listen outside the room, to any possible movement near the door. If anyone tried to crash in, he wanted to be prepared, to do what he could, although tied up. He wiggled his toes, stretched his feet, his arms, his hands. Nothing eased.

"What makes you tick, Brannon? How come you're so predictable? A friend's gone. You've got to save him. You're wound up. Maybe Tom Wiseman deserted his duty. Or ran off with a woman. Or took a bribe and escaped to Argentina. Did you really want to risk your life to dig into another man's dirty business?"

"That's slander. Tom's a good friend of mine, one of the best. I know what he would or wouldn't do."

"Slander? This is my court. I can say anything I want."

Brannon thought he might be able to twist and roll. Then what? At least it was movement. But he couldn't try it out until the critical moment. "But wouldn't you do the same for a friend? You do have one, don't you? You surely haven't shot them all. Wouldn't you be there for them?"

"I like to let life happen, to grab the next opportunity. I don't pay attention to people much . . . except for gals like Sylvia."

"Without thought to the consequences?" Brannon strained his ears and tried hard not to look at the door. He thought he heard a scraping sound.

Lanigan leered as he tried for a grin. "Did you notice how they like me? They respect me. They look up to me, those people in Gearhart. A lot in Portland too. I'm changed, Brannon. I'm not the same guy you knew in Arizona. And I think Sylvia Wiseman's warming up to me. Lady Fletcher was going to talk to her. She knows the real me."

Sylvia Wiseman . . . one man's dream, another man's tornado. Lanigan's stepped into a total delusion, a very dangerous state.

Lanigan was wistful, almost boyish in his longing. "Does the President know my name?"

"I'm sure he does. You want to feel important." Brannon kept talking, just to say something, anything. "You've almost reached your goal. Let the kids go and you can be a hero."

Lanigan snapped to attention. "You're desperate to be important yourself. You can't deceive me. I know the tricks guys like you play. Pretend to be a champion and down deep inside you're evil, watching for a chance to take advantage." His eyes cleared. A filmy kind of peace mixed with power took over. He twisted around to the boys. "No heroes today with these two. No awards given. No speeches by the big man."

How in the world did Tom, then Rebozo and now me get caught by this guy? In Tom's case, he trusted God. Why did He let him die?

We've always had the upper hand, kept control, managed to get free eventually in any tight situation. Sure, he appears to be one way, but is really another. No different than other scoundrels. Maybe it's because he's evil smart. Or lucky.

Brannon felt like he teetered on a mountainside about to give way to an avalanche. Not knowing when the slide would come, he waited for an opening, a misstep by Lanigan. His only chance was to keep Lanigan talking . . . about himself. "But you don't want to ruin that reputation you've developed. You add any more murders, that's gone forever."

Lanigan roared until the tears came. He grabbed a kerchief. "I did not kill Tom Wiseman. He shot the Frenchman and then fell in those tree roots. It was an accident."

"So, you admit you were there and left Tom to die."

"I don't admit anything."

Brannon tried a different track. "Sylvia's out there. She'd sure like to know what happened to her father."

Lanigan rushed to the window and flung aside the tattered curtains. "Sylvia!" he shouted. "I've got to talk to you." His head swirled back and forth.

"I'm right here, Lanigan." It was almost a whisper, yet Brannon heard it. A floor board moved.

She's under the house.

"Sylvia!" Lanigan yelled again from the window, then stomped over to creak open the front door.

This would be a good time for some action from my crew.

The floor board moved again. Lanigan swiveled around and stalked over to the wooden floor. He kicked up one of the boards and shot twice.

"Why did you shoot her?" Brannon bellowed.

"I didn't. There's no one down there except the snakes."

But I heard her voice. Where is she?

CHAPTER FORTY THREE

Brannon forced himself to not shift or roll. He knew he'd be a helpless target. His main concern turned to what or who was under the boards. He strained for a sound, but heard nothing. If one of his friends had been wounded, he or she needed help. If they were dead, Lanigan had a growing list of victims . . . and he may be next.

Lanigan shoved down the board with his shoe, then stacked the blanketed pile of guns on top. "You know what I see for my future, Brannon? I see a change in my fortunes, both social and financial."

Brannon twisted his arms, hands and legs again. "And you'll do anything to make that happen."

He chuckled, deep and low. "You see that stack of papers over there? You think you're the only one who can be a hero in novels? I'm going to be the main character in my own series, a sophisticated, refined and inspiring character. I'll use a pen name for the author. In fact, until Hawthorne Miller showed up, I thought you wrote all those stories yourself."

He's so far gone, he talks like he thinks he has a chance for a normal life.

"That's not my style. You don't know how much I've disliked Miller for what he's made of me, because of all those pack of lies."

"So, you and I can agree on something. I hate what he's made of you too. Everywhere I go, it's Stuart Brannon this and Stuart Brannon that. I'm going to obliterate your existence off the face of the earth. I'll be doing the world and you a favor. No more *Brannon of the Wild West Series* dime novels. I think I'll burn them all. Yes, that's my next project."

"Won't hurt me none. Suits me fine." Brannon searched for another topic. "Quite an honor to be a Rough Rider, don't you think?"

He clenched his teeth and almost stammered in a sudden rage. "You poisoned Tom Wiseman against me."

"What are you talking about?"

"He fired me on the first important mission. He wouldn't believe my explanation for why I didn't show."

News to me. Never heard this story. "Is that why you had a grudge against him?"

"I had witnesses. Didn't make any difference to him." Lanigan ground out each word. Some infected nerve had been touched. "I had been hit on the head by two different women. Lay unconscious on a street in Phoenix for two days."

"The same old Wax Lanigan, seems to me."

Lanigan's face turned a splotchy red. The veins in his neck protruded. Every ounce of energy he possessed exploded in his words. "That's . . . a . . . lie! Are you so dumb and blind? I'm a changed man. You refuse to recognize that fact. You and Tom Wiseman, all your ilk. You're the fools."

Brannon regretted riling his captor. He watched for that possible split second in every deadly confrontation that might open a pin hole of opportunity. *It's been more than ten minutes. Where are Sylvia and the guys?* "So you've changed. I'd like to hear about that."

Lanigan's eyes narrowed in contempt. "Look at these clothes. The way I can talk to a crowd. The smiles I get from the ladies. That's all different, all new."

Brannon tried to keep calm, almost monotone. "But inside, how you think and feel, how has that improved?"

"Sylvia will find out. I'm going to treat her right, do good things for her. She'll be the most loved and cherished woman who ever lived . . . right after I kill you."

I hear bells. The *clop, clop-clop* of hooves paced the rhythm of the dings. *Miller's back.*

Lanigan stormed to the door, glowered into the distance, then raised his gun. Ecstasy penetrated the glare. A perfect show of madness.

The mules trotted into view through the open

door. "Miller!" Brannon shouted. "Duck down."

Miller hopped off the wagon and sprinted to the woods.

Lanigan squeezed off a shot then rushed towards Hawthorne Miller's wagon. He climbed into the seat, fussed to untangle the reins and slapped the leather to the teams of mules.

Someone grabbed the tailgate and ran along behind. Hair flying. Long skirt swaying. Sylvia grabbed a fallen pine branch and jammed it into the spokes of the right rear wheel.

The wagon braked, jerked left and right, then teetered over. Four mules toppled in a scramble and chorus of pitiful brays that faded into whimpers and whines.

"You ruined my wagon," Miller screamed. A hole pierced one jacket sleeve and a stream of blood rolled down.

Lord Fletcher and Tanglewood scurried from out of the trees to tackle Lanigan who came up swinging. Fletcher's right uppercut sprawled him back to the ground. Lanigan went for his holstered revolver, but the toe of Tanglewood's boot caught his hand and sent the gun flying. Fletcher shoved a fist hard underneath his chin.

Sylvia grabbed Lanigan's revolver, got it aimed and cocked.

Brannon scrambled with all his might to free any part of his limbs from the ropes. Lanigan spit a stream of curses and threats. Sylvia fired three quick shots at Lanigan's position. Hawthorne Miller scrambled into his wagon, pulled out his photography equipment and began the setup.

"Come help me," Brannon yelled.

Lord Fletcher motioned to Tanglewood who ran into the house and had Brannon and the two boys untied in two minutes flat. Bueno and Hack grabbed up boards from the floor and dashed towards Lanigan and beat him until Brannon held their arms back.

Then shots were fired. The first cracked over their heads. The second hit Sylvia. She fell in a heap.

"Run to the house," Brannon ordered as he hauled Sylvia away by the arms.

The third splattered into Miller's camera and tripod which collapsed around him.

Brannon tucked Sylvia into the house, checked her for pulse and injury. "It's my leg." She pulled up her skirt. Brannon noticed a gash above the tattoo. "Where are the boys?" she asked.

Brannon took a quick glance at the room. He yanked up the blanket full of guns and scooted them over to Sylvia. "Pass these out," he said as he crouched at the door.

The gunfire kept up a steady *pop, ping, pop* as Tanglewood and Fletcher tried a scatter chase towards the fallen mules. The boys had cowered underneath the over-turned wagon. *What are they doing there? Why didn't they flee to the house like I said?*

Then he spied Lanigan underneath the wagon with them, an elbow hold on Bueno's neck, a gun in the other hand. "Don't think I won't shoot them. I have nothing to lose," he hissed at Brannon.

Then he leaned out and called towards the woods. "It's me, Lanigan. I've got some orphans with me. Hold your fire."

He positioned them as a shield. He held them both with one arm and had his gun to Bueno's head.

Tanglewood and Lord Fletcher ducked behind some trees. Brannon pulled a table out of the house to scoot in front of him as he eased forward. He pushed the table down the trail as far as he could, then assembled his take-down rifle and readied his revolver. Lanigan crawled out from under the wagon, both the boys squeezed tight against him and hiked forward. He raised his gun into the air.

"Get rid of the kids," a man ordered.

Lanigan slammed the two boys to the ground, trekked across the dirt trail and towards the trees. A shot rang out, from the woods. Lanigan staggered and fell.

The boys raised up and ran. Tanglewood and Lord Fletcher rushed towards them as Lanigan aimed his gun in their direction. Another shot rang out, this time from behind the table.

As gunfire followed from the woods, Lanigan crawled back to the wagon, mouth open, breathing hard. Brannon provided a steady stream of cover for Tanglewood and Lord Fletcher as they scurried the boys to the house. Brannon scooted the splintered table behind Miller's wagon. He inched towards Lanigan as bullets splayed around them.

"What are you doing?" Lanigan rasped.

As Brannon got closer, he could hear Lanigan's labored breathing, a wheeze like the chug of a slow train. "I'm hurt bad. I guess you win."

"No one's won anything," Brannon said. "Can you crawl to this table?"

"I can't move at all."

"Just like Tom Wiseman."

"You going to leave me here?"

"Nope. Not unless I'm forced."

"I would leave you." Lanigan gasped for air. "You know I would."

"Yep, but that's your way, not mine."

The shooting stopped. The scene echoed with silence. *Could be a reload. Can't tell if there's two shooters or just one. All I know is whatever I do, I must do quickly.*

He slammed the table against the wagon and stretched as far as he could near Lanigan, his guns on the ground. Lanigan slowly raised his revolver, hand shaking, and aimed at Brannon.

"You goin' to shoot me?" Brannon asked. "Don't make much sense. I'm tryin' to get you back to the house. Might save your undeservin' hide."

His words came in spurts. "I can shoot you . . . if I want. I can kill you . . . right here . . . right now. I'm the author . . . of your story . . . this time . . . Stuart Brannon."

"No, God's the author of my story. If you shoot me dead, it's only because He allows you to."

"You're gone." Lanigan strained to squeeze the trigger. It clicked on an empty chamber as he passed out.

CHAPTER FORTY FOUR

Lord Fletcher provided cover for Brannon from the porch while Tanglewood and Sylvia threw lead from the windows. He dragged and weaved Lanigan through the hail of bullets. Some zinged close. Others whizzed farther away. Finally, he lugged the unconscious Lanigan up a few steps and into the house, with Fletcher's aid.

"I used Wyatt Earp's and Buffalo Bill Cody's guns," Fletcher announced. "That'll make quite a story in England."

"That's quite an event anywhere." Brannon stretched Lanigan out on the floor.

Lanigan turned chalky, as if bleached out. His eyes deepened in his head, like the hollowed, sunken sockets of a malnourished or starving man. Brannon had never seen a living, breathing man look more like a corpse with the spirit sucked out.

As a man of action, Brannon despised indecision. He also dreaded to watch anyone suffer, even a man like Wax Lanigan. If he was a horse, he'd shoot him to put him out of his misery. As a man, he'd shoot him to gain vengeance for Tom Wiseman . . . and Tally Rebozo . . . and also for Argentiferous Jones.

The quality of mercy is not strain'd . . .

Sylvia's leg had been bandaged with the torn hem of her skirt and she now leaned over Lanigan to study his wounds. "Why'd you do it? He may not survive anyway."

It droppeth as the gentle rain from heaven

"It's who I am," Brannon replied.

Upon the place beneath. It is twice blest:

"My father would do the same." She burst into tears as she dabbed at the wounds of the man who let Tom Wiseman suffer and die.

It blesseth him that gives and him that takes.

"I can help. I've had to cut out bullets, arrowheads and porcupine quills," Brannon stated.

Sylvia heated a knife with some matches from Lord Fletcher, then tore the hem of her skirt into rags. Lanigan was still unconscious. "Did anybody happen to bring some liquor or morphine?"

"He's got no struggles with pain," Tanglewood observed.

She seared the wound to prevent infection. "If he gets a high fever, I'll need more rags to help cool him down."

Bueno and Hack Howard turned away. Tanglewood started tearing the sleeves and hem of his shirt.

"Where's Miller?" Brannon asked.

"Out there." Lord Fletcher pointed out the window.

Hawthorne Miller had reset his camera and

tripod on a grassy area in front of some trees to the right. He waited for the next action.

"You can't say the man doesn't have bravado," Fletcher surmised.

"You going to go get him too?" Hack Howard asked Brannon.

Brannon considered the absurdity. Miller risked his life to record this event for posterity, but Brannon jeopardized his for the man responsible for the danger. Would he do the same for Hawthorne Miller?

Yep.

It felt good to retrieve his Colt revolver again and hold his new rifle.

I value the ability to protect the innocent, provide a fair shake for those attacked. Injustice must have penalties.

But words from the good book assailed him.

"Vengeance is mine; I will repay," saith the Lord.

But that doesn't mean we do nothing, that we don't fight for what's right.

The laws of the twentieth century and the principles of scripture coincided. He wrapped his fingers around the grip, pulled back the hammer with his thumb then held it back as he pulled the trigger. He slowly let the hammer fall. It still fit his hand well, after all these years. *Great investment for seventeen dollars.*

"Is the shooter still out there?" Brannon asked.

"There are two," Fletcher reported. "One of them's the deputy. The other's the one you called Slash."

"The thief on the train? What do they want? They could have ridden away with their loot scot-free."

"We'll know soon enough. The deputy is rummaging through Miller's wagon," Fletcher said.

Brannon got to the window just as two shots rang out in rapid succession. Brannon ducked down. In a moment, Miller crashed through the door and into the room.

"I do believe they wanted him in here," Fletcher observed. "They shot over his head."

"Barely missed me," Miller huffed. "And as anyone can see, I'm an impartial spectator."

"If you're going to fight, grab a weapon and stay in the front," Brannon advised. "But if you're a witness only, stand back there with the boys."

Several bullets hit the door and windows. Miller hunkered down in the corner with Bueno and Hack.

"My word," Fletcher exclaimed. "They're throwing something burning at the front."

Brannon popped his head up and fired a shot, clipping Barranca's arm, just as the whole front porch exploded into flames. Brannon and Fletcher both fired off several rounds through the flames.

Miller jumped up and screamed at them. "That's the collodion solution. It will give off poisonous gases." He raced to the back of the house. "We've got to get out of here."

"The back doors and windows are all boarded up," Sylvia reminded him.

A flare of fire sailed through one of the windows. They ran and shoved once, twice, three times at the back door. Not a splinter budged. Brannon grabbed up the floor boards and pounded the windows. The glass shattered, but the two-by-fours covering the outside wouldn't give.

Brannon knew it was time to tend the herd. "Everyone cover their mouths," he yelled as Fletcher and Miller coughed.

Brannon yanked up floor boards as the house sweltered with rising heat. The fire was spreading. Tanglewood, Fletcher and Sylvia followed suit. Brannon slung aside two dead snakes with his rifle. He dropped down, spread out on his stomach and crawled through the wide hole.

"Be careful, Stuart," Fletcher warned.

"We've got no choice," Brannon replied. "I can see an opening. Follow me."

"What about Lanigan?" Sylvia called.

"Leave him. I'll come back," Brannon said.

"By Jove, he'll melt before you ever reach him," Fletcher cajoled.

Brannon pawed and scooted his way in the

dark underside of the house through a muddy moat of pine needles, leaves and substances he couldn't begin to name. He moved as steady and fast as he could towards the light and pushed through some rotting planks.

After the others inched out, Sylvia begged him not to go back for Lanigan. Brannon considered to her pleas.

She's being reasonable, not vindictive. No one can blame me or anyone if Lanigan burns up in that house. I don't have to try to save every villain I come in contact with. He sighed. *However, by God's will, I am who I am.*

CHAPTER FORTY FIVE

Brannon scrambled back through the muck to the floor gap. Sparks showered the room. The roof smoldered. A thick, dark smoke hovered. Brannon covered his face with a muddy bandana and yanked off his shirt to cover Lanigan's head. Brannon couldn't tell if the man was alive or dead, but he hauled him to the floor cavity, just as two arms reached out and yanked him through.

"Edwin! Harriet would never forgive me if . . ." Brannon began.

"Come on, man. This is no time to exchange chitchat."

With Brannon straining to shove from the back and Fletcher pulling from the forward position, they got Lanigan out from the house and over to their comrades before the whole structure burst into roiling ash and charred timber.

Bueno's eyes reflected the fire as he stretched his arms towards the inferno. "We forgot the gold."

Brannon swiped mud and gunk from his clothes and face. "What gold?"

"We saw Mr. Lanigan hide a box under the floor. He showed us the gold inside. He said it had been the Frenchman's, but he didn't need it anymore."

"You mean this?" Sylvia cracked open a rectangular box filled with gold colored nuggets and dust. "I bumped my head on it coming out."

Lanigan's eyes suddenly gaped wide open. He made a kind of screeching sound. "That's mine."

"That's the same box Bois DeVache showed us at the Lewis and Clark Exposition in Portland," Hawthorne Miller reported.

Brannon wheeled around. "When?"

"On opening day. He was trying to find investors for a gold mine in Panama. I didn't fall for it, no sirree, but those Lazzard women sure took him under their wings. They introduced him to all sorts of men. I even saw him talking to Tom Wiseman."

"Stuart," Fletcher interrupted. "I've been watching those two men who started the fire. They haven't moved or raised up from the ground."

"We must have hit them with our bullets." Brannon and Fletcher marched over to the sprawled deputy and Slash Barranca.

They turned the bodies over. "They're dead, all right." Brannon searched them all over with care. "But not a bullet hole anywhere, except for a possible graze or two. I'm real sorry I didn't get a chance to talk more than business with the deputy . . . for his father's sake . . . for his sake. Sure hope he made his peace with God."

Miller had tied a large bandana around his nose and mouth. "We'd all better be careful. There are still many toxic fumes."

A woman screamed behind him. As Fletcher and Brannon covered their faces, they rushed to the grove where the others huddled.

"I turned my back for only a moment," Sylvia said.

"Mine," he repeated. Lanigan's voice had a whooshing edge, a sacrifice of diminishing breath. He clasped the box of gold between his knees. Each hand grappled with a firearm.

"What are you doing?" Brannon aimed his rifle at Lanigan.

"Earp . . . Cody . . . are they here?" Lanigan wheezed.

"No, they're in Gearhart." Brannon turned around to the photographer and dime novel author. "But Hawthorne Miller's here." A bullet zipped past him. Brannon whirled towards Lanigan, ready to fire.

Both Lanigan's arms crumpled, spraddled across his chest. "God . . ." His face relaxed into a ghoulish grin. "I'm the hero . . . I am *somebody*." His last word was a hiss. His eyes shut into slits. Two long gasps escaped him.

Brannon walked over and waited a moment.

A couple more jerks shook Lanigan's shoulders. "He's gone."

Sylvia stared down at the shell of the man, as though mesmerized. "It doesn't help. I thought it would. This death doesn't bring Papa back. That's the only real victory. Maybe there is no way to experience true justice. That is, to *feel* vindicated."

"Not always. That comes later. In the next life."

"Lanigan tried so hard to gain respectability, yet remained a rake. Selfish. Depraved. It led to murder and his own destruction. End of story."

"He couldn't break the greed habit on his own."

"I do not understand a man like that." Sylvia's words shuddered with force, slow and deliberate.

Brannon closed Lanigan's lids. "Only God does."

CHAPTER FORTY SIX

Neighbors of the region gathered by foot, horseback and wagon to help contain the fire to the clearing. Soon, Sheriff Linville and a posse from Astoria arrived. They took down statements from all of them and hauled off the bodies.

"Hope you're leaving my region soon," was the sheriff's parting barb at Brannon.

Miller tried to rescue the remnants of his photography equipment. Brannon picked up Lanigan's Kodak that had been left on the lawn nearby.

They prepared for the long ride back to Gearhart. They took it slow, steady, to save their mounts. Bueno and Hack both rode close to Brannon. "Boys, I know you're weary. You've been troopers."

He looked over at Tanglewood. "Brave warriors," he affirmed.

Hawthorne Miller rode one of the gray mules they had recovered, paper and pencil in hand. "So Tom Wiseman suspected that Lanigan skimmed monies from his various enterprises."

"Miller, are you goin' to try to get the details right this time?" Brannon said. "Actually report the facts?"

"I always do," Miller retorted. "Then Wiseman planned to confront Lanigan after the meeting with the Panama engineers. He told the President he'd send him a report right after, but it never came."

Lord Fletcher chimed in. "Your President may have imagined intrigues of an international sort. With the Exposition as a perfect cover."

Sylvia sounded close to tears. "Ironic, isn't it? So many possibilities, yet the motive for Papa's death amounted to plain old thievery."

Miller kept reciting. "Lanigan devised many ways to gouge the railroad. He forced men like the Rincon brothers to give him a part of their take or he'd turn them in."

"That's conjecture," Brannon said. "Don't accuse him until you can prove it."

"Brannon, one trait of yours both irritates and thrills me," Lord Fletcher began. "Your inability to ever, under any circumstance, back away from confronting evil."

"There's some things in life a man's got to do." Brannon scanned the horizon. The Tillamook Lighthouse beacon slivered a warning through the shrouded mists. "I've learned something though. In the old days we tried to tame an uncivilized land. But we never could purify a heart. Not a single one. And that hasn't changed."

"Why does a man like Wax Lanigan happen?" Sylvia asked.

Brannon didn't know if the question was addressed to him or not, but he gave a stab at the answer. "One fertile ground for evil to me is a person who only and ever looks out for himself. No one else matters."

Lord Fletcher pulled off his hat and fanned his face. "May God have mercy on us all."

Later that night when they returned to Gearhart, Lady Fletcher hustled the boys to a hot meal and bed. She wrapped a fresh, tight bandage on Brannon's arm. "Mr. Earp and Mr. Cody are eating and playing cards in the lobby," she reported. "They tied the tournament, 101 to 101. It lasted longer than usual, because Mr. Earp kept breaking his clubs over his knee and the caddie had to scout for replacements. He claims Mr. Cody purposely harassed him with ill-timed, loud comments, jingling coins, coughing and taking practice strokes when he tried to swing or putt."

"We missed quite a show," Brannon noted.

"Stuart, I don't suppose I could talk you into doing a make-up game tomorrow afternoon?"

"If you can get enough other players."

Brannon pounded boot heels across the wooden floor to return weapons to Earp and Cody. Smoke from Earp's cigar rippled over their table. Half-eaten plates of sirloin steak had been pushed aside. Cards were scattered around.

"Hello, Wyatt, Buffalo Bill," he greeted.

"I'd prefer you call me Will," Cody said. "Never have liked the name Bill."

"Okay, Will, honored to know that. Here's your guns." He laid down Cody's .36 caliber Colt pistol and handed Earp his Buntline Special on the table. Then he recounted the story of Lanigan's demise.

"We knew you could do it," Cody said. "No one can outsmart Stuart Brannon."

"And it's so nice that we don't have to be the heroes anymore. We can rest on our laurels, tell our stories, enjoy life," Earp remarked. "Come join our game. It's friendly and low stakes."

"Sorry, I've got a previous appointment. Thanks for your participation in that tournament. The orphans and the rest of us are grateful. See you tomorrow?"

"No, we're both leavin' at dawn," Earp said. "My brother, Virgil, is sick with pneumonia in Goldfield. He don't seem to be gettin' better. I'm goin' back as quick as I can."

"And I've got to catch up with my show," Cody said.

Brannon waved to them and headed out the front hotel door.

He could hear music from the gazebo at the park, the strains of *After the Ball* and *Maple Leaf Rag*.

"Go to the dance with me?" Tanglewood had asked Laira.

She was adamant. "Only if Nicholas invites Darcy."

Brannon decided to take a peek at the event before he gravitated to the golf course.

Curious whether Laira will dance with Tanglefoot or Yancy more. Maybe I'll see The Cakewalk number she was so excited about.

Cordelle Plew had been waiting for Sylvia on the hotel deck when they returned. Brannon now caught them in a hug and kiss. He turned his head and scurried past them, but with an inner smile.

One thing Brannon had learned through the tragedy and trial of life: the earth heals quickly. Not so soon the human heart. But shared laughter, the labors of love and the grace of God help mend the wounds.

The real tragedy of Tom Wiseman filtered down to the frustration of no opportunity to save him and no satisfying, proper way to tender a last farewell.

Even in the twilight, with the blessing of the full moon, Brannon could detect the golf ball pull to the left. He rolled another ball in front of him and regripped his club. This time the ball jumped off the clubface with a crack and sailed into the dove gray sky.

As did the next one.

And the next.

Harriet got the bandage just right. Hardly feel the wound.

One after another, he brought the club back low and slow, twisted his hips, then slammed down through the ball.

I don't like anyone dying . . . not Tom Wiseman, not Chuy Carbón, not Tally Rebozo, not even Wax Lanigan. Not the man washed up on the beach. It doesn't seem right.

Like a slow metronome, the repeated *thwack* of the ball kept steady time as the green grass merged to gray, then black.

But it's more than agony over the loss of friends, foes and strangers. I should be doing something that's more eternal.

Thwack.

I don't know my goal. My heavenly one, that is. I accept some things I don't understand.

Thwack.

I just can't figure out why You left me here on this earth without Lisa and our baby.

Thwack.

She's had another life with You these thirty years. Her life here stopped that day. But I will go to her someday.

Thwack.

Each day I have managed to find a purpose to go on.

But some days can sure play out lonely.

Thwack.

And if Victoria was part of the purpose . . .

Thwack.

I really messed up.

Thwack.

By the time a man figures out what's really missing, what's of true importance, it's too late. Or is it?

He could no longer watch the ball in flight, but could feel and hear the crack of the club every time he swung. He didn't know if they flew straight. He didn't care.

If I can get one good golf shot in a round, I'll have a good game overall. One last shot before I go.

Later, after a bath swim in the ocean and lying warm in clean clothes beside the dying embers of his campsite, his gaze was drawn to the rim of Tillamook Head. He jumped up and looked more intently. A flaming torch moved forward across the rim. Brannon watched until it reached the cliff edge and slowly faded away.

Catcher-Of-The-Sun.

A victory run.

One story's end.

Others still left to complete.

CHAPTER FORTY SEVEN

Sunday, June 18

Brannon loved Sundays. On this day he could rest or play, could forget the relentless routine of the rest of the week and not feel guilty. Sundays meant church. He had grown over the years to appreciate churchgoing and the community of believers.

And now he sensed a really good day about to happen.

He hoped the date was already logged into God's book, a day worthy of eternity's notice, as well as his own.

The whole town had been invited to a Sunday School picnic at the Gearhart Park after their own services or family activities, sponsored by friends of the orphan farm. Deer meat was announced for the main dish. Besides the make-up golf tournament there would be games of "catch the duck," a boys' swimming race, plus comic diving contest, tub race, single and double paddle canoe races.

Lord Fletcher met up with him there. "I couldn't sleep last night, as exhausted as I was. I was in no mood to adjourn."

Brannon chuckled. "You've missed the adventures, haven't you, old boy? But just think, you and I have the opportunity to saddle up this very day and ride it into our memories. But that means staying awake."

Lord Fletcher yawned. "I'm bushed."

"You wear your Sunday best everyday," Brannon opined. "I feel like a struttin' peacock, like everyone's gawkin' at me, ready to roll in the grass over the way this ole cowboy is dressed."

"You take it too personal. Keep in mind why you're doing this, then hold nothing back. Every time you swing a club or hit a ball in that tournament, you're providing an overnight stay for an orphan."

"The funny thing about those dime novels. Puts everything out of proportion. When they take the great photograph of mankind's family reunion, I'll be the one in the tenth row from the back, fifth from the end, partially blocked by the lady in the feathered hat. I'm the one who stares down at my scuffed, dirt-colored boots, the one listed as 'unknown.'"

"But that doesn't mean you haven't had a shining moment or two."

"Yes. Every once in awhile, we catch God in action, directly involved. By mistake, we get the credit."

At the after-church picnic, Sam Smythe introduced social worker Cordelle Plew as a special friend, then surprised Brannon by asking him to give the grace before the meal.

"I can tell from your prayer you have a big view of God," Sylvia whispered.

"He makes the rules. This whole earth and beyond is his ranch."

"I'm just surprised that a man like you seems so at ease talking with the Almighty."

"Maybe that's 'cause I talked to Him before I knew His name. Long before we were properly introduced."

A large birthday cake had been prepared for Sylvia, at Lady Fletcher's direction. The Royal Hawaiian Band played hymns. They had a concert later that evening at the Chautauqua. As Sylvia cut the cake, Cordelle Plew announced that she had agreed to be his wife.

"Here's my birthday present from him." She showed off a simple, but sparkling ring. "We're eloping tonight."

Sylvia opened several other gifts . . . a travel bag from the Fletchers, a brush embedded with gems from Brannon. The one from her father: a small model of the U.S.S. *Maine* ship. Tears flowed.

"He knew," she whispered. "He knew all along."

Applause and congratulations were extended to the happy couple.

"She's going to start training, as soon as we

return to New York, to become a social worker," Plew affirmed.

"It's one way I can become a sort of mother," Sylvia said. "But after we get married, we're returning to Tillamook Head to place a marker on my father's grave, before the location's lost."

After she hugged the couple, Lady Fletcher declared, "There will be another golf tournament to benefit the Willamette Orphan Farm this afternoon, starting in one hour. Get your tickets at the golf course. Buy tickets for the team you think will win. At the end of the tournament we'll randomly draw a name from those who picked the winning team."

Lady Fletcher looked straight at Brannon. A mischievous grin crawled across her face. "The prize will be dinner with Mr. Stuart Brannon and a picture with the famous gunman taken by none other than the esteemed photographer Mr. Hawthorne Miller. And since his own camera is under repair, he will be using a modern Kodak instead."

Murmurs of approval and excitement buzzed through the crowd. Brannon wanted badly to protest, but Lady Fletcher had that look in her eyes that let him know it would be futile. Besides, he felt that he still owed her for all the ripped jackets, dirty faces, bloody lips and tardy appearances in recent days.

"And please don't tell anyone the Kodak

belonged to Wax Lanigan," Lady Fletcher whispered to Brannon. Aloud she said, "Pass the word around town. All the money is for a worthy cause," she paused for effect, "and will be in honest hands."

Before the crowd dispersed, Lady Fletcher yelled above the din, "Because the rest of our players are gone, we will play only twosomes, who will be chosen from the following. Those who are called please step forward: Lord Edwin Fletcher . . . Stuart Brannon . . . Deedra Lazzard . . . Darrlyn Lazzard . . . Hawthorne Miller . . . and Lady Harriet Reed-Fletcher."

"My word, Harriet, you have the ladies playing?" Fletcher fussed.

"We practiced yesterday while you and Stuart were out playing hero," she replied. "Ted Fleming gave us lessons. There's really nothing to it. Hit the ball. Get the ball to the hole. Repeat. Repeat. Oh, I did forget to mention we're only playing three holes. We ladies determined that the others are redundant."

"Redundant! It's how a full game's played."

"Oh, posh, this is for charity. It should be fun, not work. Now, let's get started. The caddies will be Keaton Tanglewood for Stuart, Darcy Lazzard for her mother, Laira Fletcher for her father, Nicholas Yancy for me, Bueno Diaz for Deedra and Hack Howard for Mr. Miller. We will do that scramble game. After teeing off, both players on a team hit from where the best ball lands."

She turned to Edwin. "I forget. Is it highest or lowest score that wins?"

Lord Fletcher grumbled something to himself and pointed his thumb down. Brannon didn't know if that was to signal that the winners had low points or to indicate his opinion of the whole proceedings. Perhaps both.

"But who will be the teams?" Deedra Lazzard asked.

"I'll pick them from a hat . . . Stuart's hat."

Brannon handed her his Stetson and she tossed in six pieces of paper. "Here's the teams, drawn at random." Lady Fletcher pulled slips of paper out one by one. "Let's see . . . myself and Edwin . . . Mr. Miller and Deedra . . . that leaves Stuart with Darrlyn."

The players looked at each other as if searching for a reason to object to the team assignments, but Lady Fletcher plowed forward.

"Please head over to the golf course straight away. We want to be there to shake hands and help sell tickets. Remember, the more tickets purchased, the more money raised for the orphans." Lady Fletcher herded them along, without verbal protest.

After thirty minutes of shaking hands and smiling for prospective ticket purchasers, Brannon's patience was gone. *Let's get this over with, Harriet.*

CHAPTER FORTY EIGHT

A signal from Lady Fletcher brought the players to the first tee. The crowd, which began as a couple of dozen, but now swelled to two hundred or more, filled in behind. A man walked up to the players and Lady Fletcher introduced him as "Portland outgoing Mayor George Henry Williams, who will officiate."

Mayor Williams gave a slight bow. "The teams will tee off in the order they were selected. After three holes, the team with the lowest score wins. In case of a tie, the tied teams will play additional holes until there is a winner. Good luck."

As Mayor Williams moved to the edge of the crowd, Lady Fletcher stepped forward and teed up her ball. She addressed the ball, made an awkward swing and bobbled it several feet. Without pause, she marched to the ball, picked it up and placed it back on her tee.

"You can't do that," Lord Fletcher objected. "It's not in the rules."

"That was my practice shot." Lady Fletcher turned around to all the players. "I forgot to mention that you each get a practice shot from the tee for every hole, if you so choose."

Lord Fletcher glanced at Mayor Williams with

a hesitant look, but the mayor shrugged his approval.

This time Lady Fletcher hit a solid shot that sliced into a bank of trees. She turned with a bow to her husband.

Lord Fletcher hit hard at the ball's center. The long drive landed well down the fairway, and just a short distance from the green. "Oh, Edwin, that was so good," Lady Fletcher gushed. Her effusive praise flustered him.

"Quite, quite," he said as though such a shot was expected.

Next came Deedra Lazzard and Hawthorne Miller. Deedra's shot came low off the club, but it rolled a long way so she declined it as a "practice." Miller placed his ball with great care and fanfare on the tee. Then he set and reset his stance and club position several times with exaggerated movements until he settled into a stiff, statuesque pose.

Brannon watched with great curiosity, as did the other players. *I've seen peacocks preen less. But can he play?*

Miller had a slow and deliberate backswing, but brought the club through the ball at lightning speed. The crash sent the ball sailing so high, so far that not many watching were able to detect where it landed.

Hack Howard cried out, "On the left, just past that big bush," as he pointed with excitement.

The ball passed Lord Fletcher's. The crowd clapped in approval.

Lord Fletcher, who had shown nonchalant interest in his drive before, blustered with an excuse when he heard the report about Miller. "Maybe my brassie isn't enough anymore. Time to upgrade to a play club."

An intense competition brewed.

I can't allow Hawthorne Miller to beat me at golf. That just can't happen. He tried to remember everything Ted Fleming and Tanglewood taught him, but only bits and pieces came to him now.

To Brannon's great surprise and relief, Mama Darrlyn proved to be an able contender. She landed a smooth, straight shot midway down the field. "Darcy's father built golf courses as a hobby," she answered his quizzical look, "although his main occupation was in oil fields. He and I played a lot."

The pressure was off to produce every good shot. Brannon's ball veered a little left but stayed in the fairway. He considered that a success even though it did not match the distance of Mama Darrlyn's.

As the players and crowd moved up the fairway, Brannon noticed a lad boosted on his father's shoulders. The boy's eyes bored into Brannon's. He chuckled as he heard the boy say to his father, "Is that really Stuart Brannon? He's an old man."

The father tried to shush him. Brannon gave him a wink and a smile.

The next shots for each team left them on the green. Mama Darrlyn had hit hers smartly and a little long. Brannon topped his. The ball bumped straight but short, yet closer than his teammate's.

Miller hit his ball clean and right up to the cup. Fletcher also hit a nice arching shot that stopped abruptly near the hole.

Not sure we stand a chance. His putt sailed past Mama Darrlyn's short attempt and rolled to the other side of the green. *I've got to pull it together to beat Miller.*

Mama Darrlyn's next putt was successful.

Lady Fletcher hit her putt way too hard, but it was straight and it hit the back of the cup, bounced up, and landed in the hole. The crowd loved that and clapped, as Lord Fletcher tried to hide a scoff.

Deedra easily tapped her ball in.

Pars are not going to win this. The other teams made birdies seem normal.

The next hole pounded away the same, except this time it was Mama Darrlyn who took a "practice" off the tee. Again, all three teams hit the green on their second shot, but this time Mama Darrlyn's ball rolled right next to the hole. The Fletchers both missed their putts, as did Miller and Deedra.

Darrlyn did not.

A birdie! We're tied back up. Stuart Brannon hated to lose, whether tracking a stray calf or trading blows with an outlaw. He found golf to be no different. Once challenged, he wouldn't back down. *I've got to find a way, even if my arm's aching.*

The third hole ranged much shorter, but Brannon wasn't sure if that was to his advantage or not. There was a pond on the right, a large sand trap on the left.

The Fletchers were on the green from the tee, though Lord Fletcher's ball rolled back down to the front of the sloping green.

Deedra hit hers straight into the pond, called out "practice," and hit her second tee shot straight into the pond also. The crowd chuckled quietly, but when Deedra declared, "Oh my, I'm not properly dressed for a swim," the crowd roared. Deedra preened.

Miller's tee shot hit near the hole. The back-spin sent it to the front of the green, past the Fletchers'.

"This is our chance, Darrlyn," Brannon encouraged his partner.

Mama Darrlyn's first swing off the tee looked wrong from the beginning, and netted a ball sliced violently to the right and out of play. She teed up a second shot, took deep breaths, then clobbered it. The ball pulled to the left. It rolled off the green, into the sand.

Well, it's up to me. His first swing felt great, but the ball sliced into the water. *C'mon, Brannon, you can do this.* He focused on his stance, kept his swing slow and steady and hit through the ball. This time the ball sliced so far to the right that it was in some trees and unplayable. *How can that be? I swung the same as last time. Must be my left arm.*

"Just relax," Keaton Tanglefoot said.

"What I need is more patience." *More something.*

The crowd murmured as the whole group walked to the final green. Brannon stole a look behind him and took a quick count of the crowd. The herd certainly hadn't dwindled, and in fact it looked to have a gained a few head. *These will not be fruitless deeds in the dark, but they'll be done for all to see.* Brannon heard a few people making side bets. None wagered on him to win.

At the green, Darrlyn was up first. She lightly stepped into the trap and, careful not to let her club scrape the sand in advance, hit a nice spraying shot up onto the green about eight feet from the hole. The audience applauded and, with grace defying her years, she curtsied daintily.

Keaton spoke low to Brannon as he handed him an odd-looking club. "Use this rake iron. Remember, don't touch the sand before you hit the ball."

Brannon inspected the club head. It looked more like an iron grate for cooking over a fire. Brannon frowned at Keaton, unconvinced.

"Trust me, it's the latest thing from England. It will help you in the sand."

The horizontal fingers did make sense for gliding.

Brannon made himself relax as he stepped up to the ball. *Reminds me of the Arizona desert, minus the scorpions.* He set up for his shot. *If I can improve on Deedra's shot, at least I won't embarrass myself.*

The crowd was silent as Brannon raised the club back and struck the ball with a sandy *thwack*. The ball shot forward in a low trajectory, much lower than he intended. Heading straight towards the flag at a pace way brisker than it ought to have been, the ball made a loud whack, directly against the pole, stopped in its path, then fell straight down into the hole.

Brannon didn't know a couple hundred people could make so much noise. The crowd hooped and hollered as the other teams shook their heads in disbelief. Mama Darrlyn rushed to his side, gave him a big kiss on the cheek.

"You always come through, Stuart Brannon," she purred in his ear.

Brannon gave a quick wave to the crowd. Mayor Williams waved his hands in the air and shouted, "It's not over yet. It's not over yet."

CHAPTER FORTY NINE

As the crowd quieted down, the mayor reminded the onlookers, "the other teams can still tie by making their next putt and force a playoff."

Miller and Deedra had been eyeing their putt line, but the read was made difficult by the slope of the green and the drop-off to the left. Both teams remaining had very long, snaking putts to make.

Deedra's putt missed to the left by over two feet. Miller, sweat now beaded on his forehead, stroked the ball smoothly and at a solid speed, but he had overcompensated for the leftward lean. The ball stopped to the right of the hole. Some in the crowd sighed in relief. Others groaned. Miller cursed. Brannon tensed up.

The Fletchers' balls landed in front of where Deedra's and Miller's halted, so their putts would be on the same line. Lady Fletcher's ball followed much the same path as Deedra's and stopped even further from the hole. This was not a putt for the inexperienced.

Lord Fletcher squinted in deep concentration. He strolled to the spot, gently put the ball on the green, lined up his stance. Brannon could hear his heart beat. Nothing else.

Lord Fletcher hoisted the club in a slow loft, moved it forward through the ball. A perfect pendulum swing. The ball rolled up the green, angled down the slope towards the hole. The crowd gasped. The ball rolled closer and closer. Two turns away. One turn away. Two inches. One inch. It stopped.

The crowd presented a collective moan, then burst into applause with chants of "Brannon, Brannon" and shouts of "great match."

Brannon finally exhaled and began to relax. *Boy, I got way more intense than I thought I would.* He congratulated his partner, then shook hands with the other players.

"Well done," Lord Fletcher declared. "Good show."

Miller shook Brannon's hand cordially. "You've done it again. I'll see you at the picture session."

The crowd gathered around to shake the hands of the winners, though many men seemed more interested in congratulating Mama Darrlyn than Brannon. She didn't mind one bit.

Lady Fletcher was pulling a man with a small canvas bag into the middle of the crowd. "May I have your attention please?" she shouted. "We'll now have the drawing."

Lady Fletcher asked the mayor to pick the winner. Mayor Williams stuck his hand in the bag, rooted around for a few seconds, then pulled out a ticket. Squinting at the paper and moving it closer, then further in front of his face like a trombone player, he patted his pockets. From the left breast pocket of his jacket, he pulled out a small pair of reading spectacles and focused again on the paper ticket.

"And the winner is," the mayor intoned, "Mrs. Jedediah Acorn."

Stuart Brannon had endured many difficult encounters . . . outlaws, uncooperative steers, droughts, and disease. At the moment, they seemed preferable to the task he now faced . . . allowing Hawthorne H. Miller to set up this photography shoot.

Mrs. Jedediah Acorn, widowed, rich, bored with life, but an avid reader of dime novels, was to sprawl on Brannon's lap. The worst of it was, she acted as though she'd won a husband. Effusive squeals of delight. Too-familiar hugs. Pokes in the rib. Pecks on the cheek.

He began by signing every one of her Hawthorne Miller novels, but there was a line to be drawn and this was it. For the third time, Brannon nudged her to move off his scrunched legs and to scoot beside him on the bench.

Meanwhile, Miller fussed with the Kodak camera, then called out, "As soon as you two hold still, we can forever memorialize this momentous occasion."

Snickers could be heard around them as Mrs.

Acorn consented to cuddle close to Brannon. Her ample shoulder against his chest. Her husky hand on his. She beamed the joy of the starstruck. Brannon grimaced. The photo was snapped.

He saw Lady Fletcher's frown.

"Mrs. Acorn," Brannon began.

"Patricia," she corrected.

"It was a pleasure to meet you. I wish you many blessings in the future."

The woman hugged him with a vise-like squeeze. He had to use a fair amount of force to break free.

The Fletchers burst out in raucous laughter, as did most of the crowd.

"Quite liberating, actually," Lord Fletcher later told Brannon.

Mrs. Acorn grabbed Brannon by the face and looked him square in the eyes. "You still owe me dinner. You're not going to back out on the deal, are you?"

A hundred excuses crossed Brannon's mind, as did a hundred punishments for Lady Fletcher for roping him into this. But Brannon replied, "No, ma'am."

CHAPTER FIFTY

Later that evening, after a very public dinner with Mrs. Acorn at the Gearhart Hotel Café, in which he gently, but firmly assured the woman that he was not interested in pursuing a further relationship, Lady Fletcher sauntered with Brannon out to his beachside camp. "It was so sweet watching Hawthorne Miller walk Mrs. Acorn on the Ridge Path after your date."

"No date. Doin' my duty."

"Laira and I will be staying in Gearhart and Portland through the summer. Edwin's going to Turkestan, to be with young Stuart. I know he wants to be there and I have no compelling reason to make him stay."

"That's great. He can be the interpreter for the expedition party."

"He so fits the role."

Brannon cleared his throat and plunged his hands into his pants' pockets. "Harriet, I have a very special favor to ask of you."

Lady Fletcher stopped to look at him closer. The hush of stillness punctuated the *whap* of the waves, the squeal of fighting gulls. She folded her arms as she waited, her face pensive, as though she sensed the unveiling of a life-changing event.

He slipped his hands out of the pants' pockets, slid back his coat and wiggled the fingers of his left hand in the inside pouch. He snagged the end of a chain and slowly tugged it out until the locket dangled free and clear. A carefully inked letter, folded in half, came out of another pocket. He reached for one of Lady Fletcher's arms, spread out her hand, dropped in the locket and spread out the note.

"Harriet, would you please package these up and mail them to young Elizabeth, my granddaughter?"

"Are you sure, Stuart?"

"I'm as positive as the day I said, 'I do.' "

"I'm . . . so . . . greatly . . . honored, to accomplish that for you," was all she could say.

They stood in the calm, watching the incessant movement of the breakers, glowing in the bonds of friendship, drinking in the peace of the Pacific.

Lord Fletcher joined them with a plate of razor clams in garlic sauce. "Taste these," he stretched out a fork full. "They're quite good."

Brannon shoved them away. "I've done my duty."

"You just don't have a sense of adventure, Stuart," Fletcher remarked. "You've got to get out and try things."

Brannon nudged his old friend with a kick from his boot. "I have been thinking about taking a vacation. A real one, with no agenda.

Before I collapse on my Arizona porch. I'm off to Montana to throw a hoolihan to Tap and Pepper Andrews. Then down to Goldfield to meet up with Everett Davis' niece and her family. I've also been invited on a huntin' trip near Carson City with T.R. and Todd Fortune of the Black Hills."

He watched Lord Fletcher's face as he teased, "And maybe I'll take a little trip to Panama, to do some gold mining."

"My word, Stuart, without me? How beastly of you."

Brannon gave him another kick.

"I wish you moments of true joy, Stuart," Lady Fletcher said. "To make all the harsh memories of the past finally flee."

"As my schoolteacher friend Rose Creek once told me, I'm going to finally retire from public life and spend my days doctorin' sick cows, breakin' frolicky horses and watchin' sunsets. And I anticipate all the seasons of my grand-children's growth."

He pushed down his black hat, grabbed up his satchels, and winked at Lady Fletcher. "And did I tell you? I asked Victoria to save a date for a very special dinner at our favorite restaurant in Prescott."

Lady Fletcher looked startled, but intrigued. "And what will be the topic of discussion, may I ask?"

"It won't be about guns or golf."

Lady Fletcher hugged him as though she'd never see him again. Lord Fletcher pushed up his hat with a cane and flipped around with a jaunty stroll beside his wife. Brannon watched them until they became two silhouette specks, a man and woman partnered together in an honest match of wits, a fair and equal fondness.

Was it real love? Yep.

He pulled from his bedroll the mashie wooden club Tanglewood had crafted for him, with the carved boot at the top of the handle. He plucked out a ball, his last one and balanced it on a plug of moss he'd taken from a tree.

He took several practice swings. He imagined for a moment what it would be like to stretch in the Arizona desert, sun boiling down, wind whipping his gray hair.

Then he smacked the ball, just below center, with the full force of a near perfect curve.

It arched high and long, stretching over heaving whitewater, into the orange-drenched sunset.

NOTE FROM AUTHOR

I'm often asked, "Who's your favorite character in all those many stories you've created?" Hard to say. They're all part of me and I've gotten to know them so well. They're friends, even family. But Stuart Brannon's special.

He's not my first western protagonist . . . that distinction belongs to Sandy Thompson, the Confederate veteran in *The Land Tamers*. Nor is he the last. There's Tap Andrews of *The Code of the West* series. There's Brazos Fortune with his sons and grandchildren in the family saga of *The Fortunes of the Black Hills* series, which included Sam Fortune of *The Long Trail Home* and received a Christy Award.

And I can't forget the host of heroines in *The Belles of Lordsburg* series and *The Heroines of the Golden West* series, plus feisty Judith Kingston in *The Carson City Chronicles*. Or long-suffering Dola Mae Skinner in *The Skinners of Goldfield* series. There's quite a slew of them.

But Stuart Brannon's my most well-known. He's become a legend, in my mind and in the minds of my most faithful readers. My wife, Janet, claims he's just like me, only different. "After all, look at his initials—same as yours."

Here's a secret that many ardent fans have already discovered: most every Stephen Bly novel, whether historical or contemporary, has some sort of reference or cameo appearance by this hero of mine. Some propose that all my fiction is one huge revolving series. The main characters interrelate in one way or another.

I reckon there's some truth to that.

Why, some enterprising soul with nothing else to do with his or her life could put together quite a genealogy to prove that fact. Maybe they could use such tidbits to stump players in a trivia game some day.

However, that's not my calling.

I'm too busy writing more stories.

On the trail,
Stephen Bly
Winchester, Idaho
December 2010

IN MEMORIAM

STEPHEN BLY

August 17, 1944 – June 9, 2011

Center Point Large Print
600 Brooks Road / PO Box 1
Thorndike ME 04986-0001 USA

(207) 568-3717

US & Canada:
1 800 929-9108
www.centerpointlargeprint.com